YOU DON'T BELONG HERE

TIM MAJOR

SNOWBOOKS

Proudly Published by Snowbooks in 2016

Snowbooks Ltd.
email: info@snowbooks.com
www.snowbooks.com

British Library Cataloguing in Publication Data
A catalogue record for this book is available from the
British Library.

Paperback 9781909679788
Ebook 9781909679795

Printed in Denmark by Nørhaven

To Rose

Farewell to the gold that never I found
Goodbye to the nuggets that somewhere abound
For it's only when dreaming that I see you gleaming
Down in the dark deep underground.

– Paul Metsers

ONE

The time machine in the back of the van shifted as Daniel pulled off the motorway. He grimaced as the contents of the vehicle scraped and lurched before settling.

The sky had only begun to lighten during the last hour. Daniel's jaw ached from the effort of concentration. He coughed and cursed himself for not bringing water and being too afraid to stop and buy a bottle.

The journey north from Oxford had been close to unbearable. Having avoided the toll road—which would have been far faster, but cameras surrounded its toll booths—he had taken his place in a procession of truckers cursing roadworks. At Lancaster the traffic had melted away, but on open roads Daniel had discovered that speeds above fifty produced horrendous noises from the rear of the van.

Was it safe back there? He pictured the straps and buckles holding the tarpaulin-wrapped panels of the time machine. Everything had seemed secure when he had set off, but with so little time to prepare, who could tell? He should have planned ahead, should have brought pillows and duvets to pad the sides.

His legs ached. His bladder, too. He stretched in his seat, and jolts of pain shot up his spasming right leg. The van kangarooed forwards as his foot jabbed the accelerator. He flinched at a flash of light from the roadside.

Shit. Was that—?

He swung onto a narrow grass verge. The time machine moaned, pushing against its restraints as the van juddered to a halt.

As he placed one foot onto the road, a passing truck screamed at the intrusion. Daniel retreated back inside the driver's cabin. His fingers skittered across the dashboard and finally located the button to operate the hazards. He crouched in the footwell, breathing deep, forcing his heartbeat to match the steady tink-tink of the indicators before he reopened the door.

The cold air stung his skin. It had been warm when he had left, even though it had been late at night. It was as if the journey had taken weeks, not hours, as if the seasons had changed while he had been trapped in the driver's cabin. He hurried to the safety of the verge as more cars passed. Drivers craned their necks to see what was the matter.

The sky had turned the same dirty grey as the road. Daniel rubbed his eyes, and sparkles danced at the edges of his vision. Thirty metres behind the van, the yellow box of a speed camera hovered, visible only in the on-off illumination of the hazard lights.

Abruptly, bile rose up in his throat. He dropped to his haunches, retching. When the feeling passed, he remained there for a minute, rocking back and forth with his arms coiled around his knees. After all those hours he had spent driving, putting hundreds of miles between himself and the lab, he had been caught out. And he had been so close, too.

He spat onto the ground. He couldn't allow himself to give in. He was a thief now. There was no changing that.

He rose. As vehicles swept past, the air tugged at his thin T-shirt. Edging between the van and the steep embankment slope, he approached the passenger-side door to the cabin. His hand trailed along a deep, ragged gouge in the van's side. Hundreds of miles away, its paint must also mark the gateway to the lab.

He rifled through the contents of the holdall on the passenger seat but found nothing weightier than a shoe. Casting around in the dark of the grass verge, his fingers closed around a large, irregular lump of concrete. Its sharp edges dug into the scrapes that already lined his palms. He carried the concrete to the yellow speed camera perched on its narrow stalk.

With difficulty, he raised the concrete above his head. It wavered there, heavy and cold.

Had a photo and data already been transmitted to some central database? Perhaps. But if there was any chance he could prevent himself from being traced, he must take it.

The concrete smacked against the metal side of the speed camera before he had fully committed himself to the action. He closed his eyes against the rock shards.

He hit and he hit and he hit. The reverberations shot along his arms, shaking his entire body. When he had finished, both the camera and the concrete were mangled and misshapen.

He dropped the rock, pissed onto the embankment, then climbed into the driver's seat.

There could be no going back.

~

A white flag appeared alongside the curl of the driveway. A golf course stretched away towards a hillside the colour of butterscotch. Daniel flinched as a rabbit emerged from the bushes and onto the road. Instinctively, his foot went to the brake pedal, but at the last moment he held back. A jolt might endanger the time machine. He checked the wing mirror to see the rabbit bound away unharmed.

The driveway led through an iron archway to the crumbling tarmac forecourt of a large building. Daniel parked the van beside a silver MG, the only other vehicle.

He sat for a moment, rubbing life back into his legs. Sweat had drawn salt orbits under the armpits of his T-shirt.

Breathe. Act normal.

Close up the Manor appeared vast, far bigger than the pictures in the welcome pack had suggested. Ivy laced its walls, fluorescent against the grey Cumbrian stone. All of the windows were dark. Perhaps the house was already empty.

He hopped down onto the tarmac. He paused at the rear doors of the van, but stopped himself from opening them. The most important thing was to ensure that the building was safe. He checked and rechecked the van's door lock.

He rummaged in the holdall on the passenger seat, pulled out a sheaf of papers in a transparent plastic wallet, then crossed the forecourt to the Manor. Through a wide window he saw a high-backed armchair at a wide desk. Both were covered with clear plastic wrappers, as if packed for transportation. Loose flaps of sheeting rippled in the breeze from a partially-open window.

The ornate doorbell produced only a dull clunk. The twin glass panels of the front door were dark.

He pushed lightly at the door. It swung open. Security must not be much of a concern in rural Cumbria. That would have to change.

He felt around for a light switch. A wide lobby bloomed beige around him. Enormous, gilt-framed mirrors reflected each other from opposing walls. Daniel flinched at the sight of his reflection and its double, one creeping behind the other. His white T-shirt had become streaked with dirt, and his hair stuck upwards in a clump at one side. Hardly the image of a master thief. Or of a time-travel pioneer, come to that.

"Hello?" The echo made his voice unfamiliar.

Beyond the foot of a curved staircase he saw a huge lounge lined with dark wooden panels. He stepped inside. Despite its size, the room had only one entrance, which made it ideal for his purposes. There was too much furniture, though. He'd have to shift the sofas in order to assemble the time machine. The area in the lab had been larger, and the machine had still sprawled to touch the walls.

His skin prickled at the thought of the time machine left outside in the van. Perhaps somebody was already on the forecourt, trying the locks. He must bring it into the building, fast.

He turned, then yelped in surprise. A shape now filled the doorway, blurred-edged against the soft light from the lobby chandelier.

It cleared its throat. "You must be Faint?"

"Yes. Daniel Faint. I'm the house-sitter." Daniel's tension made his own voice unrecognisable. He glanced down at the names on the front sheet of the welcome pack. "Mr Benfield?"

The man strolled into the room, shaking his head. Though he couldn't be much older than Daniel, mid-thirties perhaps, capillaries had broken in his cheeks and nose. His eyes peered out from fleshy puffs of skin.

"Harrigan. The old fellow's my father-in-law."

Daniel smiled. He must feign friendliness. It wouldn't be for long.

"You look like you've seen a proverbial," Harrigan said. He paused. "Perhaps you're feeling *faint*-hearted."

Laughing at his joke, Harrigan slumped into a low three-seater sofa, somehow taking up more than half of it. Daniel remained standing. He looked out of the window, where croquet mallets and hoops had been arranged in a neat pile at the edge of an immaculate lawn. A tall hedge hid the forecourt from view. He slipped a hand into his pocket and gripped the van keys tight.

"Has Mr Benfield gone away already?" Perhaps a reference to leaving might spur Harrigan into action, get rid of him sooner. He forced himself to smile.

"Uh-uh. Hasn't lived here in donkey's."

"And you...?"

Harrigan snorted. "Bit quiet for my liking. Our liking. We're used to the distractions of the capital."

Daniel was suddenly struck by the idea that the wave of short, wiry hair was the exact style that Harrigan had had since he was a boy. People who began life wealthy had no incentive to review or reinvent.

Harrigan lifted a decanter to fill a sherry glass, then arched his eyebrows in an offer. Daniel looked around but saw no other glasses. And this early in the morning? He frowned a refusal.

"Can't imagine what one'd do out here in the sticks," Harrigan continued. "For more than a few days, I mean. I'm not a golfer myself. What is it they say? A good walk spoiled. Except—ha!—the walk's not much fun either."

The muscles in Daniel's mouth began to ache from his fixed smile. If only he were more assertive, he ought to bundle Harrigan out of the door. Why couldn't this idiot appreciate that he had vital work to do? If, that was, the time machine were still intact. And if the machine was irreparably damaged, what then? He had abandoned his former life and his most recent menial job, for all that was worth. He possessed no skills. No future, other than the time machine.

He removed his glasses and wiped fingerprint smears with the fabric of his T-shirt. He kept his fingers folded over his palms, hiding the grazes and cuts he had received while dragging the components of the time machine to the van. Last night, his blood had pumped so loudly in his ears that he kept mistaking the sound for sirens.

"What's your line of business?" Harrigan said.

"No business," Daniel replied. He winced, realising that he hadn't prepared a lie. "I mean, nothing you could call business, as such. I'm a... student."

"Little old for that, aren't you? Pushing thirty? Which university?" Even a fool like Harrigan could see immediately through a lie as blatant as that.

Daniel's mind blanked. "Oh, none. Independent studies. A thesis."

"Ah. Hence the need for free digs, I suppose. Not a lucrative life, the knowledge-and-understanding game." Harrigan's speech had begun to slur. He downed the sherry and stifled a burp. His attention travelled to a point above Daniel's head. "Ah, the lady wife herself." He half-rose, then slumped back into his seat. "Daniel Faint, meet my wife, Florrie. And vice versa."

How many other people might be hiding in the dark of the Manor, ready to leap out and obstruct him from testing the time machine? Daniel turned to see a young, slim woman in pencil skirt and blouse leaning against the doorframe. While her outfit was as tastefully neat as her husband's, her hair was a wild, dark bundle. A large, beak-like clip bit into the centre of its mass. Typical privileged type, underplaying her perfect breeding. Women like her understood that their beauty could penetrate an unkempt appearance. Her long face contained a constellation of freckles.

"Florence," she said, correcting her husband. She scowled as her eyes flicked towards Harrigan, then she held out her hand. She didn't flinch at Daniel's damp palm. "Perfect timing. I'd hoped we'd see you before we leave. It's a peculiar feeling, leaving a stranger to prowl around your house."

"Oh. I didn't think—"

"Sorry, bad choice of words. No, there'll be no need to prowl, in any capacity. No patrolling the grounds or culling the peacocks. Just turning the lights on and off every so often will be enough, and I'd have thought you'll be doing that anyway. Come on."

She swept out of the room. Her husband, still supine on the sofa, grinned, belched and refilled his glass. Daniel wavered for a moment, then followed Florence. Of the two of them, she at least appeared functionally human. He tried not to stare at her neat buttocks encased in the tight sheath of skirt.

"The place is a bit of a mishmash," Florence said. "Might take some getting used to."

She grunted against the weight of a thick plate-glass door that led from the rear of the lobby. A wave of moist heat swept around them. Daniel's glasses misted up immediately.

"When Dad bought this place four years ago, it was still a working hotel," Florence said. "He kept the staff on for a while, not wanting to let down the locals. This part of the house was open to the public until last year. The golf course still is, technically. Do you swim?"

Baffled, Daniel shook his head. Couldn't she see that he had no interest in the Manor, or her and her soused husband? He glowered at the back of her neck. A wisp of her hair had come free, forming an inverted question mark with a freckle as its dot.

They waded through hot, thick air to reach a curved reception desk in the centre of a perspex conservatory.

Through a condensation-streaked patio door Daniel saw a paved path and more golf holes. To his right, beyond the reception desk, the white lane guides of a swimming pool wriggled lazily.

"I had no idea," Daniel said. "The whole place, I mean. It's a lot bigger than I expected."

Florence paused with her hands flat on the reception desk, as if he were a customer making a difficult request. "Is that a problem? The agency said that you'd been fully briefed."

"Oh, they did. I mean I have been. It's no problem." In fact, he hadn't made it past the front page of the welcome pack. The only aspects that mattered were the remoteness of the building and the distance from Oxford. The Manor was a safe hiding place where he could test the capabilities of the time machine. Everything else was a triviality.

He recoiled as he realised that Florence was watching him closely. Nobody had a right to that level of confidence. It smacked of arrogance. You could tell in an instant that she'd always had money. Her father, Benfield, was an indulgent old fool, no doubt.

"You'd think anyone'd be happy to have such a big house to themselves for the summer," she said.

"I really am very happy," he replied. If he demonstrated a convincing level of joy, might she leave sooner?

"Good. So that's the pool, anyway. And over there—" She pointed over his shoulder, almost touching him.

"You'll find changing rooms and officially the tiniest gym in the entire world. You'll not be... Well, use it if you like."

Involuntarily, Daniel glanced down at himself. The sleeves of his T-shirt barely grazed his thin arms. No, he wouldn't be using the gym.

Florence sidestepped past him. Her expression suggested an anthropologist observing behaviour at once fascinating and distasteful. England's class structure had never died, at least for those at its upper end.

She paused before the doorway. "You were told that you can't have parties, weren't you?" But her single raised eyebrow, her body language, even her freckles seemed to suggest that, rather, parties should be encouraged.

"I know. There won't be any parties. I don't know a soul in the area. There'll be nobody here."

She frowned. "Well, you don't have to go that far. Just use your common sense." She led him out of the humidity and into the house proper again.

In the lobby, three heavy-looking suitcases made a fat tower. Muffled snores came from the lounge.

Upstairs, Florence led him from bedroom to bedroom. There were six of them, all identical, large and crimson-wallpapered, with matching bedspreads and poky ensuites. The windows seemed secure enough, so it was only the ground floor he had to worry about.

Some of the Harrigans' possessions still cluttered the sideboard in the final bedroom. A shaving kit, a copy of *Zeno's Conscience*, a small bottle of pills. Daniel blushed furiously as Florence saw him notice a pair of tan stockings draped on the bed. Was that a smirk?

"You should definitely take this room," she said. "It's the same as the others, of course. But if you're anything like me you'll enjoy waking up to the sound of the breeze swaying the monkey puzzle tree."

If you're anything like me. What a joke. Daniel looked again at the stockings, then his eyes flicked to Florence's legs as he tried to determine whether they were bare. Embarrassed, he blundered from the room, then lost his bearings in the dim corridor. He aimed towards a door at random.

"Not that way," Florence said.

"Oh. I—"

Florence's face scrunched. "Sod it." She pushed open the door. "It has the best view, but you won't want to spend any time in here."

The bed had been pushed to one side. Most of the space had been filled with a variety of surfaces: shelves, a park bench, a Black and Decker Workmate. Each surface held dozens of unfinished sculptures. The more complete appeared to be figures, although few were recognisable as fully human. They bent double with limbs that encircled their own bodies. An enormous mound of clay on one work surface suggested a primordial goo from which they had all crawled.

"You'll have to excuse all this," Florence said. "It's a whim brought on by boredom. I always start new hobbies in the summer. My husband says I'm faddy and that it's just something in the air."

"You made all of these?" Ugly though the figures were, Daniel found himself fascinated.

"I'm afraid so. Just ignore this room. Or throw them out, if you like. I don't mind a bit."

She picked up a nearby figure, around six inches tall. Its features had been carefully sculpted but appeared distorted, as though viewed through ancient glass. As she turned it in her hands, Daniel saw that it had more than one face, each varying in expression. Florence gave a lopsided grimace, as if the object had been made by a close relative that she didn't want to offend.

"They're impressive," Daniel said, meaning it.

Florence's eyes lifted. She scrutinised his face. "Like I said. Do what you like with them."

She placed the figure down. Daniel winced as part of its base chipped away.

"Daniel Faint!" The shout echoed through the building. Daniel drew away from Florence and stumbled from the room.

"Ah, there you are." Harrigan's eyes had become even more bloated with sleep. "Give me a hand loading these bags, would you?"

In the lobby Harrigan pushed the largest suitcase towards Daniel with his foot, taking only a satchel himself. Daniel staggered out to the forecourt, half-dragging the enormous case. Despite the indignity and Harrigan's clear enjoyment of putting him to work, it was best to keep on his right side. It couldn't be much longer until Daniel would be left alone.

"You'll have a ball," Harrigan said as he surveyed the open boot of the MG. "A rent-free life of luxury, for a time."

"Yes. But I'll be working."

Harrigan grunted. "Ah, studying, of course." He eyed the white van. "Got a lot of kit for a student, haven't you?" He sidled over to the back doors of the vehicle, trying the handle.

Daniel dropped the suitcase. It sprang open, shedding Harrigan's shirts onto the tarmac. Harrigan sighed but only watched as Daniel scrabbled to collect and replace the items.

"No kit. Just books," Daniel said.

By the time he had jammed the suitcase closed again, Harrigan had already re-entered the house.

~

Now that he was outside again, Daniel's resolve weakened. With Harrigan safely out of sight and Florence busy in the kitchen, he returned to the van. The gravitational pull of the time machine increased with every step he took.

The rear doors opened with a whisper. At first the interior of the van appeared empty, until his eyes adjusted to the dark.

Tightly-bound tarpaulins still covered each of the eight panels. The straps and buckles had held, more or less. Two of the panels had come loose, only a little, to lean off-kilter against each other. They might have been scraping together for most of the journey. He leant in to grasp a large wooden crate and dragged it towards him along the dusty floor of the van. Something within tinkled. He shuddered. Were the contents damaged?

What time was it—eight? Nine? Somebody must have entered the lab by now and found the empty space where the time machine had crouched. Panicked. Called superiors. Tried to check the CCTV footage, then found the hard drive missing. And after that? Crisis talks, no doubt, and blame, but perhaps not yet. For a while it would be just anger and confusion. But soon enough somebody would be knocking at Jimmy's door.

A muffled but insistent sound pulled him away from his thoughts.

A phone.

The sound came from within the van, echoing through the metal partition wall of the driver's cabin. At first he felt paralysed with confusion. He didn't own a phone.

Of course. He had taken it from Jimmy's bedside table while he slept. Using any other phone to call the police would have been too risky. But he was a fool for bringing it up north with him. Didn't modern phones allow the police to track the location?

The phone has stopped ringing by the time he found it in the side pocket of the holdall. He had no idea how to determine who had called, but it hardly mattered. He prised off the back of the casing with a fingernail but hesitated before removing the SIM card.

One more time. He could allow himself to watch the video one more time, before destroying the phone.

There were only three video clips stored on the phone. The first showed Jimmy and his friends downing shots. The third was from Jimmy's point of view as he encouraged two inebriated, partially-undressed women to dance for the camera.

Daniel clicked play on the second clip.

The child's teddy bear seemed symbolic, as endearing and oblivious as a dog or monkey shot into space. The graininess of the footage was exacerbated by being filmed through thick glass and at a peculiar shooting angle above head height. Digital zoom artefacted the image.

The first time he had seen the video clip, he had snatched the smartphone from Jimmy, squinting to make out the details.

"Nothing's happening."

"Watch. Wait."

The time machine itself remained invisible apart from a black curve that obscured the bottom of the screen. The first time he had watched the video, Daniel had swiped at the phone settings to adjust the brightness.

"Stop messing with it. Just watch. It'll be any second now, swear down."

The glow increased, washing out the muzzle of the teddy bear in a wave of white pixels.

Then the bear was gone.

"How do you like them apples?"

Daniel had frowned to mask a surge of excitement. No need to show his real reaction.

"So you're a dab hand at video editing. Big deal."

And yet he had still found himself watching the tiny screen intently. Less than a minute later, the teddy bear reappeared in the same position.

Common sense had told him that it was a fake.

But still.

If you want something bad enough, why let common sense get in your way?

~

The time machine, still lurking within the van, exerted an unwavering pull on Daniel. He dug his nails into his palms in an attempt to withstand the gravitational force and to stop himself from bellowing at the Harrigans. Florence had insisted that they would all breakfast together before she and her repellent husband left for London.

Florence sat at the head of the kitchen table. Harrigan and Daniel took a longer side each, facing each other like distorted mirror images. Harrigan tucked into the selection of cold meats and cheeses with gusto, barely looking up from his plate. Daniel only picked at the food, carefully avoiding the parts of the cheddar that Harrigan had infected with stilton.

As she ate, Florence glanced between Daniel and her husband. She cringed at each of Harrigan's noisy slurps. Narrow lines marked the corners of her eyes. Who wouldn't feel the strain, being married to that oaf? With difficulty, Harrigan was trying to pour orange juice from his glass back into its Tetra Pak container. He topped up the glass with murky liquid from a hip flask.

"Did you find the old bar?" Florence said in a low voice. Daniel realised that she was speaking to him. "Help yourself to whatever you like. I mean it. You'd be doing me a favour." She blinked rapidly.

"I don't drink, usually," Daniel said. He almost added, 'Gambling is more my vice' but was relieved that the words didn't spill out.

Florence's eyes glistened. Harrigan began to hum a tune to punctuate the silences between chewing noises.

Why couldn't they just leave, taking their tawdry marital problems with them? The contrast between the triviality of their bickering and the world-changing importance of the time machine hidden in the van was dizzying, comical. And yet, here he was, brokering an uneasy peace between two strangers.

Breathe. Act normal. They would leave in due course. He must find the strength to bear their presence, for now.

Steer the conversation back to safer topics. Try not to think about the clinking sound that came from the crate in the van.

"I'm a little confused," he said. Florence smiled sympathetically, as if this were evident. "Mr Benfield—your father—why doesn't he live here himself?"

Florence's expression softened still further. "I'm not sure he ever believed he would. I mean, buying this place... I don't know what he was thinking. And now there's no chance of him coming back, really. His mind had already begun to deteriorate, even then. He wasn't happy."

Her husband reached across the table to take the cow-shaped butter dish from beside Florence's plate. "Bet he is now though! That sanatorium costs enough. And those nurses—"

Florence swatted his hand away. "Jesus. It's a home, not a sanatorium. And as for the cost, it's not even your—" She rubbed at one eye, then turned back to Daniel. "Shit. Sorry."

Daniel glared at his plate in embarrassment. "Your father never intended to run the Manor as a hotel? You said it was still operational when he bought it."

"Oh, barely. No, he had no interest in that. Dad had grand plans for the place. A proper family pile, with everyone under one roof. Him as the grand patriarch, I suppose, and the two of us, and then, in time... Well, who knows what he was hoping for."

"But you live in London? That's where you're going now?" Daniel wondered whether this sounded too obviously a demand for them to leave. He realised that he was gripping his knife in a tight fist. He released his fingers. The knife clattered to the table.

"Yes," Florence replied with a sigh. "We live in London. Not my idea."

A few seconds passed in awkward silence.

Finally Florence spoke. "So, Ian tells me that you'll have your head buried in books while you're here?"

Daniel blinked, taking a moment to realise that Ian and Harrigan were one and the same person. He nodded.

"It's good to find someone interested in bettering himself." Her eyes remained fixed on Daniel, though his own flicked towards Harrigan. "Dad was a student, too, in his way."

"I saw a study at the front of the house," Daniel said. "With plastic sheets over everything."

Florence's smile thinned. "It's hard. It meant a lot to him, setting up there, with the view of the Old Man—" She registered Daniel's confusion. "That fell you can see beyond the golf course? It's called the Old Man of Coniston. I always thought it was a fun image, the Old Man of the Manor staring out at the Old Man of Coniston, like neighbours waving over the garden fence. Anyway. It was all part of Dad's vision. We Harrigans scampering around the house and Captain Benfield tucked away at the front like a pilot or a—I don't know, a bus driver or something."

She rubbed her eyes again. "Christ. Sorry, I'm rambling. Dad was a historical researcher, there's the short answer. I can't even remember if you asked me a question."

If Harrigan noticed his wife's discomfort, he ignored it. "Florrie whacked on the plastic sheets the very day the old fellow checked out." A cough became a guffaw. "Sorry, Florrie. That sounded a bit bleak. Checked out."

Florence watched her husband dispassionately. It was hard to imagine them ever having had much in common. Their marriage was a transaction, no doubt, with other, financial benefits.

Abruptly, she turned her attention back to Daniel. "What subject are you studying?"

Daniel found that his mind had become blank.

Before he had time to formulate an answer, Florence said, "I dream of turning back the clocks."

Daniel gripped the edge of the table, amazed at how closely her thoughts echoed his own. What did she know about his plans?

"If I could justify going back to uni," she continued, "I'd get deep into literature."

Sweat prickled on Daniel's forehead. He wiped it away as unobtrusively as possible. Florence knew nothing. He was paranoid, that was all. Nobody in their right mind believed that time travel was possible.

Harrigan's chewing had reached an almost intolerable volume but Florence seemed to be doing everything she could to ignore it. She raised an eyebrow as a reminder of her unanswered question. "So, what subject?"

A piece of cracker lodged in Daniel's throat so that his next word came out strangled. "Physics," he lied.

"Wow. Weighty. Go on, hit me with your thesis title. I bet I'll not be able to make head nor tail of it. I should note down your name, in case you win the Nobel Prize. Actually, Daniel Faint? That should be easy to remember."

Daniel cursed himself for not using a false name in his application. Even at the van-hire company he'd used his real name. Hopefully, though, only Jimmy could possibly be in a position to make the link between Daniel and the time machine, and he was an imbecile.

"I don't know my thesis yet," he said in a weak voice.

Florence's face fell. Daniel realised that she had been expressing genuine interest. She dabbed at the hummus on her plate with a crisp.

"It's about time," Daniel said, without thinking.

Florence glanced at her watch.

"No. I mean, my studies. They're about time."

She smiled wistfully. "Then you've come to the right place. There's almost literally nothing to do here. You've all the time in the world."

TWO

An hour later, Daniel watched the MG slide through the iron archway and disappear behind the trees. He exhaled a breath he had been unconsciously holding in. It smelt of pungent cheese.

Beyond the golf course, shadows of clouds gave the fellside the appearance of being bruised or mottled with liver spots.

He placed a hand on the side of the van as if any disturbance might be felt from outside. The metal wall of the vehicle seemed to have darkened, as if its contents had corroded it from within. He fumbled for the keys and threw open the doors.

"Looks like it's just you and me," he said to the time machine.

The wooden crate seemed heavier now. Perhaps adrenalin had given him extra strength when he had bundled it into the van. It was hard to believe that that had been only a matter of hours ago. He grimaced as the contents of the crate tinkled again. He staggered into the house, heaving open the front door with his backside. He deposited the crate in the centre of the lobby, regained his breath, then carried it the rest of the way into the lounge.

In contrast, the wrapped panels were far lighter than he remembered. As he trudged with each one from van to house, van to house, he imagined the panels as wings. If he only jumped into the air while holding one horizontally above his head, even the slight breeze might be enough to lift him clear from the ground and away over the fell. He walked slowly and bow-legged to avoid bumping the panels against the door frames.

The engine of the van cut out twice, a half-hearted refusal to limp any further, before he coaxed it into life. He drove at a stately pace to the corner of the Manor, where tarmac gave way to loose gravel in the shade of a monkey puzzle tree. He parked before a rusted garage door, out of sight from the driveway.

As he made his way back to the entrance, something flickered at the edge of his vision. His head jerked to follow the motion.

Nothing. It must have been just the shifting of the light through the trees.

The lounge still stank of Harrigan's alcoholic belches. At the edges of the wide windows, exposed stonework revealed the thickness of the walls. The Manor was safe, impenetrable. Outside, someone had removed the croquet equipment from the lawn. Florence must have tidied them before she left.

He spent the next few hours shifting bulky furniture from the lounge to the bar, which until now had been hidden from the lobby by a heavy curtain. When he finished, the sofas, armchairs and coffee table provided an extra barricade against a fire exit. He leant against a chair arm, panting and rubbing his aching back. Beyond the pile of furniture, a monkey puzzle tree cast tentacled shadows criss-crossed by the window panes.

Something moved outside. Shielding his eyes against the light, Daniel peered through the window. Something squatted low in the shade of the monkey puzzle. It shimmered, slick and dark.

It reminded him of another figure, long ago. Crouching, then head over heels into darkness.

He leapt back as the thing burst from its hiding place. It seemed to raise a cowl over its head as it moved. It squealed as it ran.

Finally, Daniel identified its head and body, its fanned tail feathers. A peacock. Its pace slowed as it approached, cocking its tiny head to watch him.

He gasped for air and steadied himself against the chair. Breathe. Look. See the creature for what it really is.

The peacock halted and turned, as if pirouetting for Daniel's benefit. They were like butterflies; dramatic from a distance but up close as ugly as hell. The peacock watched him. Its tail feathers rippled, the pattern of blue eyes separating and coalescing.

~

The tarpaulin slid away from the final panel with a whisper. Daniel kicked the sheet, along with the straps that had held it tight, towards the pile beneath the window.

While they had been covered, he had remembered the panels as black monoliths. Now he saw that they were a pale grey. All identical, sleek and sheer, they each measured two feet in width and perhaps five in height. Daniel pressed a palm against the nearest panel. The heat of his hand left no trace on its surface. He shuddered at the cold that seemed to creep along his arm.

He tried to visualise how the panels had been arranged in the lab. Could that really have been only last night? With difficulty, he jostled the eight panels into a rough circle, twelve feet in diameter with wide gaps between each one and its neighbour. Upright, they had become less manoeuvrable, despite his ease in carrying them from the van. Each panel curved slightly along its longest length. The concave surfaces faced towards the empty centre to make segments of a ring. Standing in the centre of the ring, it appeared almost as if they tilted towards him. The effect persisted as he moved from side to side.

Carefully, he prised open the lid of the crate. He lifted out a thin sheet constructed from a light, hard material, more like porcelain than metal or plastic. He yelped in alarm as it suddenly became slack in his hands. Hidden hinges swivelled open, making the object fluid and formless. Within moments Daniel found himself holding a hollow tube, roughly three feet in diameter and the same in height. Holes riddled the curved surface, like the drum of a washing machine.

He bent double to reach inside the crate to retrieve the remaining items. Something came free and he lumbered backwards, almost stumbling into one of the panels. Glittering dust burst up from the carpet as, clumsily, he set the heavy object down. It was a thick quarter-circle, smooth and dense. He pulled out others until four identical black quarters made a hollow circle in the centre of the ring of panels. Daniel wiped the sweat from his forehead. How had he managed to lift them all together within the crate? The slatted tube fitted onto the black base with a sharp click. He gasped, hand over mouth, as a section of the tube swung open. A door.

He worked carefully to pull out a bundle of wires without snagging them on the splintered edges of the crate. They were thin like strands of silk, but rubbery to the touch.

Each year at Christmas, his father and his twin brother, William, had made a routine of sorting the fairy lights before decorating the tree. The lights were wired in series and each bulb needed to be checked and tightened. It was frustrating work but William enjoyed it. Daniel only watched on, having been correctly judged too impatient for the task. Inevitably, it would be the last bulb they checked that proved to be the culprit. With the final twist of this bulb the lights would become dazzling, magical specks of colour.

He fed the wires into holes at the foot of each panel. They held tight as if gripped by something from within. When he had finished, the time machine resembled a giant spiderweb with shimmering lines of silk radiating from the fat black beast at its centre.

One thicker cable remained. At one end was a red, oval ring, the size of Daniel's hand. It was made of cheap plastic, like the handle of a child's stunt kite. His fingers fit within its hollow centre. This must be the means of operating the machine. A section of the plastic handle had cracked so that sharp edges protruded; a dark slot seemed designed to hold some missing piece within the ring.

He groaned. His luck had been due to run out. He prayed for the pieces to still be inside the crate. There could be no going back.

With shaking hands he tipped the crate to rescue the fragments that had fallen within. He discovered a trigger shape, contoured with four divots to accommodate fingers. It slipped into the slot in the plastic handle. Gently, he pushed the trigger in and out with bent fingers. It moved without resistance. Perhaps some smaller, intricate mechanism had been lost in the lab, the van or elsewhere. Could the handle be fixed? More importantly, could he, an unskilled thief, fix it?

He left the room, still holding the disconnected plastic handle, squeezing the loose trigger.

~

A door led from the rear of the kitchen to the garage. Inside, a flickering strip light illuminated a sit-on mower with gleaming red trim. On the wall behind it, jars of screws and nails filled haphazardly tilted shelves. There were racks of hanging tools: rusted saws, pliers and hammers. In a metal cabinet Daniel found a roll of silver duct tape.

He wrapped tape around and around the broken top of the trigger handle, strengthening and swelling it. There was no way of telling whether the damage had loosened something vital inside. Nothing for it but to have a go.

He remembered the teddy bear in the video. He should start small, then work onwards and upwards.

Choosing a suitable object seemed important. This was a historic moment, after all. He found himself upstairs in Florence's converted workshop, examining the rows of half-finished sculptures. Bingo. Test subjects in a queue. By accident or design, no two figures looked alike. Some had spindly arms that wrapped twice around their bodies. Others had more than one face. At random, he picked up one of the more complete statues, then replaced it. On reflection, he found that he preferred the less obviously human ones. He selected a pyramidal lump of hard clay, little more than a stone cairn, but with dark smears that might be eyes.

The time machine sighed as Daniel connected the trigger cable to its base. He edged away from the ring of panels, as far as the cable would allow, and lay flat on the ground with his chin resting on the carpet.

One small step. Daniel Faint is making history. How do you like that, William?

He pushed the trigger, just a tap. To his surprise, it no longer felt totally loose, giving slight resistance as it slid inwards a fraction. Using his fingernails, he pulled the trigger back to its open position.

The machine hummed softly. Daniel's stomach tightened.

The clay figure remained in place.

Daniel's head drooped. Perhaps the machine really was broken.

But the humming increased in volume. Light played and flickered on the panels of the machine. Daniel glanced at the window and frowned; the afternoon sunlight was steady and unchanging. Rather, the light seemed to come from somewhere within the panels themselves, although the closer he looked, the less he was able to make out any differences in shade. The panels highlighted in sequence, their intensity growing and diminishing. The strobing effect accelerated.

Then he realised that the clay figure had disappeared.

He leapt to his feet and burst forwards, only at the last second holding himself back from entering the ring of panels.

It was real. The pumping of his pulse matched the hum of the machine.

Then, a blink of an eye later, the statue reappeared in its original position. Daniel gazed at the streaked eyes pressed into the clay. Impassive, the eyes gazed back.

~

Two peacocks watched as Daniel crunched along the gravel, passing the patio doors of the conference room and the monkey puzzle.

Against the outer wall of the garage, he discovered a pile of discarded fenceposts and hedge cuttings. A flurry of movement came from within as he prodded at one of the sticks. Perhaps hedgehogs had made their home there, as well as insects and mice. He drew back slightly to allow sunlight to pass over his shoulder, illuminating the rotten pile. His hand hovered an inch above the sticks.

A shrill yelp from behind him made him flinch. He spun around to see that one of the peacocks had approached from behind. It called again, its thin head raised to project the sound further, and watched Daniel with glinting marble eyes. He hissed and lurched towards the bird with both arms raised over his head. It backed away a couple of steps, then paused. Soft clicks came from its throat.

The peacock dashed towards the pile of sticks in a blue blur and Daniel tottered backwards to the ground. The bird's wings produced a dull thud of displaced air as it passed. It disappeared around the corner of the garage.

He turned back to the pile. Again, something darted within. He thrust in his hand.

The mouse made only a whimper as he pulled it free. Its dangling body became bulbous as it pivoted, its tail trapped between Daniel's fingers. He strode back to the house, spitting on the ground near to a peacock that sheltered beneath the monkey puzzle.

Now that he thought about it, the round perforations in the slatted tube were wider than the body of the mouse. It would escape in moments. In a kitchen cupboard, he found a tall, wide-bottomed vase. He dropped the mouse in. It scritched and scraped at the glass.

He placed the vase within the slatted tube of the time machine, repositioning it so that it sat exactly centrally inside the black base ring. The door to the tube closed with a click. With the trigger in hand he scurried away through the gap between two panels. He was Wile E. Coyote laying a fuse, ready to demolish a rocky outcrop. But instead of Road Runner, Daniel had only a trapped mouse. And instead of a rocky outcrop...

He crouched low. The mouse darted back and forth within the vase.

He tapped the trigger, then pulled it back to an open position.

The machine hummed.

The mouse paused, then continued to scrape at the glass, the only sound in the room.

It paused again. It seemed to look directly at Daniel. He waited, lying on his belly, watching the mouse flit from side to side. It showed no signs of discomfort.

There had been a delay during the previous tests. He forced himself to wait.

Minutes passed and nothing happened.

Finally, he set down the trigger and stepped into the ring of panels.

The mouse became more animated as Daniel opened the slatted door to retrieve the vase. He tipped the mouse out onto the palm of his left hand, cupping it with his right. It wriggled in his grip, pushing at his fingers with its nose. He shuddered at the sensation.

The mouse nipped at a barely-healed scab on his finger. He grunted and loosened his grip. The mouse dropped to the ground, sniffing at the black circular base of the time machine before scurrying away into the corner of the room. Daniel leapt to his feet in time to see it push its way into a dark hole between the skirting board and the ragged edge of the carpet.

He realised that he was still standing within the ring of panels. He darted through a gap in the circle to stand outside its circumference.

Not that it mattered. The time machine hadn't worked.

He waited for more than ten minutes beside the hole in the skirting. As soon as the mouse's head protruded he nipped it by one ear and pulled it out.

Under the monkey puzzle, he crushed the mouse with a rock.

~

He reverted to the clay figurines. Each statue disappeared, then reappeared. The time machine hummed. Daniel imagined it smacking its lips.

It still worked. So why hadn't the mouse disappeared?

Stepping sideways to protect the contents of the tray in his hands, he pushed aside the heavy curtain to enter the bar. He placed the tray on a stained round table, then lifted the fractured pieces of one of the clay statues, fitting them together along the cracks. Even though Florence placed no value on her creations, he felt unexpected guilt at having destroyed one.

But he was being a scientist now, even if it was only a charade. And scientists did experiments. Scientists changed conditions and parameters in successive tests. It might only have been a sudden impulse that made him toss the statue into the air before pulling the machine's trigger, but the results had been extraordinary. The statue had dematerialised midair. When it reappeared thirty seconds later, it was in exactly the same position before it fell to the floor and shattered.

Science in action. Undeniable, dizzying proof of the capabilities of the machine.

He placed the dusty clay pieces back onto the tray and turned his attention to the plateful of cheese on toast. Gingerly, he prodded with a finger. It was still hot, twenty minutes after he had prepared the meal. Twenty minutes in which the cheese, toast and plate had all disappeared from sight within the machine's slatted tube. He lifted the toast, raised it to his lips, then replaced it on the plate. Bad idea, Mr Scientist.

Not that he felt hungry, anyway. And cheese on toast hardly represented an adequate celebration of a historic event.

He wished he felt more joyful. But, in addition to having had no effect on the mouse, the time machine appeared to have one fundamental limitation. A squeeze of the trigger controlled the time travelled, but there seemed no way to dictate direction. The subject could only be sent forwards in time.

He had been a fool to believe Jimmy's description of the machine's capabilities in the first place, of course, but he had been proved right. Now it seemed doubly unfair that Daniel's assumption—that the machine might transport a subject both forwards and backwards in time—had been wrong.

All those months of planning, all that risk.

There could be no going back.

The skin around his eyes itched. He thought of wasp stings.

For the first time in as long as he could remember, he needed a drink.

Three pump handles stood in the centre of the wooden bartop. Only one still retained its label, advertising a beer named Homunculus. At a tug of the handle, a cough escaped from the nozzle, followed by a mist of dry, flecked foam. Below the counter Daniel found a three-quarter-full bottle of whisky. He pulled the cork from the bottle and swigged. He had never had much of a taste for whisky. It was his father's drink. His father's and William's, for a time, but never his own. The sour liquid clogged and burned at the back of his throat.

'Onwards and upwards,' his father had always said. That and, 'Experience maketh the man.'

The mouse was a problem, but there was still a hope that the time machine would work on living things. What use had the development of the time machine been for, from a scientific point of view, if that wasn't the case? The levels of funding must have been astronomical. So it was the secondary problem—that the time machine only sent its subjects forwards in time—that most concerned him.

He would have to embrace the opportunity he had been given. Rather than travelling to his own past, he could simply push ahead to a time beyond his own natural lifespan. Wouldn't that be a fresh start? Nobody would know him. Nobody would link him to the time machine or his mistakes.

His mind reeled at the thought of hurtling into the future. The possibilities were vast and, at the moment, unknowable. Caution must be his watchword. A machine this powerful required scientific rigour. He must take stock. Work methodically.

The effects of the whisky had already mutated from giddiness to a dull headache. He needed to sleep. Just a couple of hours to recharge.

He retrieved a bundle of T-shirts and underwear from the holdall in the van. Upstairs, he selected the Harrigans' recently vacated bedroom as his own, in order to remain close to the van parked directly beneath its window. He lay on the bed. To his surprise, his thoughts weren't of the time machine, but the memory of Florence's draped stockings.

He slept fitfully, half-waking often at the unfamiliar sounds from the old house.

~

When he awoke, he had no sense of time. Was it even the same day? Something thumped behind his forehead. Whisky residue slimed his gums.

A sharp, metallic sound echoed in his memory. It must have woken him.

He darted from the bed and gripped the stone window sill. The shadow of the monkey puzzle now fell over the white van, making it zebra-striped. Hours must have passed. He craned his neck to check the narrow gravel strip from the corner of the building to the garage, but saw nobody.

The walls pushed at him as he stumbled downstairs. Even after sleeping for several hours his body felt weak.

A grandfather clock stood at the foot of the stairs, outside the study. Its pendulum was only visible as it passed its central point; at the extremes of its arc it was obscured by an ornate plate. The name *Benfield* was inscribed on it. Florence's family had an illustrious history, it seemed.

It was three o'clock.

He found himself wavering in the lobby. He stood at its centre, turning on the spot to reorient himself. His multiple reflections in the opposing mirrors spun, too.

THREE

"Hold... it..." Daniel said between gritted teeth.

The wings of the peacock strained against his grip. He twisted awkwardly so that the bird's beak stayed clear of his face. His bare arms were already marked with red nips. The peacock had punctured the tarpaulin that he had used to trap it, and had fought him all the way from the monkey puzzle to the lounge.

The bird's sleek neck feathers shimmered in the light from the wide windows. The peacock squirmed as Daniel struggled with the straps laced through the holes in the slatted tube.

He stepped backwards out of the ring of panels. Held captive, the peacock looked even more ridiculous. Its long triangular neck tapered to a stupidly thin head. Was any other animal quite so bottom heavy? Its clump of tail feathers, barely restrained by a second strap, swished back and forth against the slats.

Daniel squeezed the trigger.

The peacock cried out. Its indigo neck glistened like water from a shaken hose. Daniel waited, willing the bird to stop shouting as it struggled in its cage. He glanced down at the trigger and pressed it a little further in. The trigger eased into the hollow handle with treacly resistance.

Nothing changed, except a slight alteration in pitch of the machine's hum. The peacock, though shifting and straining against the straps, appeared no more or less frantic than before.

It was possible that the mouse hadn't been substantial enough for the time machine, so Daniel had thought bigger. Was the peacock still not a suitable enough subject? He wished that he had been able to steal notes from the lab, in order to continue where the scientists left off.

He thought of a science kit that he and William had been given at Christmas one year. His twin brother had revelled in the experiments, working carefully with their father to change the colour of liquids and produce puffs of powder from test tubes. Daniel had, in a fit of pique when William had left the house, mixed together all of the powders, then tried and failed to set light to them in an ice-cream tub. When he returned, his brother had been surprisingly calm. He read and reread the scribbled notes in his jotter, reliving earlier experiments. If he were here now, William would have approached these tests methodically.

Daniel sighed. He still felt his twin brother looking over his shoulder, constantly.

Abruptly, the bird stopped struggling. Its glassy eye turned to meet Daniel's. For a brief couple of seconds, it stood utterly still, as though stuffed. He stared at it, willing it to disappear just as the statue had done.

Instead, somehow, the peacock's tail feathers freed themselves from the straps. Accompanied by a sharp displacement of air, the feathers sprung upwards, fanning out, pushing through the slats of the tube.

Daniel stood transfixed in terror, as motionless as the bird had been only moments before. The eyes on its tail feathers watched him. The feathers curved inwards so that he became the object of every gaze.

A noise from behind released him from paralysis. He spun around and yelped in surprise.

A figure pressed up against the window, framed against the queasy, vivid green of the croquet lawn. One hand was cupped over its eyes.

The hollow, panicky feeling in Daniel's stomach rose up, jabbing at his throat.

William?

He stared, uncomprehending, for a moment. The shape at the window shifted. Its face turned, looking first at the spread feathers of the peacock and then at Daniel himself. The face was nothing like William's.

Get a grip. Deal with this.

As Daniel bounded from the room he saw the peacock spasm, its tail-eyes shuddering, accompanied by the sound of a kite in strong wind. He imagined that the bird followed close behind him, shadow-like, as he darted through the lobby.

The stranger met him at the corner of the building, beside the croquet lawn. He appeared to be in his late fifties and wore brown cords and an ancient wax jacket, despite the morning's warmth.

"Everything aright in there?" the man said.

Daniel felt sweat dampening his T-shirt. Was the tone unfriendly, or was this just a standard greeting? "Of course. Everything's fine. Perfect."

The man looked back along the path to the lounge windows.

"I'm Daniel Faint. I'm the house-sitter."

The man squinted. Despite the fact that he must be taller than Daniel, his back bent dramatically, giving him the appearance of some kind of woodland animal barely able to rise from all fours. The man gave no impression of having heard him. Daniel wondered whether he ought to repeat himself.

"Heard about you," the man said, finally. He held out a hand. "Tosh."

Daniel recoiled from the extended hand. "Excuse me?"

"Everyone calls me Tosh."

They shook hands. Tosh's grip was surprisingly strong.

"And you're the... gardener?" Daniel said.

Tosh nodded. "Gardener, guardsman, builder, kew-rator. Whatever needs doing. I feed the boys and all. Seven days a week."

"The boys?" Daniel said. He frowned. "Oh! I see. The peacocks. I— You must be wondering what all that was about in there."

Tosh responded with a raised eyebrow.

"I'm the house-sitter," Daniel said again.

"Aye."

"But... not just that. I'm a photographer too." First a student, now a photographer. The lies flowed more easily all the time. "Harrigan was keen for me to capture the house and everything. Not capture but, you know. That's why I'm here. And I thought that I ought to include the peacocks. He loves those boys, doesn't he?"

Tosh rubbed his chin. His stubble produced a rasping sound. "He does, does he?"

Daniel fought a rising, lightheaded sensation. "I've set up my studio in the lounge. But the boy, I mean peacock, I've chosen doesn't seem to want to play ball. I suppose I'll have to resort to photographing outside rather than in studio conditions."

Tosh processed this information. The lie was ridiculous, no doubt. Why would the peacock need to be strapped down in order to have its photo taken? But the gardener appeared no more or less sceptical than before. Perhaps he was biding his time before making an accusation.

A shrub at the corner of the lawn seemed to have taken Tosh's attention. He rubbed a leaf between a thumb and forefinger before bringing his hand to his nose to inhale the scent. He stood in contemplation while Daniel shifted uneasily.

"So you'll be bringing him back outside then?" Tosh said at last.

Daniel's body jerked like a puppet. "Certainly, yes. Right away, in fact."

Chewing his cheek, Tosh sidled away in the direction of the garage, apparently satisfied that their conversation had ended. Daniel watched his broad back. Then, flustered, he darted back into the Manor. He fumbled with the straps to release the peacock. It complained with angry squawks and beating wings.

When he returned to the doorway with the bird jammed under one arm, the gardener was in the shade of the monkey puzzle, revving the mower.

~

Daniel drew the lounge curtains shut. The time machine seemed to glow faintly, as if from some internal source.

He must keep it isolated from now on. He was a fool for leaving it visible from outside.

Tosh's unwelcome presence changed things. There must be no trace of any wrongdoing from outside the Manor.

The van.

He imagined Tosh glaring at it as he squeezed the sit-on mower out from the garage. No matter how secure Daniel made the Manor, the van remained visible to all. It linked him to Oxford, the lab and the theft, the destroyed traffic camera. He had made countless mistakes already, using his real name when arranging the van hire and the house-sitting. He couldn't afford to make his trail any easier to follow. The van had to go.

He found himself at the front door. A chisel he had found in the garage pulled his jeans low at one side.

The gardener sat astride the mower at the crest of the golf course, dark against the pale flank of the fell. Daniel scuttled around the corner of the Manor to the van and started the engine. He winced at its volume.

He manoeuvred the van slowly around the building to the iron archway, watching Tosh to reassure himself that he didn't turn around. It was only halfway along the length of the driveway that he remembered that the time machine was no longer in the van and the speed bumps posed no danger.

Soon, the roads narrowed. Daniel reminded himself not to drive too far. He would be returning to the Manor on foot.

He pulled into and then discounted two overgrown laybys and a field before settling on a final resting place for the van. He cruised past the entrance to the farmyard twice before plucking up the courage to enter. The yard looked abandoned. The barn was partially derelict and the farmhouse windows were all boarded up.

The van jolted and lurched to one side. Daniel's head knocked against the window. He grunted and pushed at the accelerator again. The van remained in place, seesawing from side to side with the momentum of the spinning tyres.

He dropped out of the cabin, and his trainers sank into soft mud. The rear tip of the vehicle still protruded into the road. As he knelt down, muck transferred to his legs.

He groaned. The rear axle of the van had become lodged on a thick, mud-covered branch. The back-right wheel no longer touched the ground; the left pressed only against the branch itself. He steadied himself with his hands to kick awkwardly at the branch, but it held fast. Back in the driver's seat, he gunned the engine but the van only creaked and juddered.

He put his head in his filthy hands.

At a sharp sound he whirled around to see a spectacled face peering through the window, hand raised mid-tap. "Need any help?"

Shaking, Daniel wound down the window. His voice came out as a dry croak. "I got stuck. Just need a shove, I think."

The man laughed. He wore a tartan cap over thin blonde hair, a fashion choice at odds with his youth. He rummaged in a pocket and fished out a pair of gloves.

Daniel gulped with relief when the stranger disappeared from the window. The van resettled slightly as he felt weight placed against the rear doors.

"All right, knock yourself out!" the reedy voice shouted. It was only now that Daniel recognised that the accent wasn't British. Australian, perhaps. A tourist. The stranger probably had no ties to the local community.

The van broke free with a crunch. With difficulty— the axle must have been badly damaged—he steered the van to come to rest beside the barn. The blonde stranger still stood at the gateway, hands on hips. Daniel waved to dismiss him. The man waited for a moment as if expecting Daniel to approach. Then, with a shrug, he turned to make his way over a stile and into the neighbouring field.

Once he was certain that he was alone, Daniel used the chisel to prise away the registration plates. He placed them and the chisel itself into the holdall, which already contained a bulky CCTV hard drive, the phone and SIM card, and the black peaked cap he had worn at the lab. The interior of the van contained no trace of the time machine, only dust. He turned his attention to the driver's cabin, stuffing the contents of the glove compartment into the holdall. At least the van was decrepit enough that there was unlikely to be any tracking technology on board. The woman at the hire company had wrinkled her nose in apology as she had presented the vehicle to him. When he failed to return it in a week's time, it was difficult to imagine them launching a nationwide search. The traffic camera was another matter, but the police could only send fines and threatening letters to his old, abandoned address.

He locked the van and shouldered the holdall. At the gateway to the farmyard he watched the blonde man continue to pick his way slowly across the field.

He thought of the chisel in the holdall. There was only one certain way of ensuring that the man wouldn't present a threat. A single blow with the chisel might do it. Was it a necessary precaution?

He shook his head, hesitated, then shook it again.

~

The sun had dipped down towards the fell by the time Daniel reached the road to the village. *Broughton-in-Furness*, the sign read. *Welcome, any time.*

Mud caked his boots, leaving a dark trail and making each step awkward. He had buried the registration plates, hard drive, phone and cap in four separate holes in different fields. His right hand stung where his cuts had reopened. He had been a fool for bringing no digging tool other than the chisel.

The route to the Manor wound between a smattering of houses at the outskirts of the village. Children played in a garden beside the track, five of them surrounding one in the centre, all singing. *The farmer's in his den, The farmer's in his den, Ee-I-Addio, The farmer's in his den. The farmer wants a wife...*

The path emerged into a wide, grassy space. Daniel stood, disoriented, in the shadow of the fell. The cloud shadows shifted, producing a rippling effect on the fellside that matched the floaters dancing at the edges of his vision. He walked along the length of the golf course. A dense, circular copse located between two of the fairways reminded him of the slatted tube of the time machine. The afternoon light through the trees produced a strobing effect as he passed. The right side of his face warmed and chilled, warmed and chilled.

Beyond the copse the Manor reappeared, framed by the tall iron archway. When it had still operated as a hotel, smoke would have poured from the chimneystacks, reminding golfers of the roast dinners that awaited them, the barman ready with jokes about the nineteenth hole. It was a grand building, and even Daniel could see the shame in its uncertain future. Presumably, when Florence's father died, the Harrigans would inherit the place and sell it on. Until then it would remain a shell. A box filled with other people's memories.

The beauty of Cumbria as a hiding place had been its openness, its blank, pointless surplus of space. The same applied to the Manor itself. By occupying only a tiny portion of the huge building, its emptiness ought to have provided a buffer. But the Manor was already occupied. Watched.

He approached the sand pit that Tosh was busily raking. He trod heavily in the hope of alerting the gardener without having to call his name. The old fool must be deaf. Daniel was nearly upon him when Tosh raised his head to watch him with a level gaze.

Daniel floundered under the scrutiny. "Looks like it'll be another nice one."

Tosh glanced up to the sky, then met his eyes again. He bounced the handle of the rake lightly between his hands. Daniel saw malice in the dark crease between his eyebrows. He wished that he had the stamina to force Tosh to be the one to break the silence.

"I'm an awful golfer, I'm afraid," Daniel said.

Tosh nodded.

"But even so, it's wonderful to see these bunkers so neat. Shipshape. Until some clot like me comes along and hacks holes in them!" He sounded like Harrigan, a fool. "Must make you livid," he concluded in a weak voice.

The gardener sighed. "It's my job. That's all."

"Well. Yes. And I salute you for it." Daniel considered actually doing so, just to fill time. His hairline prickled. Get to the point, then get out.

"Tosh. There's something I wanted to speak to you about."

Tosh said nothing.

"It's very important that I work quietly while I'm here. And alone. I don't mean to accuse you of anything—"

"All right then." Tosh cleared his throat.

Daniel hesitated. "No, but what I mean is, I hadn't realised that you'd be here quite so much."

"Seven days a week," Tosh said. Was that a sly smile? "No rest for the wicked."

"Exactly," Daniel said. "Look, I'll ask you a blunt question. Do you have a key to the main house?"

Tosh folded his arms and balanced them upon the tip of the rake. He chewed his lip for what felt like minutes before answering. "Just the garage and the leisure centre."

Daniel tried to picture the layout of the Manor. Both the kitchen door and the glass door to the leisure centre reception had locks. He could still make the main part of the Manor secure, if he just kept the doors to the other areas locked tight. He tried to read the gardener's expression. Was there any reason to think that he might be lying?

"Okay," he said, unable to mask the relief in his voice. "Good. I mean, thanks. What's most important is that I'm undisturbed."

Tosh chewed on something, waiting for him to speak again. Daniel tried to resist the temptation to over-explain. There could be no benefit in returning to his flimsy story of photography sessions.

The gardener cleared his throat. He produced a grimy handkerchief from his breast pocket and spat into its centre, then folded the linen carefully into quarters before replacing it. "Undisturbed. I see. Hope the peacocks ain't too loud for you, then?"

Daniel saw a glint of malevolence in the gardener's eyes. He took a step back.

"They're fine. I won't be taking any more pictures of wildlife, I shouldn't think. Just landscapes and skyscapes for me, from now on." He grimaced, realising that he was gabbling. "What I'm trying to say is this. Do you think you could make sure nobody comes calling? It's so peaceful around here, and I've no taste for visitors."

Tosh regarded him for a few seconds.

"I'm not your butler," he said.

Swinging the rake, the gardener strolled down the slope towards the garage. Daniel waited until he reappeared at the corner of the Manor. Tosh glanced in his direction, then set off along the driveway. His posture appeared straighter and his pace quicker, now that he was off duty.

Daniel exhaled with relief and set off towards the house.

After a few paces, he froze. The sun had dropped below the treeline, but enough light remained for him to make out the front of the building. He saw a dark shape against the window of the study that contained plastic-covered furniture. No, not just a shape. A person. He glanced along the driveway, where Tosh remained visible for a second before disappearing at the road junction.

His pulse quickened. At first it looked as though the figure might be inside Benfield's study but, as he squinted to see better, he saw one limb still visible against the outer wall. It reminded him of something from his past. When he and his twin brother had been young the family had once holidayed in the north of France, hiring a draughty gîte. He and William had clambered in and out of the

57

shuttered windows that reached almost to the ground, using them like doors. They had both been fascinated by the bronze shutter latches. Each one had been a different, tiny, caricature of a man.

The shape moved towards the door. Measured against the doorway it seemed small, childlike. It hovered there, just as Daniel hovered uncertainly beside the copse.

Don't jump to conclusions. Don't let your nightmares take over.

He crept towards the building, skidding on the sloped fairway. He kept his gaze fixed on the dark shape at the door of the Manor. His fingers curled around the iron archway for balance as he forced himself to tread carefully on the tarmac. The shape didn't move. Ignoring the tight knot in his stomach, he tiptoed closer.

He was no more than ten feet from the door when the security lamp, an ornate Victorian-style lamppost on the opposite side of the forecourt, lit. He gasped but didn't turn to look at the lamp. Instead, he stared at the front door.

The doorstep was empty.

But his fear remained. He stayed rooted to the spot, feeling the veins in his arms pulse. After precisely a minute the lamp flicked off again. The dark, human-sized patch reappeared on the door. It swayed very slightly. It must be a shadow of some outcrop of trees, a trick of the fading light.

He turned. The lamp lit again.

He clucked his tongue against his teeth and re-entered the Manor.

~

Only thin knives of daylight snuck in at the edges of the closed curtains. Swarms of dust motes danced in the vertical strips. Daniel flicked on the upturned wall lamps behind the panels of the time machine. The panels absorbed the yellow light without reflection, remaining pale grey with no variation of tone across their surfaces.

In his hand he held a peacock quill that he had found in the lobby. It was undamaged. Unharmed.

There were all sorts of reasons why the time machine might not have worked. All sorts of reasons why a mouse or a peacock wouldn't do. And hadn't he heard the machine hum, showing that it was operational?

So.

The lab scientists had had time on their side. No doubt, their approach to testing the machine was methodical and exhaustive. William would have taken a similar approach.

But the time machine now belonged to Daniel alone. And he possessed something else, an attribute that none of the others had. Impulsiveness.

This was the way that people changed the world. By taking a risk. By taking yourself by surprise. A quick push into a wasp's nest, and hang the consequences.

Even so, the time machine's gravitational influence fluctuated. He bobbed in its orbit. He turned to leave the room, pulled at his hair with both hands, then spun on his heel again.

His fingers were thick and heavy as he fumbled with the catch of the slatted tube. It felt as though his body was being controlled by some clumsy, remote operator. He found himself crouching within the curved walls of the tube. There was just enough room for him to lower himself to sit cross-legged. The panels that surrounded him now seemed impossibly tall. They curved like satellite dishes, focussing on his position. In his hand he held the plastic trigger handle, still attached by its cable to the base of the slatted tube. He turned it in the palm of his hand.

Minutes passed. He stared at the handle. His fingers seemed unwilling to curl into its contoured trigger.

Wait. Think. Wait.

If it did work—and despite the tenuousness of that 'if', it still warranted consideration—wouldn't the plastic trigger be stuck in a closed position? Mightn't he be unable to pull it out again, whilst in the grip of the machine?

He clambered out again, accepting the delay with relief. He unplugged the trigger cable from the base of the unit.

In the kitchen he ransacked drawers. Finally, he pulled out an oversized, green potato masher made of two pieces of moulded plastic and a metal stem with a tough spring. He couldn't prise it apart with his fingers. After a minute of fumbling, he entered the garage and returned with a hammer. Soon the potato masher lay in pieces on the kitchen counter. He flexed the freed, thumb-sized spring between his fingers.

The spring fit perfectly into the space between the trigger and the hollow slot in the plastic handle. Now, even with great effort, he found it difficult to maintain the pressure to hold the trigger down for more than a few seconds before it flicked back to its open position.

So there were no more obstacles. He submitted to the gravitational pull of the time machine.

After reconnecting the handle to the black base, he sat cross-legged within the slatted tube. Sweat prickled in his palms.

He waited for nothing and nobody. He gazed at the contraption in his hand. Looking without thinking.

When he had been a student at university he had struggled to wake for lectures, with no mother to force him out of bed. A member of his study group had given him a tip: to simply tell himself that he would continue sleeping, and to enjoy the sense of indulgent comfort. Then, just as he was on the cusp of slipping into a doze, he would leap out of bed. The more he had tried it, the better it worked. His body could be given a headstart on his mind, as if they were unconnected. The trick was simply not to think directly about what the body was about to do.

So.

He tapped the trigger, little more than a graze of the fingers. The pressure of the spring popped it out again immediately.

His ears popped. His stomach growled.

He blinked rapidly and looked towards the slivers of light at the curtained windows where the dust danced. For a brief moment, he had sensed brightness, but it hadn't seemed to come from that direction, or any direction in particular.

Had anything actually happened? The effects might easily have been a trick of mind. Or had the machine worked to some degree but, like the mouse and peacock, had he been unaffected?

He leapt up, expecting disorientation but finding none. He felt healthy and alert. Outside the ring of panels, he performed a couple of clumsy star-jumps, as if that might prove something. But he felt absolutely normal, other than the first rumblings of hunger.

He snorted with laughter. He had ignored one vital element. In adulthood, he'd never taken to wearing a watch. What time had it been when he'd finally pressed the trigger, anyway? He giggled. He was hardly the image of a time-traveller.

Shaking his head in disbelief, he opened the lounge door. Benfield's grandfather clock stood directly opposite, at the foot of the staircase. Once he had propped open the lounge door with one end of the single remaining sofa, he could see the clock from the centre of the time machine.

He ought to wait before testing again, of course. A real scientist would take time to observe the results. Detailed notes were required, control experiments and double-blinds.

He allowed his body to drift from room to room, standing before each window to stare out over the grounds and fell.

But the time machine pulled at him and his body returned to it. On an impulse, he pulled open the lounge curtains. The low sun made an orange halo just above the trees.

Cross-legged within the slatted tube, he kept his eyes fixed on the grandfather clock in the lobby. It was two forty-three in the afternoon.

He tapped the trigger with the same amount of pressure as before. The compressed spring pushed back against his grip.

The time machine hummed. The tone was so low as to be almost inaudible, like a cat's contented rumble.

The panels seemed to highlight in turn. This produced a sense of motion that became more and more pronounced until he could no longer identify which panel flashed. The effect became dizzying, as if he were spinning at the centre of a vortex, whilst not moving at all. He felt both weightless and hopelessly, heavily inert at once. His breathing quickened, or stopped.

In an instant, a hollow complaint in his stomach became a heavy churning.

He watched as the brightness-but-not-brightness, aura-but-not-aura, transferred from panel to panel, slowing like a giant zoetrope or roulette wheel. He imagined himself as the roulette ball and half-expected to ricochet outwards to come to rest against one of the panels.

Then the panels became uniformly grey once more.

His ears popped. His stomach growled.

A strobing light filled his vision. He thought of blindness and tumours. He had experienced this sensation before, having suffered from occasional migraines since childhood. Back then he had been terrified of the episodes, never once telling his parents. When the migraines began he simply retreated to his bedroom. The first episode had hit him during a school day, when he was aged nine or ten, and he had expected the tunnel vision to creep in further and further until it absorbed him and he would die. In later years he had lashed out at the people around him without explaining the cause of his panic. William had taken the brunt of his rage. As always.

He leant to one side and his vision cleared. Orange light from the window now illuminated the wall behind him, a bright patch where his head had been. Within a few more seconds, the sun dropped totally behind the treeline and the room darkened.

The grandfather clock confirmed that four minutes had passed in what had seemed only moments. But that was nothing compared to the experience of seeing the sun jump in the sky.

FOUR

It was the voice that woke Daniel, rather than the calls of the peacocks.

He lay rigid in bed, holding his breath. He had slept badly, dreaming of William, his body twisted. All limbs as he fell forwards and away.

The voice was little more than a murmur. It came from outside the window.

He found that his arms had gathered around his knees. Protecting himself rather than William.

"Ain't done this to yourself, have you?" the voice said, from somewhere far away.

Daniel roused himself. His feet thudded onto the floor. He edged to the window to pull aside the curtain, then winced at a pain in his hand. The cut in his right palm had reopened. Elastic, gluey pus pulled tight as he flexed it.

Below the window, a ghost crouched in the shadow of the monkey puzzle.

Cold crept from the pane and along Daniel's arm. He squeezed his eyes tight, shook his head, and reopened them. Please let him be gone.

The ghost remained. It shifted and moved partially out of the shadows. Daniel exhaled gratefully.

Tosh.

But his relief was short-lived. Now he saw that the gardener was bending low over one of the peacocks. The bird lay on its side with its neck curled awkwardly, like a question mark with a fat dot.

It looked dead.

He struggled to locate the exact horror of this fact. The eyes of the peacock's tail feathers were hidden from view. He wasn't sure that he could bear being the object of their gaze again.

If it was dead, it was the time machine that had killed it.

And Daniel had used the machine himself, only hours later.

Tosh shifted on his haunches, working his way around the peacock's body. He cradled the bird's limply hanging head while his free hand worked over its indigo flank, patting and pushing.

Daniel bunched the curtains in his fist. For the first time, he realised that he could hear, faintly, the ticking of Benfield's clock from downstairs. It sounded almost like padding footsteps.

He leant forwards so that his forehead touched the cold glass of the window. With an agility surprising for his age, Tosh dropped again to a crouched position. His hands scoured the gravelled path. He turned to the monkey puzzle and placed both hands on its trunk. The great tree shook as he pressed against it with his full weight. Perhaps he supposed that something had fallen and hit the peacock. He gazed up into the branches then stood back, rubbing his chin.

Then Tosh scooped the peacock into his arms and plodded along the gravel path towards the garage. After a few steps he paused.

Daniel let the curtain drop again as the gardener turned to look up at his bedroom window.

~

He didn't dare leave the Manor until Tosh had disappeared over the horizon. He clung to the stonework like a shadow as he made his way to the rear of the building.

Two peacocks shuffled backwards under the shelter of the monkey puzzle as he crunched along the gravel path. Daniel squinted into the shade. How could anybody tell them apart? The tail feathers of one of the birds appeared thicker than the other, but he struggled to remember any particular details about the one he had used in his tests.

Another peacock strutted in the sunlight refracted through the windows of the leisure centre. It pecked at the ground, then raised its head to regard Daniel. Proud and indignant. Was this the one? Perhaps it remembered him with distaste. But it seemed healthy enough, that was the main thing.

The bird opened its beak and emitted a shrill shriek. A mating call, perhaps. Daniel frowned. All these birds, with plumages equally stunning, were male. Where were the females? The peacock called again. Daniel fought the impulse to rush forwards and kick or spit at it. Any louder and it might attract Tosh's attention.

He heard a faint, low hiss, as if in response to the call. He edged towards the source of the sound. A row of bushes separated a small lawn from the golf holes beyond. Something within shuddered. Daniel thought of William, struggling to free himself.

Whatever was in the bushes hissed again, a low, fluctuating sound like the drone of wasps. He crept forwards and pulled aside a branch.

A fourth peacock lay on its side on the ground. Its flank shuddered and its claws scrabbled into the loose soil as if trying to find purchase.

"Oh God," Daniel heard himself say. His voice sounded distant and not his own.

The bird pushed at the ground again. Despite its efforts the long neck lay coiled on the soil. One side of its head pushed into a hollow as if it were too heavy to lift.

"Get up," Daniel said. "Please get up."

He shook the branch, producing a ripple that spread through the leaves. The bird's uppermost eye moved sluggishly to follow the motion. When it came again, the hiss sounded more like the mewling of a cat. The peacock's claws pushed at the ground in a frenzy, sending up a rain of dry soil. Finally, it raised itself upright. Its head still hung down, swaying like a loose pendulum.

The bird froze. It looked like a product of expert taxidermy. Then it shivered, its tail feathers thumping dully on the soil. It slumped once again to the ground.

The time machine had all but destroyed it. And it would destroy Daniel too.

His head felt heavy, his neck barely strong enough to hold it upright.

~

Beneath the plastic sheet in Benfield's study, he discovered an ancient beige computer and an old rotary phone pushed to one corner of the desk. He lifted the receiver to hear the dial tone, then replaced it. He mustn't call for an ambulance until he was certain it was necessary.

The hiss of the injured bird echoed in his ears. What had the time machine done to it, exactly? More importantly, how long did he have before the same thing struck him? He tried to remember how many hours he had spent getting rid of the van yesterday. It was now late morning, several hours after he had first seen Tosh tend to the peacock below his bedroom window.

The plastic wrappers sputtered in the breeze from the open window.

Would he feel anything when it came? Would he be pushed to the ground, like the peacock?

And was he just going to let it happen?

No.

A thought, familiar from years past, pushed into his mind. *Where can I get a gun?*

Benfield might have one stashed away. In the countryside, everyone had a gun, probably.

Of the three desk drawers, two were locked. The upper drawer contained pens, rulers and a pair of compasses alongside a battered, cloth-covered folder. Already forgetting about the gun, Daniel lifted the folder out and flicked through its contents. A spidery shorthand filled sheets of paper. Diagrams too, abstract and mathematical, mandalas of data plotted on unlabelled axes. Hadn't Florence said her father had been a historian? Despite the contents of the folder being illegible in coded scrawl, the level of expertise and hard work was clear to see. Some people were prepared to put in the hours rather than taking short cuts.

He leafed through the pages blindly, lost in his own thoughts. William had been the hard worker of the family and, as a child, had teased Daniel about his impatience. Although not identical twins, their roughly similar appearance made criticism doubly hurtful, as though coming from within himself. In response, Daniel had smashed William's Lego creations, copied his research for school projects, or worse.

He dropped the open folder back onto the desk. Dimly, he realised that some of the text on the page laid out before him was legible. Dark, oblique handwriting cut across the faint shorthand underneath.

NO! No good. No time.

He flicked through the papers again, but the short phrase was the only text that he could understand. He pushed the folder back into the drawer. Benfield must have been some kind of obsessive, lost in his research. Wartime secrets and conspiracy theories, no doubt. The Enigma code. Nothing that concerned Daniel.

The past was the past. People formed their own futures. Experience maketh the man.

He returned the folder to the drawer. What did his own future hold, now? How many hours did he have left?

The waiting was the worst part of it. He had always hated suspense. He remembered another time, another enforced wait. He remembered dialling and redialling a phone number, with no answer.

The view caught his attention as he reached over the desk to pull the window shut. It was easy to see why Benfield had chosen this room. A gap in the trees opposite seemed designed to allow a view through the foliage to the pale hump of the fell beyond. What had Florence called it? The Old Man. The *other* old man.

~

He succumbed to the instinct to flee.

Onwards and upwards.

The world around him failed to acknowledge the urgency. A tractor spluttered ahead of the bus, its driver refusing to pull into any of the few passing places. Daniel massaged his forehead. A migraine, or worse? Either way, it made the journey even less bearable. Already, the decision to climb the Old Man seemed rash. He was wasting his remaining hours, in the same way that he had wasted most of his adult life.

The roadside trees thinned to become sparse woodland, then disappeared entirely as Coniston Water came into view. Its vast grey expanse absorbed the sunlight that filtered through the low clouds. Daniel thought of the grey panels of the time machine. He heard the machine's soft hum within the Manor, miles away.

As he embarked, the bus driver handed him a folded timetable and warned him that return journeys left every two hours and didn't run after dark. Not that the timings mattered. If he made a return journey at all, that would be enough.

A queue of cars bearing canoes turned at a crossroads, following a road signposted 'boat landings', past a row of houses clad in slate matching the colour of the clouds overhead. Beyond a BP garage, pedestrians approached a white-painted pub. Daniel thought of families crowding the bar lounge, demanding Sunday roasts before their weekly hike. If indeed it was Sunday. The days had begun to merge.

A steep, narrow road formed the opposite limb of the crossroads. As Daniel set off and left the residential properties behind, the butterscotch-coloured lumps of the Old Man of Coniston rose into view. The road wound in tight turns, with tributary lanes peeling away to deliver tourists to car parks. It narrowed and became corridored by scrub, then bare grassland. The shadows on the Old Man shifted and undulated.

He was struggling for breath by the time he reached a concrete area that contained two unoccupied cars. Panting, he leant against the bonnet of a blue Mini. Had the peacock become weak, too, before it finally collapsed?

The fell now looked more blunt, its peak reduced to a nubbin above the crooked skyline. From Coniston village it had appeared as a substantial climbing challenge. Now the Old Man was less a sleeping giant than a low hump barely distinguishable from the surrounding fells.

Nevertheless, Daniel's mind cleared a little as he set off along the trail leading towards the eastern side of the fell. The air tasted tangily fresh and became even more chill as he began to ascend the fell. The cagoule he had discovered in the Manor's garage billowed out with the wind from behind, like a kite being drawn upwards. Despite the cloud shadows visible on the slopes ahead, it was difficult to judge whether he stood in a dark or light patch. Things lost focus, up close.

As he climbed, he kept his mind resolutely blank. His body trudged onwards, while he simply watched. He marvelled at how many of his physical processes were automatic.

A teetering cairn marked the apex of the fell. The lake, visible for the first time since he had set off, coiled around the village below. Its dark mirror reflected ghosts of the clouds above.

With one hand resting on the top of the cairn, he walked its perimeter, trying to orient himself. To the southwest he saw the thin smear of the Irish Sea, with the Isle of Man little more than a fingernail speck. He traced the route towards Broughton-in-Furness. Beyond a sparse collection of houses, he identified the green splash of the Manor's grounds. The building itself was all but hidden, a fat ghost visible only in part through the clumps of foliage. Daniel squinted at a shifting dot to the left of the copse on the fairway. A golfer? He bit his lip, thinking of the time machine, vulnerable inside the building. There were countless numbers of people between him and it. He watched the dot flit against the green for a few minutes, but then lost track as it moved behind or within the copse.

He waited. He slumped against the side of the cairn, facing the Manor. Gusts of wind whipped through his cagoule. Overhead, the wings of a kestrel produced a heavy, skidding sound. Its snub head ducked and disappeared behind its feathered cape. Perhaps it had spotted a potential kill, something darting for cover on the blank fellside.

He waited. The shadows that slipped over the fell marked the passing time. A phrase repeated in his thoughts, an echo from the past: *You have to promise it's the end.*

Anybody possessing the knowledge that they will die that same day might expect their last hours to seem momentous, or even tragic. But some things just stop.

He waited.

Other than queasy anxiety, he felt fine. He wished that he had thought to bring sandwiches.

Perhaps he was different.

The shadows lengthened. It must be late afternoon. If he was due to be struck in the same manner as the peacock, it ought to have happened by now.

The wind's chill had lessened. With each minute that passed, he felt more confidence that he might survive. He replayed the events of the day before in his mind. All this fear had blinded him to the fact that he had participated in something world-changing.

He must think like a scientist. Concentrate on the facts. Either he had travelled forwards in time by four minutes, or time had travelled forwards faster than it ought. The latter seemed grossly self-centred, as if he, Daniel Faint, sat at the apex of time in the same way that he now rested at the apex of the Old Man. Was it possible that beneath him, rather than fells and lakes, minutes, hours and days passed while he remained immune? No. He had been the one inside the machine. The machine had worked its spell on him, its panels focused only on Daniel Faint, not on the world outside. He had entered the time machine, squeezed the trigger, and skipped forwards in time by more than four minutes.

Why didn't that feel nearly as astounding as it ought? Granted, arriving four minutes in the future earlier than scheduled was hardly the stuff of science-fiction blockbusters. But even so, it had worked. It really had worked. His obsession with the time machine had been vindicated.

He thought of the time machine's gravitational pull and its hum as he pressed its trigger. It had felt like a welcome. It was as if the time machine had chosen him as much as he had chosen it. Already it seemed strange to think that it had belonged to others before him. A team of scientists had built it—over how many years?—hidden in their nondescript building in a featureless Oxfordshire industrial estate. It seemed only reasonable to assume that he hadn't been the first to let himself be the test subject. He wished he could meet them, these people who had experienced what he had experienced. A round of pints in the pub below the Old Man. Pioneers comparing memories of the spinning, sickly sensation as the panels of the time machine swung into life.

Except that could never happen. He was a fugitive. Those same scientists, if they had an inkling who he was, would despise him. There could be no going back.

This thought filled him with fatigue. For years, he had attempted to escape his past by being constantly on the move. In the last few days he had added genuine pursuers to his imagined ones. But now, using the time machine, he really could escape. Why shouldn't he leave everything behind, once and for all? Even if he kept moving from place to place, there would always be a risk of being traced. Scooting decades forwards in time would allow him to hide totally.

But what about the time machine? It had remained, while the clay figurines had disappeared. If he sent himself into the future, to a time when the machine might have been removed from the Manor, he would be trapped there. It would be a one-way ticket.

Relief mingled with disappointment as he realised that he had already discounted the idea. He knew himself well enough. He was a coward, not a true pioneer.

So. If the machine wouldn't allow him to travel back in time, and he wasn't prepared to risk sending himself far into the future, what remained?

Only one thing. Money.

There must be others who wouldn't suffer the same qualms as him. People who would pay to use the machine. People fascinated with the possibilities, or with little to lose. People with diseases that were currently incurable, who would do anything to travel ahead to an era when they might be treated. People who needed to escape the present.

The plan, and the future, became clear. He would use the time machine to accumulate wealth.

But he mustn't get carried away. This new idea didn't change the situation. So far, he had only proved that he could send a human subject a few minutes into the future. It was an irrelevance, a rounding error.

Two challenges remained. Firstly, he had to achieve greater ranges of time travel, with jumps of hours and days indicating the possibility of years and decades. Secondly, he must find a way of predicting in advance the scale of each jump, at least roughly.

He pushed against the cairn and set off, downwards.

~

His body felt looser and lighter. He was alive. He had cheated whatever fate had befallen the peacock. The time machine had spared him.

He took a different path down the fell, picking his way carefully on loose gravel. The path wound north, then declined towards a shale quarry nestled between two rust-orange hillocks. A yellow JCB indicated that the quarry was still in use. Two men in hard hats surveyed the hole, appearing tiny beside the vehicle. One man's hand rested on the digger as though displaying an owner's pride. Daniel slowed his pace to a creep. First one, then both of the yellow-hatted men turned. The taller man raised an arm.

Daniel froze. Was it a warning of some nearby danger? But the waving man didn't appear alarmed. He turned to his neighbour to make a comment, then turned back again. Now Daniel saw the man's wide smile.

An instinct told him that, in fact, the wave was not directed at him. He heard a noise from behind and spun around to see somebody skittering slowly downwards along the same route he had taken. The person alternated between skeletal and bulbous as its coat billowed in the wind.

The wind whipped across Daniel's cheeks. He remembered William, wearing Daniel's own jacket, heading out into the night instead of him. An instinct told him to hide.

He was trapped between the descending figure and the waiting JCB workers. He looked from side to side. To his left a clump of rock had fallen away, probably many years ago, to reveal the strata beneath. Daniel abandoned the main path, taking long strides to avoid slipping on the wet grass. The folds of rock strata appeared to slide from horizontal to vertical as he passed, as though in slow fluid motion, like geological time travel. Where the strata became vertical, a dark cleft split the rock.

He peered into the hole. He glanced back at the yellow-hatted men who still faced upwards along the path, then stepped into the opening. He expected to find only a shallow hollow in the rock, but once inside it was impossible to see a rear wall. He waited for his eyes to adjust to the darkness.

The cave walls glowed faintly orange, reflecting the little sunlight that entered. He edged forwards with one hand trailing the smooth, cold surface. The walls opened into a wide, bowl-shaped space. Bottles and empty cans littered the side of the cave most sheltered from the wind that rushed in from the corridor.

Flush against the rear wall, a wide stone slab stood at waist height. Piles of stones, like small copies of the cairn at the summit of the fell, had been arranged upon it. Beside these piles was a larger rock with smooth, almost sculpted, surfaces. Daniel kept his distance, trying to make out its details. He saw the rock as a man, bent double with his face buried behind one bare bent leg. It stared down at the slab like Dali's Narcissus gazing into a pool.

"That's not an altar, if that's what you're thinking."

Daniel whirled around. A thin figure stood in the opening of the cave. He shielded his eyes with a hand. As the stranger moved into the cave, he saw that it was a woman. She wore a pink storm jacket. Her tightened hood revealed wild, loose strands of fair hair. Her booted feet appeared comically large.

She shone a small torch around the cave, settling its beam on the stone slab. "People—kids, I suppose I mean—always think it's an altar. It's a hotspot for wakes, that sort of thing. Whenever there's a hit-and-run or overdose this place is packed to the rafters."

Daniel found that his throat had become clogged. He spluttered incoherently. The woman shone the torch directly at him and he recoiled from the light.

"You all right?" she said. "It looked like you were having some trouble making your way down the fell."

"No," he said, frowning. He had felt light and free on the slope. "I was just taking my time."

"Seems to me that once people reach the peak, they most often can't wait to get down again. The Old Man promises plenty, but in the end he's just a slightly bigger lump amongst all the other lumps."

Daniel watched her carefully, trying to determine whether she might be a threat. Yesterday he would have avoided speaking to her entirely, but after seeing the injured peacock he had expected to be dead by the end of the day and now here he was, alive. The woman wasn't unattractive, either, despite her matted hair that showed signs of repeated bleaching. *The farmer wants a wife.*

"Let me guess," the woman said. "One, this is your first time visiting Coniston. Two, you wish you'd bought boots with better soles. Three, you thought you'd take some excellent photos from up here, but you didn't even get out your camera. And four, you'd rather be in the pub."

"Close enough," Daniel said. He smiled. "Except I didn't even bring a camera."

The woman grinned. Incredibly, his banter appeared to be working. His last serious relationship, with Lorna, had been more than six years ago. Since then he had pursued few women. No longer being able visit Lorna or her son contributed to the guilt that he carried. The whole relationship had been messy and unnecessary. This woman, on the other hand, would never see him again.

He flinched as the torch shone into his eyes.

The woman said, "Hey! Don't I know you?"

"No, you don't."

"I've seen you walking through the village. The other village, Broughton. You're the house-sitter at the Manor."

Daniel stumbled back against the stone slab. In the torchlight he saw that the large, smooth rock was nothing like a man, after all. "Have you been following me?"

She laughed. "Why, would it be worth my while? I've seen you around, that's all. And it's a small place, you know. People stand out."

He glared at her. One brief pass through Broughton, and he had somehow become a local figure. He had been an idiot to imagine that he might remain incognito in a place like this.

The woman huffed and turned back to the opening. "Look, if you've come to bury treasure, or wank over a creepy stone altar, that's your business. I'll leave you to it."

Daniel lurched forwards to put a hand on her shoulder. His flesh looked gangrenous against the vivid pink of her coat. She didn't flinch.

"You surprised me, that's all," he said.

She shrugged his hand away but then turned at the cave opening. Her body made a cats-eye pupil against the light. "Fair enough. I'm heading back down. Are you coming with?"

He shook his head. Lesson learnt. He couldn't allow himself to become close to anybody who lived so close to his new home. What was the phrase? Don't shit where you eat. She seemed like a talker, too. "I'll slow you down. I'll be hanging around up here for a while longer."

Her head cocked. "Suit yourself. Maybe I'll see you in the Cradle some night? The pub on the square, I mean. I'm there all the time."

Daniel stopped himself from speaking, from making a commitment.

The woman left to become absorbed by the flare of daylight.

He waited several minutes before emerging from the cave. The woman must be a quick walker; she had already reached the JCB at the edge of the quarry. One of the men turned as she passed. Even from here, Daniel could see the foolish expression on his face. The man's hard-hatted companion thumped him on the chest and said something to the woman. She chatted to them briefly as she walked backwards down the path for a few steps, apparently unflustered by their attention.

Daniel nodded at the JCB men as he passed. One of them responded with a grunt. He felt their eyes on him as he continued along the path.

The woman slipped away ahead, skipping effortlessly, whereas his own feet caught repeatedly on the uneven rocks. He forced himself to breathe more slowly. She was no threat. Nobody in a jacket that pink could have sinister intentions.

When she reached the foot of the hill she crossed the concrete to the only remaining car, a navy-blue Mini. She swung herself into the driver's seat.

Daniel ducked down. Cold crept up his thighs from the damp grass.

A minute passed and the Mini hadn't moved. An arm emerged from the open window and swung high and wide, beckoning.

He sank lower to the ground. His haunches ached.

The hand swivelled and the beckoning motion became a farewell wave. At this distance, the engine of the Mini sounded like a wasp's buzz. The car pulled away and slipped into the corridor of trees that led towards the village.

On autopilot, Daniel's body delivered him safely the rest of the way to Coniston village. Despite his misgivings about the pub, he bought a pint of Bluebird and drank it standing at the bar. His feet throbbed from the effort of slowing his descent.

The bus arrived twenty minutes late, by which time the drizzle had turned to a downpour.

~

Back at the Manor, Daniel braved the rain to prowl the grounds. He counted four peacocks. All appeared healthy. There could be no way of determining which was the bird that Tosh had found injured or whether it was the same he had tested upon.

But he was alive. That was all the proof that he needed.

So. No excuses.

In the lounge he examined the trigger mechanism. If only the cable wasn't moulded to the handle, he might stand a chance of replacing the mechanism with something more precise. A dial, a computer-controlled plunger, anything. The snapped part of the handle clicked in his palm. He wrapped the duct tape tighter.

How far had he pushed the trigger during his first tests with the statues? Only a fraction, a few millimetres at most. With the cable disconnected from the base of the time machine, he applied light pressure to the trigger. At its full extent, it could be closed by around four centimetres. Possibly the squeeze pressure acted as a multiplier. If a few millimetres sent the subject forwards in time by a minute or so, what would that make the maximum jump? An hour per centimetre, perhaps. So four hours, tops.

But the ability to jump into the future by four hours was worthless. It represented only time lost, rather than anything gained. The question was whether the time machine had a practical upper limit, or whether it was only the trigger that caused a restriction.

He selected a clay figurine from Florence's workshop and set to work.

The time machine hummed happily. Its panels flickered with warmth as it received its new subject.

When the figurine disappeared, Daniel marked the squeezed distance on the trigger handle with the point of a pair of compasses taken from Benfield's desk drawer. The spring he had fixed behind the trigger pushed it back to an open position. The statue reappeared a minute and fifteen seconds later. Daniel scratched numbers above the line on the handle.

He squeezed the trigger to twice the extent, then marked the handle and watched the clock. He rapped his fingernails on the plastic handle. One problem with time travel was all the waiting involved, if you weren't the one travelling. He collected another two figurines from Florence's workshop. The first was a squat lump with eyes on both the front and back of its head. The other was more human in shape, with legs that seemed too spindly to hold the weight of its belly. He placed one into the slatted tube and squeezed the trigger, just moments before the previous test subject rematerialised.

An hour later, he sat at Benfield's desk, transcribing the marks on the trigger handle to a sheet of graph paper. Five millimetres equalled seventy-five seconds. A centimetre equalled ninety seconds, give or take. He tried to recall lessons from school. Two points of data meant nothing, but three could show a relationship. Label the axes. Science in action. His old teacher, Mr Madden, would be proud of him. Proud of his pupil, and giddy with amazement at the experiment.

One and a half centimetres equalled...

He marked the point on the graph. Two minutes and five seconds.

He traced a faint line between the points. His heart rate accelerated to become twice as fast than the ticking of the grandfather clock.

How would Mr Madden have phrased it?

The relationship between trigger squeeze and time travelled was exponential.

The third statue hadn't yet returned. He had pressed the trigger three whole centimetres. Daniel looked at the line he had drawn, which veered sharply upwards.

The statue would return in roughly five and a half hours.

His palms became clammy as he scribbled calculations at the margin of the graph. He looked again and again at the graph line, which reached a near-vertical angle at the edge of the paper.

Three and a half centimetres equalled one thousand, nine hundred hours. Eighty-one days.

So the full extent of the trigger, four centimetres, would send the subject forwards in time by...

Surely not.

More than two hundred million hours.

Nine million days.

Twenty-five thousand years.

FIVE

The stench of beer belched from the entrance to the Cradle. Inside, a scruffy young man in a ripped green jumper perched on the back of a sofa, tuning a guitar. Daniel ordered a Guinness and took an empty table in the opposite wing of the pub, where only a handful of older customers played dominoes or sat in comfortable silence.

He stared at the tabletop as he downed his pint. He bought and drank another, then switched to whisky without fully understanding why, until a shadow in his mind's eye became his twin brother, tumbler in hand. His thoughts settled on William rather than the time machine. He remembered the time William had once brought home a cactus from primary school, having been tasked with tending it over the Easter holiday. He had been horrified when he discovered the plant jammed into the boiler, extinguishing the pilot light, but had accepted Daniel's claims of innocence. He remembered the time he had lured away William's first serious girlfriend, despite disliking her; their dismal weekend of nightclubs and room service. He remembered the times that he had taken William's money, even before he genuinely needed it. William had been too gullible, that was his problem. He had been too easy a target, whenever Daniel had needed a scapegoat.

He was surprised, and a little shocked, to find that the memories seemed less tangible than they once had been. Vignetting marked their corners, like old photographs. Something else unsettled him, too. He pictured a scene of himself reading a storybook to William, but saw not just his twin brother but also his own seven-year-old self. The effect was further confused by the similarity of William's face to his own. Why did he see himself in the third person? It must be a memory inspired by an old home video, rather than his own experience. Those videotapes must have been packed up to leave with his mother.

The folk singer, perched on the sofa back, reached the chorus of his song. A group of drinkers clustered around him sang along. *Farewell to the gold that never I found, goodbye to the nuggets that somewhere abound.*

Somebody blocked Daniel's view. Blearily, he peered upwards.

"Hey Georgie," the newcomer said, "I think one of your horses has got loose."

The barman laughed. Evidently, he was Georgie.

"Scratch that," the voice continued, "I was just fooled for a second by this guy's long, long face."

Daniel recognised the woman from the Coniston cave. So she was as true as her word.

She slid gracelessly into the chair opposite his own. Her sand-coloured hair had been tied in two short bunches, despite the fact that she must be near thirty. Fashion sense clearly wasn't a priority in these parts. Unlike most of the other pub customers she had dressed for a night out, though her pink storm jacket still lay on the back of the chair. Despite his drunkenness, Daniel managed to avoid staring at her bosom.

"Seriously, fella," she said, "It can't be all that bad, can it? Whatever it is."

Daniel shrugged and stared at his glass where the images of William rippled and dispersed. Don't appear too enthusiastic. Don't scare her off.

She held out a hand. "Nic."

"Daniel."

As they shook hands, he upset Nic's half-pint of cider, which seeped beyond the beermats and onto the already-stained carpet.

"Shit. Sorry," he said. He was drunk already. William would have been ashamed.

Nic smiled. An eyebrow raised.

"Sorry," he said again. "I'll buy you another?"

Georgie served him with a smirk. Daniel scowled and returned to the table with another cider and a whisky for himself. The singers had arrived at the end of the chorus once again. *For it's only when dreaming that I see you gleaming, down in the dark deep underground.*

"You made it down all right, then?" Nic said.

Daniel thought of her waiting for him in the blue Mini. He should have accepted the lift and started working on her sooner. Now that he understood the full potential of the time machine, it was far too dangerous to conduct more tests on himself. He couldn't risk accidentally sending himself hundreds of years into the future. He needed a lab rat.

He shrugged agreement.

"Must be lonely up there alone? The Manor, I mean, not the Old Man," Nic said.

"No. At least, I don't mind it."

"So you are alone, then? Just you?"

He nodded.

"Playing golf all day, I guess?"

"Not really." He thought of using Harrigan's line about a good walk spoiled. He realised that he had inadvertently ended the flow of conversation. He would have to try harder if he was to lure her back to the Manor.

"Okay." Nic extended the second half of the word, rolling her eyes. "Scratch that off the list of conversation starters, then. You're a tough nut to crack, Daniel Faint."

How did she know his surname? The whole village must knew his identity by now. Sooner or later, he would be noticed by someone that mattered. He would have to move fast, then get out. Stay hidden, elsewhere, if he was to make money from the time machine. And when the time came, he would have to target potential customers carefully and discreetly.

All he managed to say was, "I'm sorry."

"We've established that," Nic said, stifling laughter. "You're generally a sorry kind of person, it seems. Can't we move on? I know what it's like being a stranger round here. I'm just trying to be a friendly face, all right? But this, right this moment, is your opportunity to tell me to fuck off if you want."

They faced each other in silence.

"Fine." She tapped the tabletop twice. "So I'll stay. Anyway, I guess I already knew you didn't shack up at the Manor for the golf. In fact, I heard you brought a bunch of stuff with you. Equipment. Is that right?"

Daniel eyed her warily.

"So you're some kind of big-shot photographer?" she continued. "Where are you from, Manchester? Further south? Can't imagine what there might be at the Manor to take pictures of all summer long."

Perhaps Tosh had spoken to other people about Daniel's treatment of the peacock. Daniel fought the impulse to sprint out of the pub.

"Wildlife, that sort of thing," he said. "Sunsets. That's why I was climbing the Old Man." Even as he said it, he sensed that he was gabbling, giving more information than was necessary.

"But you didn't have a camera."

"I was scouting. I use, ah, heavy equipment."

Nic's eyes moved around his face, scrutinising him, vetting him for lies. "So I heard. Still, you'd have thought the big money was in people. Portraits, I mean."

"I suppose you're right," Daniel said. He glimpsed a safe topic of conversation. "I've been known to do portraits, every so often. With the right face."

Nic leant forwards. Daniel's eyes flicked to her breasts as they pressed against the table.

"Have you photographed anyone famous?"

So that was it. The bait. Daniel felt the tension leave his body.

He drank his whisky, then another, as Nic spoke at length about photography, magazines, celebrities and gossip. He smiled and nodded, trying to mask his giddiness. His mind swam. He felt as if he were still within the machine, spinning among the tall, grey panels.

Suddenly, he could no longer bear to hear any more of Nic's trivia. The purpose of his visit to the pub became foggy in his mind. He would get her into the time machine, yes. But right at this moment he felt a growing, desperate need to unburden himself. And maybe Nic might provide clues about the type of person who might later pay to use the machine.

"'F you could travel in time, would you do it?" His mouth tangled awkwardly around the words.

Nic stopped talking and he realised he had no idea what she had been speaking about. The eyebrow raised again.

"Course. Who wouldn't?"

"What would you do?"

"I dunno. See the pyramids being built. No, too hot and dusty. Go dancing at a speakeasy. Um. Stop Marilyn from overdosing."

He snorted. She was as unimaginative an idiot as he had suspected.

"Wouldn't work," he said. "How would you get to Egypt, or... Chicago, or wherever Marilyn Monroe died?"

"I thought you said—"

"I said time travel, that's all. Not teleportation."

"Oh." She sipped her cider. "Well, I'd go back and see my nan, then. Get the train and see Lancaster in her day. She was always banging on about how much better things were."

He felt a pang of jealousy. Her first instinct hadn't been to repair past mistakes in her own life. He had assumed that was what everybody would wish for.

"You can't go back," he said.

Nic stuck out her tongue. "I'm only playing along, aren't I? But that's what I'd do if I could time travel."

"No, it's impossible." Daniel hit the table with a fist, with far more force than he intended. Now, the concept of travelling back in time seemed patently absurd. Why had he ever imagined it might be possible? "Imagine if you did go back. Think of the anaco... anachronisms. Think of the repercussions just being there would cause. Everything'd splinter. Shatter."

"All right, smartarse. If you could time travel, where—I mean, when—would you go?"

He put his glass down to gesture with both hands, describing the walls of a straight tunnel. "Forwards. The future."

"Oh! Good idea. You could see how George turns out when he's king!"

"Could do."

Nic warmed to the theme. "Or how about even farther ahead? Everything'd be like in that film with Tom Cruise waving his hands."

"Maybe not."

"Whaddaya mean, 'maybe not'? Some game this is turning out to be. You're a real sparkling conversationalist, you know that?"

She seemed to be on the verge of leaving. Daniel put a hand on her arm, gripping too hard in his drunkenness. Forget the unburdening. Stick to the plan.

"Want to have your photo taken?"

~

The journey back to the Manor took longer than it ought. Despite his haste, Daniel's limbs failed to cooperate fully and Nic supported him most of the way. When they emerged onto the golf course, the moonlight spiked long shadows across the hillocks.

"I'm not available, you know," Nic said.

Daniel spread his arms wide. "A photographer's word is his bond."

"I'm serious. No funny business."

He moved to stand before her, both arms still outstretched for balance and emphasis. What was it she wanted to hear? "I have absolutely no interest in you, whatsoever," he said.

"Jesus, all right. You don't have to go overboard. You really put those drinks away, huh?"

They resumed their trek along the fairway. "Were you following me yesterday?" Daniel said.

"Yesterday? Oh, Tuesday. Course not. Think you're the only one allowed to go scrambling up and down the fells? No need to be such a self-centred prick, Mister Daniel Faint."

But Daniel had stopped listening. Instead, his attention focused on the grey front of the Manor. It shuddered under its shifting canopy of dark foliage. He reached out a bobbing hand to quiet Nic.

"Get your hands off—" She wriggled to release her jacket from his grip, before registering his concern. "What's up?"

He pointed towards the building. Something squat moved, black against black on the tarmacked forecourt.

"Are you expecting visitors?" Nic whispered.

Daniel didn't speak. Each of his breaths stank of whisky, making him nauseous.

William.

"You go first," he said, ushering her forwards.

She glared at him, then cocked her head. "Bloody weirdo." She strode down the remaining length of the golf course and onto the driveway.

Daniel crouched low, breathing shallowly. The dense copse to his right made a blotch on his vision. It reminded him of the migraines of his childhood.

Nic slowed as she passed through the iron archway. Like him, she must be watching the object on the forecourt warily. It seemed to be crouching. Daniel bit his lip.

It was the same thing as before. Something, or somebody, prowling the grounds.

He thought of the scientists from the lab in Oxford, or somebody sent on their behalf.

He thought of a Labrador his family had once owned.

He thought of William, on his hands and knees.

The security lights blazed, painting the forecourt an artificial yellow. Nic froze. The peacock in the centre of the forecourt froze, too.

Even from fifty metres away, Nic's laughter rang out across the golf course. She raised both arms, flapping them up and down as she approached the peacock.

Daniel wiped away tears from his eyes. He had to get a grip. How much more proof would he require before he would accept that nobody was watching the Manor? He rose to his feet, his knees creaking from the effort of staying in position, and stumbled forwards to pass through the archway. The peacock stayed still as Nic skirted around it.

Giddy with relief and whisky, Daniel rejoined her on the front doorstep. He fished around in his pockets for the keys, then struggled with the door locks before finally stumbling into the lobby with unstoppable momentum. He bobbed into the lounge, ricocheting from the sofa to stand before the time machine. He turned with a foolish grin.

"Ta-da."

Nic wrinkled her nose as she examined the panels and slatted tube. "It doesn't seem like much of a studio."

"State of the art."

She hovered near the doorway.

"Come on in, take a seat." He burped abruptly.

Nic moved a little closer to the single remaining sofa. "Are you going to offer me a drink?"

"No, sit over there," Daniel said. "In the middle of the tubey thing."

"Seriously? No. Why?"

"For the photo."

She walked to the time machine but hesitated at the perimeter of the ring of panels. She turned to look at him. "Photography studios don't look like this."

"You're obviously not a model."

She grimaced. "Again with the bluntness. You really need to work on your patter, Daniel." She glanced at the slatted tube. "And your furniture, too, if you're going to run a proper studio. This weird sci-fi chic isn't going to do it for the Kate Winslets of this world, I can tell you that."

Nic moved away from the ring of panels. She sat on the sofa and kicked off her boots to reveal pink-striped socks. "Where's your camera, then?"

Daniel looked from side to side as if expecting to find one.

"You're a con. I should have known. I'm off." She made to leave.

He sighed. It was going to be a long slog, getting her into the time machine. Perhaps more alcohol might help. "Look, I'm sorry," he said, "Let me get you that drink. As it happens, I have a superbly well-stocked bar."

"Don't worry, my super-sense has already detected some." Perhaps Nic's sulkiness had been only an act. She leant over the arm of the sofa and pulled a half-full bottle of whisky and a glass from a low table tucked alongside it. Daniel frowned. He could have sworn he'd moved all the alcohol to the bar. Nic took a swig and handed him a second glass. He forced a smile as he downed the drink before collapsing onto the sofa. He patted the seat beside him.

Instead, Nic rose and skipped lightly towards the door. Her skirt flared out as she pirouetted, revealing thick thighs. Her fingertips traced the carvings of the door frame. "Just look at this place. I used to come here for the pool when I was a kid, but it's been years. Can you imagine living here? I mean, for real?"

She disappeared into the lobby. Daniel lurched to his feet. Blood rushed to his head.

"Bring the bottle!" Nic called.

Rather than venturing upstairs, she had unlocked the plate-glass door to enter the leisure centre. When Daniel caught up with her, she was bending beside the swimming pool, lifting the blue stretched cover. Daniel frowned. Tosh had a key to the leisure centre. He must have covered the pool despite there being no customers. It was just as well the glass door from the lobby to the leisure centre had stayed locked.

"It's still warm!" Nic said.

Daniel placed the bottle of whisky onto the reception desk and sighed. How long would he have to play along with her whims before she would do what he wanted?

"Yeah," he said. "The heating bills must be astro-monocle. Nomical."

Nic set about unclasping the cover, peeling it back to reveal the water beneath. When she had finished Daniel leant on the reception desk and watched as she pulled her dress over her head. She had puppy fat, but not an intolerable amount. Her bra and knickers were both black, rather than pink as he had expected. She kept on her underwear as she slipped into the pool. Daniel stared stupidly at her hand outstretched over the pool edge, only understanding her meaning when she pointed to the bottle on the reception desk. He took a deep slug before handing it to her.

Nic wiped whisky from her chin and set the bottle aside. "Not coming in? You're an odd fish, Daniel Faint."

She pushed away from the side of the pool in a graceful breaststroke.

Daniel sat cross-legged, bottle in hand, and watched her cross from side to side with ease. Without her awful pink jacket and with her hair no longer in bunches, she had become a great deal more attractive. He slurped from the bottle, muttering in a low voice, reminding himself why he had brought her here. He just needed a test case, simple as that.

Nic completed several lengths of the pool. Her skin glistened as she raised herself up the metal ladder.

"Christ," she said, looking down at him as she reached for a towel hanging from a wall rail. "You look like shit."

Daniel reached for the bottle which, inexplicably, was empty. His fingers brushed against the glass but the bottle escaped him. It plopped into the pool to bob up and down in a spreading rainbow slick.

He saw a change in Nic's expression. Faint distaste. Perhaps she misinterpreted his desire to get her into the machine for a desire to take her to bed. Maybe he did, too. He reached up, pawing at her thigh, pulling at the towel that she had tied there.

"Fuck off," she said, without animosity. "I already told you what's what."

Daniel grinned. "But I need you." He removed the grin to demonstrate his serious intent. "I can't do it on my own."

"I'm sure you can, you dirty bastard. You can do it on your own all night as far as I'm concerned, once I've left."

"You don't understand."

Nic towelled her hair dry in silence. Daniel swung around to watch. She retrieved her pile of discarded clothes, then moved past the reception desk. After an indeterminate amount of time, she returned, fully dressed. She shook her head at him. Her expression was somewhere between disdain and almost maternal concern.

Groggily, Daniel realised that she was about to leave. He staggered to his feet and followed her into the lobby.

"You're right. I'm a con," he said, dimly aware that he was countering an insult she had made more than an hour ago. "I'm sorry." A stifled burp undermined the apology. "But I promise I'm not out to get you, or whatever. Do me a favour, will you? Just stay for a minute—five minutes—while I try something."

Nic relented. He took her arm, leading her back into the lounge.

"Try what?" she said. "Listen, you seemed okay, earlier. But you do realise I've gone totally off you, right?" She followed his gaze to the time machine at the far end of the room. "Really, Daniel? We're going to go through all this again? What is all that stuff, anyway?"

Daniel's head swam. He shouldn't say anything, of course. But still.

"An experiment. Like a stimulation, I mean simulation, but real." Despite his drunkenness, he could tell he was already losing her attention. "Nicola. Nic-o-la. Listen to me. It's a time machine."

Nic stared at him for a few seconds. Then she laughed. "Of all the creepy lines I expected you to use, that takes the biscuit. You, Daniel Faint, are just about the maddest person I've ever met."

"Promise." This was all going wrong. If his hands weren't shaking so much, he might have simply forced her into the machine. "I need you to help me to test it. I need to send you into the future."

He noted a glimmer of curiosity in Nic's manner. As quickly as possible, he moved from panel to panel to check their orientation. Then he gave a formal bow and gestured towards the slatted tube in the centre.

Nic shook her head. "Not on your nelly. You do it."

His shoulders slumped. Of course. It was a rational enough response, really. And he'd done it before. What harm could one more test do, as long as he only tapped the trigger lightly? Then he could try a longer time period when Nic became the test subject.

"If I do," he said, "will you do it after?"

"Girl Guide promise."

One more risk, but it would be worth it. In fact, having Nic's testimony as a witness might be useful, too. He squeezed himself clumsily within the slatted tube. His fingers traced the compass-point scratch mark labelled '1:15'.

Nic perched on the arm of the sofa, wringing her hair with a towel.

Daniel waved with his right hand, which held the trigger. With his mouth tightened in concentration against his drunkenness, he tapped the trigger.

If the panels spun around him, he didn't notice it. He blinked slowly, trying to keep his focus on Nic at the far end of the room.

His ears popped. His stomach growled.

He slumped forwards, hitting the door of the tube. When he lifted his head again, he saw Nic's bored expression.

He stayed cross-legged within the tube. "So... what did you see?"

"What did I see?"

"What did you see? S'a reasonable enough question."

Nic yawned. "Nothing happened."

"How long ago did I last speak to you?"

"You were here, weren't you?"

"How long?"

"Stop being a twat, would you? You've just been gawping at me like a monkey in a zoo."

A cold chill mixed with the hollow feeling in Daniel's stomach, making him utterly nauseous. "Something's gone wrong."

"You're not kidding. Wrong in your head."

He stumbled to his feet, leaving the tube to touch each panel in turn. As far as he could tell, everything was as it should be.

Nic's voice floated from behind. "I'm going home."

Daniel ignored her. He gazed down at the black base of the slatted tube. The cable attached to the trigger mechanism trailed along the floor.

It was unplugged. He lifted its disconnected end and snorted with laughter.

~

"Hey, watch it!" a shrill voice said.

Daniel's left elbow dug into something soft. Shakily, he recovered his balance. He was lying on his side, propped on his other elbow. A bedsheet covered his naked body. He recognised the walls of his bedroom in the Manor. His head throbbed and his tongue felt thick. The acrid taste of whisky filled his mouth.

He jerked his head up. Nic lay beside him. Her hair still had a curl from her released pigtails. She tugged the sheets back towards her.

Daniel's eyes widened and his mouth opened and closed before he managed to speak. "What?"

"What what?" Nic rubbed at a cheek streaked with mascara.

"Just... what?" Daniel clapped a hand to his forehead and moaned at the chugging and hammering within. He squinted at the daylight from the window. It was morning. Several hours had passed.

Nic's fingers dabbed at his spine. As he shuffled to the edge of the bed, her warm arms snuck around his waist. Her forehead pressed against his shoulder blades.

Daniel's eyes closed involuntarily. Skin against skin. It had been a while. The sensation almost blocked out the pain in his head. Perhaps he might allow himself to remain here, just for a moment.

"It's okay." Nic's voice tickled his skin and rattled in his ribcage. "Shush now."

Words tumbled from his mouth. "I had awful dreams."

"Tell me about it."

"I was helpless and heavy," he began, before registering something in her tone. "Hold on. That's not what you mean. You said, 'Tell me about it.' You did a thing with your voice. *Tell me about it.*"

"Sorry," Nic said. She nestled further into his back. Her hair brushed against his skin. "Do you always sleepwalk?" It sounded like genuine concern.

"I... maybe. Yes. On and off." William had, too, as a child. It was a family thing.

"I don't mind telling you, it was a bit unnerving," Nic said. "It's just as well you're on your own here. If this was still a real hotel, the other guests would be freaked right out."

Daniel felt her lips press against the hollow of his neck. A sweet smell, mixed with chlorine from the pool, clung to her body.

Memories jostled against each other. The previous evening was a sequence of disconnected images. Flashes of drinking, talking, drinking, swimming, and the time machine, always the time machine, appeared in no discernable sequence.

He leapt out of bed, abandoning the sheets to stand naked. One of Florence Harrigan's sculptures had been placed on the bedside table.

He shivered, more from fear than from the cold. "Tell me. Tell me now. What happened?"

Nic smirked. "Was it so unmemorable?"

"I don't mean—" Another wave of queasiness made him rock from foot to foot until he found stability. He pointed to the door. "The time machine."

She rolled her eyes. "Really? We're back onto that again?" She looked down at herself pointedly. The bedsheet had slid away to reveal her breasts. "Look, Daniel. However weird your whole chat-up routine might have been, you won, fair and square. Can't we zap the weird sci-fi nerd game into the past, where it belongs?"

The past? There could be no going back.

He snatched clothes from the floor, pulling on his own and throwing the rest onto the bedsheet.

"Come back to bed?" Nic said.

He had to be alone, to assess what this all meant. "Put your clothes on."

"Come on, Daniel. Don't be a cliché. Don't be that guy. It'd be such a letdown."

"Get out."

He turned to the window and watched Nic over the shoulder of his ghostly reflection. She rose from the bed and stood, hands on hips in disbelief. Then she began to dress, slowly and sullenly. She left the room without saying a word and without looking at him again. Outside, below the monkey puzzle, two identical peacocks paraded in a tight circle as though wary of each other.

Nic's voice echoed from the corridor, underscored by the ticking of Benfield's grandfather clock. "Fuck you, then, Daniel Faint."

He waited until the front door slammed before he ventured downstairs. Halfway, a thought suddenly sent a chill through his body. He dashed into the lounge, half-expecting to see the time machine in pieces. But it looked exactly as it had the night before, inert and unthreatening. Humming and smiling.

His headache intensified. He lolloped towards the kitchen. There must be painkillers in the house, somewhere.

A blotch registered on the periphery of his vision. A marker pen lay unlidded on the carpet. Written on the wall in ragged, ten-centimetre-high letters were the words: *YOU DON'T BELONG HERE.*

~

A shower softened his hangover. As he towelled himself dry, he noticed a tender sensation in his penis. On an impulse he kicked open the bathroom pedal bin and frowned at the discarded condom. Its tip was half-filled with semen. His first time getting laid in years, and he had no memory of the event. Nic's attitude when they woke suggested that the sex had been good, but that was hardly consolation.

In the bedroom he dressed in a fresh white T-shirt, identical to the one he had worn yesterday. He discarded the soiled shirt onto a pile in the corner of the room.

He returned to the lobby to stand before the scrawled message on the golden-flowered wallpaper.

YOU DON'T BELONG HERE.

Florence Harrigan had warned him about locals' attitudes to what she called 'offcomers'. Despite her friendliness, despite whatever had occurred between them last night, it was clear that Nic hated him for the simple crime of being a stranger to these parts.

There would be no budging the marker-pen ink. Scrubbing would only make it worse. Instead, he hefted the large mirror that hung alongside the message, shifting its hanging hook inch by inch along the picture rail so that the mirror no longer pointed across the lobby towards its twin. It covered the black words perfectly. He stood with both hands still gripping the gilt frame as he stared into the mirror. He nodded and his reflection nodded too.

The time machine drew him closer. Had either he or Nic used it the previous evening? Surely that had been the aim of the drinking session, to convince her to enter the slatted tube. But memories of the evening remained just out of reach.

Nic had been his best chance to test the machine on another human. The thought of establishing a relationship with someone else, or of attempting to involve Nic again, made his skin crawl.

But if his calculations were correct, the difference of a few millimetres of pressure on the trigger might send the subject years into the future rather than days, or centuries instead of decades. Commercialising the time machine would be impossible without more certainty about the results. Nobody would be rash enough to use the machine with no guarantee of the century in which they might arrive. Even without dismantling the trigger, he might one day be able to add a device make it more precise. A pneumatic grip, computer-controlled, could squeeze the trigger rather than a human operator. But he still needed proof that a human subject travelling forwards in time followed the same rules as an inanimate object.

So. He would have to man up. A final quick shove into a wasp's nest. He had proved that he was physically safe using the machine. One more test, one more result, and then he could concentrate on the future. His own future.

He thought again of science lessons back at school. Mr Madden and his talks about evidence. Measurement wasn't the only factor.

Observation. If this really was to be his final test within the machine, he must have some kind of witness or record. In the name of science.

He flinched as a shadow flitted past the window, a dark splotch on the curtains. For a moment he entertained the thought of inviting Tosh inside. Madness.

There was nobody that he could turn to for help. *You don't belong here.* He had been labelled an offcomer, and that was that. He had no friends, nobody he could trust. Only himself.

But there had to be a way of making a record of the test.

Hauling Benfield's desktop computer from the study was no easy task. Daniel struggled to gain a hold on the huge beige box. He tripped on the carpet trim, catching the computer just before it toppled to the ground. The clunky monitor was no less unwieldy. He cursed technology in general.

The webcam appeared far newer. The thought of Benfield buying it contradicted his mental image of the old man. Perhaps Harrigan had bought it for himself. With distaste, Daniel imagined Harrigan slumped in the study while Florence slept, thumbing through ChatRoulette users and licking his puffy lips.

Daniel set the webcam on top of the grimy monitor, facing the panels of the time machine. He sat on the floor before it. He rifled through program files to find a video application. Though pixelated and distorted with noise and artefacts, the live video image of the time machine was clear enough for his purposes. From this low angle the apparatus appeared tall, as mythic as Stonehenge. He clicked the Record button and took his place within the slatted tube. With his back upright against its rear wall, the knees of his crossed legs grazed the curve of metal either side of the door. The grey panels dominated his view, their tips appearing closer together than they really were, as if leaning in to embrace the slatted tube and Daniel himself.

It was three minutes after eleven o'clock.

Here goes, Mr Madden.

Here goes, William. Where did that thought come from?

Daniel angled the plastic handle, noting the precise point to which he squeezed the trigger. Just a tap, to the scratched point marked '4:18'.

The grey panels swung around him, or he swung within their loose embrace.

His stomach growled. His ears popped.

It was three minutes after eleven o'clock.

His heart thumped. How could that be possible? No time had passed. Everything had felt the same. The mixture of heaviness and weightlessness, the disorientation. His lightheadedness, the drop in his stomach. Had it worked, even only for an instant?

The computer clock confirmed the fact. The video application window still showed the low-angled view of the time machine behind him. It was a live feed, but with no human in the frame it might as well have been a static image.

He peered at the screen. The onscreen Record button no longer glowed red. Why had it stopped? He clicked it again, then reached up to wave a hand in front of the camera lens. His gesture was replicated onscreen, a disembodied limb slipping across the frame. Software lag delayed the movement fractionally, showing a glimpse of the immediate past. He rewatched the saved clip.

With the video application set to Record once again, he returned to the slatted tube. He kept his eyes fixed on the clock face as he pressed the trigger.

Bile rose up from his belly, stinging his throat. The time machine gave a low moan. His ears blocked, temporarily erasing all ambient noise so that he felt more disconnected from his body than on previous occasions.

But this time his stomach didn't growl. If anything, it felt fuller, rather than emptier.

Through tears he saw that it was four minutes after eleven o'clock.

It hadn't worked. He had spent one minute travelling one minute into the future. Time travel, the old-fashioned way.

The computer held no recording, other than the test clip showing his waving arm.

He looked from the time machine to the computer and back again, absently rubbing at a dark mark on the thumb of his right hand. The time machine waited patiently for him to come to a decision. The webcam simply watched on.

His eyes stung due to the light that penetrated the gap in the thick curtains, or due to some effect of the machine, or just despair.

What had gone wrong? What had changed?

He thought of Nic watching from her perch on the sofa arm. She had been the only foreign element, the last time he had used the time machine. Bacteria in the petri dish. Had she tampered with the machine, after all?

No, her anger that morning had been directed only at him. A normal human concerned with normal human matters. There was no evidence to suggest that she gave a damn about the machine.

So what, then?

Hadn't he heard the time machine hum, just as before?

He watched the time machine. The time machine watched him. The webcam watched them both.

He rubbed at his eyes. He must be exhausted. But still his conviction grew.

Instinctively, he reached out to touch the nearest grey panel. Shifting light from the window flickered over it and its neighbours. The panels emitted ticks, as though cooling or heating. Did he imagine the accompanying sigh? His skin felt warm, as though the machine now radiated heat.

It knew. The time machine was reacting to its surroundings. Everything had worked correctly until he had brought in a witness. The time machine knew that Nic wouldn't understand and it resented the intrusion. And now it was offended by his attempts to record its operation on video. Perhaps its refusal had affected the computer too, somehow. Machines standing together in solidarity.

Nonsense.

No.

But was it?

Was it conscious?

Fighting a giddy feeling, he turned the webcam to face the dark wall. He returned to the slatted tube without clicking Record.

His fingers squeezed the trigger before his mind had time to object.

SIX

Daniel toppled backwards. His spine struck painfully against a hard surface.

He kept his eyes closed, fighting nausea. He concentrated on locating each limb in turn.

His hands were clasped on a flat surface. His legs hung free. He opened his eyes to see that he was slumped in a wooden chair at the kitchen table.

Somehow, the machine had shifted him in space, as well as time.

As he stood, he noticed that his legs felt as if they had gone to sleep from lack of blood flow. He stumbled and leant heavily on the door frame. A pounding sensation began at his temples and then wrapped around his head like a crown.

According to the kitchen clock it was after twelve o'clock. He rubbed his forehead. Nearly an hour had passed since he had used the time machine. He staggered out into the lobby and then the lounge. This new phenomenon required further testing.

He froze.

The curtains had been tied back, and midday sun illuminated the entire room. The three sofas and an armchair were arranged exactly as they had been on the day that he had arrived at the Manor. A sherry decanter sat on the low table.

And.

And there was no time machine.

"Jesus," he said. His own voice startled him.

At first he found himself unable to move from the spot, like a puppet with its strings severed. The dull ache in his temples became a stinging migraine. He held his hands before his eyes. They hovered there, twitching slightly.

He retreated from the lounge. He spun aimlessly in the lobby, with no clear idea where to go or what to do.

None of this made any sense. The only time that he had been alone here, with the Manor in this state, had been directly after the Harrigans' departure. The time machine had still been in the van outside.

But that wasn't how the time machine worked. There could be no going back.

Could there?

A face appeared in his mind, before the name did. It looked a lot like his own face, but with a rounding error.

William.

William, irretrievably lost. William, his twin. His missing reflection.

His pulse quickened. Perhaps it was possible to travel backwards in time, after all. Perhaps he might go back and undo the mistakes in his life.

But wait. This couldn't be the point in time when the Harrigans had left. If it was, wouldn't he, Daniel Faint, already be here in the Manor?

In Benfield's study, the plastic dust sheets covered the desk and armchair. He leant over the desk to see out onto the forecourt. It was empty. He saw no van and no MG, just crumbling tarmac.

His head thumped. There could be only one conclusion. He must have travelled farther back in time. Perhaps the Harrigans weren't even here, yet. For a brief moment, he half-expected a hotel guest or leisure centre visitor to appear, clad in only a towel, as proof of the era.

Proof.

Wasn't there a calendar in the kitchen? Florence Harrigan had pointed it out during their interminable breakfast together; her cousin had taken the landscape photographs of Newcastle. He raced into the room.

June. June 2016. It was the present, still, though perhaps with a rounding error. Below the photo of the Gateshead Millennium Bridge at night, none of the dates had been marked. There were no clues to a more precise point in time.

He took a deep breath. He must start by identifying the facts. The Manor had reset itself, so he had certainly travelled backwards in time, if not by much. There might be a way to travel even farther back, if not for a more fundamental obstacle. The time machine had disappeared.

Or rather, it hadn't yet arrived.

He drifted to the lobby. With a jolt, he realised that the front door might open at any moment, heralding his own arrival with the time machine. And if it did, he mustn't be here. He *wasn't* here, the first time around.

So he must hide.

He thought of his instincts about the Manor over the last few days. His certainty that somebody, unseen, prowled the grounds. The sense of familiarity, the stale smell of family that he had taken to be William. What if it had actually been Daniel himself? Perhaps he would become that spectre, lying in wait for the younger Daniel to relax his hold on the machine. And then what? He couldn't steal it away, because that hadn't happened either. But he could use the machine himself. Only one question remained. Should he travel forwards to rejoin the present, or backwards?

Stop.

He froze. He saw a migraine blotch at the edge of his vision.

The portrait mirror was positioned too close to the front door.

His fingers scrabbled weakly against its weight. The mirror groaned as he swung it aside on its hanging wire.

YOU DON'T BELONG HERE.

Daniel stared at the block capital letters. He struggled to process the implications of the message being there. From somewhere deep within his belly something pushed against his ribs.

The doorbell rang.

He stood inert as a statue, unwilling to move any closer to the door but unable to pull himself away.

The handle turned. The door held shut.

He waited, paralysed with indecision.

The door shook with blows from outside.

He scurried back to Benfield's study and tugged aside the curtains. The stonework of the bay window obscured any view of the doorstep. He craned his neck so that his forehead touched the cold glass. A long shadow flitted outside on the tarmac, dark on dark.

The message on the wall. The message meant that this *couldn't* be the past. So whoever was outside couldn't, after all, be himself.

So who, and when, was this?

He crawled away from the window on his hands and knees. He sat in the centre of lobby with his legs tucked inside his arms.

The door handle rattled again. Daniel moaned. Whatever malevolent spirit this was, couldn't it at least wait until he'd got his bearings?

Once again, he saw William's face in his thoughts. William spoke. *You have to promise it's the end.*

"Open up!"

Despite his shock, Daniel gulped in relief. The voice, deep but muffled by the thick oak, could be any man's. But at least it was real. Human.

A grunt came from the other side of the door, then the sound of footsteps moving away.

Daniel pressed his ear against the door. The footsteps were moving southwards, towards the garage rather than back along the driveway.

He raced to the kitchen, ducking low beneath its wide window. A crunch of footsteps on the gravel outside signalled the stranger's approach. Was the garage still locked?

He heard the garage door rattle. He raised himself slightly to see out of the window. The intruder faced the metal door, with his hands on hips. William had been of slight build, like Daniel. This man's shoulders were twice the width of William's.

The man rattled the doors of the garage. Then he strode past the monkey puzzle and towards the front of the house again. In passing, he aimed a vain kick at a peacock.

The voice echoed again from the forecourt. It was louder this time. "Open up, Faint! You've locked me out, you old bugger!"

Rather than relief, Daniel felt only lightheaded.

With a sense of hopeless inevitability, he returned to the lobby, pulled back the deadbolt and opened the front door.

Harrigan was gazing at the upper storeys of the Manor with his hands cupped to his mouth.

"Finally!" he bellowed. He galloped back to the entrance.

Daniel accepted his fate. He bowed his head and stepped backwards into the lobby as Harrigan's meaty hand clapped onto his shoulders.

~

"Never too early in the day, am I right?"

Still standing, Harrigan downed his glass of sherry. He glanced around the lounge with a bloated, uninterested expression. The skin at the back of his neck had cracked into red, chafing furrows. He must spend half his life abroad, or yachting, perhaps. Despite his distress and confusion, Daniel felt his loathing renew all over again.

Daniel glanced around the lounge. Its contents really were exactly as they had been the day Harrigan had left. How had that happened?

His voice cracked as he found words, finally. "I didn't expect so see you back so soon."

Harrigan harrumphed and pushed back his sleeve to reveal a watchless wrist. "Might have teased the top end of the speed limit a tad. Rolex is in the car."

"No, I meant—"

But Harrigan had already marched out of the room. Daniel scurried after him towards the kitchen.

"Any food in the offing?" Harrigan threw open the fridge door, pulling out a clingfilmed bowl of stir fry and noodles. Daniel frowned. His stomach grumbled. When had he last eaten?

Harrigan surveyed the bowl of noodles with distaste. "Don't fancy this much. Forgot you were a bloody student. Never mind, I've sandwiches in the car. We can share them beforehand."

Beforehand? Daniel mumbled protests as Harrigan ushered him towards the front door.

"Just a minute," he managed to say, "I need to get my key."

Harrigan shrugged. "I'd have left the bugger wide open, but fair enough."

Daniel scuttled back inside, leaving Harrigan whistling on the forecourt. He raced up the stairs and threw open the door to each room. All appeared perfectly normal. In his own bedroom, his spare clothes were laid out on the blanket box at the foot of the bed. He charged back downstairs, through the kitchen and into the garage. The sit-on mower had been moved slightly, presumably by Tosh, but nothing else appeared disturbed. He pushed through the plate-glass door to find the leisure reception empty. Midday sunlight streamed through the windows on all sides of the reception desk, turning its fake mahogany surface golden.

The Manor had been returned to pristine condition. At least, given Harrigan's sudden and unwelcome appearance, he should be thankful for that.

He returned to the entrance. At the last moment he remembered to produce the keyring from his pocket, where it had been all along.

"Sorry," he said, stifling panting. "Just needed to visit the bathroom too."

Harrigan laughed. "T-M-I, my friend. T-M-bloody-I." His soft leather boot brushed idly at an oil patch on the tarmac. "Where's your ugly old van, by the way?"

"Ah. Sold it."

"Wasn't it a rental?"

Daniel bit his cheek. Harrigan was sharper than he appeared.

"Was. Ex-rental. And I didn't need it any more."

Harrigan grunted. "Until you leave, I suppose."

Daniel felt his cheeks twitch. "That's right. Until I leave."

Harrigan seemed satisfied to leave the exchange there. He waved towards the passenger door of the only vehicle in the forecourt, a Range Rover with muck-splattered sides. Daniel cast a final look at the Manor before he climbed in.

Harrigan drove as though he were the only motorist in the county. Daniel gripped the upper section of his seatbelt with both hands as the car veered around bends. Harrigan seemed oblivious of the astonished expressions of the few other drivers they encountered. He hummed and belched as he drove.

Gradually, as he acclimatised to the lurches of the car, Daniel returned to the issues at hand. Time was, after all, flowing in the correct direction. This calmed him a little, but Harrigan's appearance still defied explanation. And, of course, there was also another, more pressing concern. Where was the time machine now? It was as if the little bubble of space in the Manor's lounge had reverted to an earlier state. Might the time machine have that power?

There was another question he needed to answer, too. He had not, in fact, travelled back in time. But then how far ahead had he gone? It might not even be the same day.

Surreptitiously, he reached out to push a button beside the car's digital clock. The display changed to show the date. The seventeenth of June.

He felt like striking himself on the head. What date had it been when he used the time machine? What day of the week, even? He had stolen the machine on the night of the thirteenth and arrived in Cumbria the morning of the fourteenth. The days since then had become a shapeless mush. He was drifting aimlessly in time, even when he wasn't using the machine.

The farther they travelled from the Manor, the greater his anxiety became. He clung onto a conviction that the time machine was still within the Manor, somewhere, somehow. And if that was the case, he ought to be there to protect it. He was responsible for it, after all. A strange thought bubbled up from somewhere deep within him: *It needs me.*

The car heaved to the right. Daniel became aware once again of Harrigan's offensive presence. They hadn't spoken for more than half an hour. At least he might be able to clear up one of the smaller mysteries.

He cleared his throat and affected the chattiest tone that he could manage. "So, there'll be no Mrs Harrigan on this trip?"

Harrigan gave him a sidelong glance, a flicker of amused suspicion. "Right."

Daniel lapsed back into silence. Harrigan hummed a tune. Eventually, Daniel recognised it as the theme to the Black Beauty television series.

The car swung to a halt, skidding on the gravel of a layby beside a thickly wooded area. Harrigan's catarrh-thick clearing of his throat indicated that this was their destination. He twisted to fish around on the back seat of the car and produced a foil-wrapped parcel. He hummed in mock ceremony as he uncovered sandwiches and jammed the largest one into his mouth. Daniel accepted the remaining sandwich and peeled apart the bread to reveal meat smeared with crimson sauce. After finishing his sandwich Harrigan raised an eyebrow, noticing that Daniel's remained uneaten.

"I'm vegetarian," Daniel lied.

Harrigan took back the foil package and placed it on his own lap. He polished off the second sandwich in contented silence, then pushed his way out of the car. Daniel stepped out onto the gravel. He fought a growing certainty that he was being led into danger. He walked slowly to the rear of the vehicle, half-expecting Harrigan to clout him with a spade, and that would be that.

Harrigan only glanced down at Daniel's trainers. "Didn't I say hard-wearing?"

Daniel looked down too, feeling foolish without knowing why.

"Your funeral," Harrigan said, grinning. He pulled a bundle from an oilskin bag in the back of the Range Rover, then threw it. Daniel flinched but still managed to catch the wax jacket and trousers.

"Should be more or less your size," Harrigan said.

A sharp crack came from the wooded area beside the layby. Daniel ducked down instinctively.

Harrigan snorted. "You'll need to locate your balls, Faint. Come on."

~

Panting, Daniel leant against a tree trunk for support. His left foot, already sodden where the soil's dampness had crept through the thin fabric of his shoe, twisted as it struck a root. He grabbed at his heel as if he could protect it retrospectively. He put cautious weight onto his foot. His ankle sang with pain.

With a growl, he hurled his rifle away. It bounced dully from a tree stump. He scrambled towards it, then sat on the stump in absolute dejection.

Around him, cracks of gunfire came from hidden sources. He no longer flinched. His senses had been dulled like a soldier in the trenches.

Harrigan knew nothing about the time machine, of course. But if he had, this adventure would have been the most cruel and unusual punishment. How had Daniel ended up agreeing to join a hunt? Harrigan had ignored his last-minute protests as they had approached the hunters waiting outside the lodge. He had a knack for brushing aside conversation with which he didn't care to engage. Once Daniel had received his rifle Harrigan had melted away into the crowd.

He had expected the hunters to wear uniforms, but of course that was fox hunting, not ducks. Without red tunics, the men appeared normal enough. They must all be obscenely wealthy, just like Harrigan, though. None of them must have worked a day in their life, living solely on trust funds and company directorships awarded by others within their group. There was no way in to a crowd like that. Instead, Daniel and others like him had to rely on their imaginations. They had to be always on the alert for new opportunities.

Even so, his brief interactions with the hunters had undermined his prejudices a little. A few had stepped forward to shake his hand or clap him on the back, greeting him with convincing warmth. Only their glances at Harrigan showed their reservations: what was a man like this doing here? And yet they had all remained more or less inoffensive. Daniel found it difficult to suppress a little disappointment about that.

Still. Hunting was simply wrong. Perhaps not morally or ethically—who honestly cared about the welfare of ducks, after all?—but spiritually, somehow. Nobody had a right to declare himself worthy of destroying something else, just for the fun of it. The only justifiable reason for ending a life was sheer, unavoidable necessity. The birds of this forest had no particular reason to die today.

He prodded at the rifle with his uninjured foot. Was the safety catch engaged? Harrigan had demonstrated the mechanism, but at the time the information had seemed trivial. Daniel Faint was no hunter. He had no need for such knowledge. Now, alone in the forest, the significance of the safety catch had changed.

Fatigue and misery welled up within him. What kind of idiots would supply him with a gun?

Years ago, he had asked himself a variation of that question: *Where can I get a gun?* He had considered suicide on a couple of occasions during the years following graduation, but had been appalled at the thought of pills working slowly upon his insides, or the moments of freefall regret if he were to throw himself from a building.

William would never have found himself in that state of mind. Success clung to him. Success and self-satisfaction. Straight As, a first from Christ Church, a procession of girls resulting in his marriage to Lorna, objectively the most perfect woman imaginable. This was all the worse because Daniel saw himself reflected in his brother's face. He saw his own features smoothed and straightened. He, Daniel, was the distorted mirror image, not William.

William would never have killed himself, so somebody else had to do it for him.

Daniel swallowed hard. He was torturing himself.

He made a decision. The time machine represented the future, not the past. He had been wrong, earlier today, about its capabilities. There could be no going back. And that was for the best.

So. Onwards and upwards.

The time machine must exist still, somewhere. But before he could search for it he had to escape this godforsaken forest and its prowling lunatics. He stood up, testing weight on his injured foot.

The foliage that surrounded him was the crinkled brown of autumn. Perhaps, here in its centre, light and water couldn't penetrate the dense forest. Daniel's heavy footsteps produced regular crackling sounds that soon became hypnotic. Creatures skittering in the undergrowth added to each crunch. They produced a lag effect so that the sounds seemed to prefigure and echo his actual steps.

Which way was he heading? Glimpses of the sun ought to have offered clues, but Daniel struggled to recall what its position meant, or which direction led back to the hunters' lodge.

Something burst from the bushes to his right. Acting on instinct, Daniel raised his rifle, even though he couldn't tell whether the arrival was animal, human or something else entirely. A sharp crack sent him bounding away, deeper into the forest. He shouted at the pain from his foot. He felt his arms for bullet wounds, as if they might only be identifiable from outside his body.

His breath came in spits. What did he imagine he was running from? He slowed his pace. It had only been a disturbed bird breaking out from the undergrowth, surely. Like Harrigan had said, he needed to grow some balls.

He realised that he had left his rifle behind. He turned and tried to retrace his steps, but the dense forest had already shifted around him, rearranging its foliage and tracks. After a few minutes, he identified a tree stump that looked familiar. But if it was the same spot, the rifle had vanished.

He felt ready to give in. He pulled his arms tight around his knees. Let the forest take him, drawing him further and further into its depths. A canopy of trees was as secure as the roof of the Manor. He might even be better hidden here. Without the machine, there was no reason to be anywhere in particular. Oxford, Cumbria, the Manor, the forest. They were all the same, ultimately. They were all empty shells with Daniel prowling within them. Haunting them.

He saw another movement in the bushes. A hint of red-checked pattern appeared among the leaves. To one side he saw a familiar, bloated face: Harrigan. Daniel looked back at the first man. Above the haze of red checks he saw the perfectly circular eye of a raised rifle.

"Faint! Get down, for pity's sake!" Harrigan bellowed.

Instead, Daniel rose to his feet. He moved with a sleepwalker's calm certainty as he raised himself to stand on the tree trunk. He barely noticed the sting from his twisted ankle.

He waited for the crackle of gunfire.

Pain bloomed in his neck. He twisted away from the impact. His body dipped backwards. A slow freefall, filled with regret, just as he had once predicted.

He fell flat onto the needle-carpeted ground. Darkness crept in from all sides. The heavy wings of a bird beat above him. It croaked a staccato call that merged with the reports of rifles close by.

The bird thudded to the ground.

SEVEN

Long limbs wrapped around him. They felt both protective and suffocating. They embraced his bent legs but also constricted his throat and covered his eyes, blocking the sunlight.

The limbs multiplied. He thought of his mother, his brother, his lovers. They pinched at his skin while he squirmed in his attempts to escape. His own arms coiled around his legs too.

He freed himself. Sunlight warmed his face. It changed in intensity. Flashes of heat spun in a circle around him. His neck ached as he strained to follow its path.

His ears popped. His stomach growled.

A bird shouted.

He shouted too.

~

"Settle down. He's coming to."

Daniel saw red shapes flit above him, framed against gold. He groaned and raised a hand to his neck.

"What in fuck's name were you thinking?" It was Harrigan's voice, but Daniel wasn't sure whether it was him being addressed.

A softer voice said, "He shouldn't have been there. We were pushing east, that was the agreement."

Daniel opened his eyes in a squint. Harrigan's puffy face turned towards another man bending to examine Daniel's neck. When the newcomer raised himself into view, Daniel recognised his red-checked shirt.

"Can you hear me, Daniel?" the man said.

"What do you care? You shot me."

"I did." The man extended his hand. His eyes had the relaxed sleepiness of a forties Hollywood star. Smug and only superficially friendly. Daniel shook his hand limply.

"Covell Jones," the man said. "Nice to meet you. And sorry about the whole shooting thing. You really shouldn't have been where you were."

The comment seemed oddly profound. "I don't belong here," Daniel said, nodding. He winced at the stinging from his neck.

"Don't, didn't, shouldn't, wouldn't," Harrigan said.

Daniel raised himself awkwardly to a sitting position. The tree stump jabbed into his spine. "You're both being very calm about this."

Covell peered again at his neck, then patted him on the shoulder. "It's just a graze. You'll live."

Daniel forced a thin smile. He reached up to his neck and tapped at the source of the pain. His finger came away bloody, but only a little.

Harrigan huffed with impatience as Covell slowly helped Daniel to his feet. Then Harrigan barged through the undergrowth ahead of them, grumbling. Covell supported Daniel as he stumbled forwards.

"Don't mind him," Covell said in a low voice. "He just doesn't get many chances to hunt, these days. They called the whole thing off when word got around that there'd been an injury."

"'Word got around'?" Daniel said, "How long was I unconscious?"

"Must've been twenty minutes."

Once again, Daniel felt the sickly sensation of the tide of time sweeping past him.

"As I say, don't fret about your bullet wound," Covell continued. "It'll prove to be a nick once you've cleaned it up. But have your head seen to, okay?"

Daniel glared at him.

"Sorry, poor choice of words," Covell said. "And me a psychiatrist! I should know better than to use phrases like that. I mean you should go to your GP, or whatever. A fall backwards onto the ground like that won't have made you any more intelligent, let's put it that way."

When they arrived at the hunters' lodge, Daniel found himself relegated to the corner of the clubroom like a child waiting for a parent to collect him from school.

The Barbour-jacketed hunters busied themselves with their equipment. A few gave him hard looks and he heard somebody mutter about a missing rifle. As Covell passed on his way to the exit he gave Daniel a smile. It seemed half apologetic and half resentful.

Half an hour passed before Harrigan emerged from the bar. His cheeks glowed and his walk had become unsteady.

"Come along, then," he said. "You drive and I'll navigate. We'll make another stop before we head back."

In practice, 'navigation' meant a series of slurred instructions followed by Harrigan crumpling into sleep in the passenger seat. Daniel wrestled with the steering wheel of the Range Rover, dabbing at his neck and wincing from the pain from his twisted ankle every time he braked.

~

Harrigan directed him into the car park of an ugly modern building. Its mock-Georgian turrets and red-brick gateposts were a philistine's version of the faded grandeur of the Manor. Daniel felt weak and confused as he allowed himself to be led inside. Was this a hospital? Were his injuries really that serious?

White-uniformed staff bustled to and fro, carrying trays and bedpans. Harrigan signed a register that lay on a table beside the door, then disappeared into an adjoining room. Daniel felt a groggy impulse to flee. Before he reached a decision, Harrigan reappeared with a young nurse. They led the way along a corridor and into a communal lounge. Three elderly men and five women sat on armchairs and wheelchairs arranged in a horseshoe around a TV showing a nature documentary. The volume had been set high and almost eclipsed the sounds from the kitchen next door. A smell of gravy filled the air.

The nurse bent low to tap the arm of one of the seated men. Daniel found himself staring at the nurse's buttocks. Out of the corner of his eye he saw Harrigan openly leering at the same expanse of stretched white uniform.

The nurse tapped the man's arm again. "Mr Benfield? Jeremy?"

Benfield wore a drab, brown dressing gown over striped pyjamas that looked like a wartime prison uniform. His white hair, though thinning at the rear, sprouted wildly from his temples as if bursting outwards to escape his head. The skin on his arms was papery and off-white and looked fragile to the touch.

The sunlight from the bay windows shifted with the swaying of trees outside. Daniel imagined Benfield sitting at his abandoned desk in the Manor. Florence had been right. Her father and the Old Man of Coniston made a neat pair. He imagined clouds casting shadows upon Benfield's dressing gown. He imagined the Old Man of Coniston lying shrouded in grubby terry-towelling.

Benfield finally registered the presence of the nurse and then the two men standing behind her. He turned from the TV with an expression of annoyance, which was only compounded when he recognised Harrigan. Daniel was surprised to see that the old man's eyes were lively and alert.

"Two men come to visit you, Mr Benfield," the nurse said, speaking in a loud voice to combat the volume of the TV. "Lucky you."

Benfield scowled as the nurse tugged at the handles of his wheelchair. She spun him on the spot and wheeled him into a corner of the room. Daniel and a swaying Harrigan followed behind. Here, the volume of the TV programme was close to bearable.

"So how the devil are you, Jeremy?" Harrigan said, slumping with a squeak into an armchair covered with wipe-clean laminate.

Benfield refused to meet his eye. His mouth worked silently before he spoke. "Where's my Florence?"

"Couldn't be here, afraid to say. She sent the scout party."

The old man scowled, then peered at Daniel. "You're a scout?" His eyes narrowed even further. "Do I know you?"

"I'm Daniel Faint. I'm just the house-sitter." He winced as the pain in his neck bloomed again.

Benfield absorbed this information, chewing noisily as though tasting it. "What house?"

"The Manor," Harrigan said. He waved a hand. "While we're not there."

"While *I'm* not there, you mean," Benfield said.

"Well, that too. While nobody's there."

"Nobody's there." Benfield examined his hands, stretching his fingers and then letting them return to their clawlike default.

Sweat prickled on Daniel's forehead. He had never visited a care home before, and the atmosphere was not as he had expected. Instead of a sense of grim finality, the residents seemed placid but floating. He and these smiling husks had a great deal in common. They were all equally directionless. They were all lonely ghosts.

All except Benfield, that was. Benfield was different. His dark eyes held real anger. He didn't belong here.

"Except me," Daniel said, responding to Benfield's earlier statement, though too much time had passed.

Harrigan coughed, then swallowed the phlegm. "They all still treating you well, Jeremy? Florrie asked me to ask."

"They hate me. They won't allow me my books."

The soundtrack of the TV documentary filled the silence. Daniel cocked his head to listen and noticed Benfield do the same. Something about parasites that compelled their hosts to climb high into the tree canopy before death. Daniel turned to find the old man observing him intently.

"I'm sorry about your books," Daniel said. The old man's attention flickered, just a little. "Florence said that you're a historian. Is that right? What do you read?"

Benfield scowled. "She said that? She never understood. History's rot."

Daniel thought of the notebook he had found in Benfield's study. Would the old man be able to decipher his own shorthand? He wished he had brought it with him. Perhaps he might return, once he had freed himself of Harrigan's off-putting presence. He glanced at the horseshoe arrangement of TV viewers. Two had fallen asleep, one lolling from the side of her armchair so that a string of drool dangled towards the floor. Perhaps he wouldn't come back, after all.

Abruptly, Benfield gripped Daniel's hand, pinning it against the arm of his chair with surprising force. Daniel struggled to free himself from the dry touch. Benfield's eyes sought his. Daniel struggled to catch a breath and felt a glint of pain from the wound in his neck.

Benfield's lips smacked silently. When words finally came they were garbled, as though transmitted via a bad phone line. He wet his lips to speak again.

"I can't even watch my shows," he said in a tone so serious as to be almost comical. Except Daniel didn't laugh or even smile. The old man's desperation was real.

Harrigan pulled a smartphone from his pocket and began to thumb through emails. He spoke without looking up. "Isn't there a TV in your room?"

Benfield shot him a look. He seemed surprised to see him. "It only shows sport."

Harrigan had become absorbed in his phone. The screen lit his face from below, adding extra undulations to his chin.

Daniel chewed his lip and watched Benfield. The old man's eyes fell. Perhaps the effort of conversation had exhausted him. Suddenly, Daniel found it difficult to imagine him ever having been young. All of his vitality seemed contained in those eyes. When they were closed, he appeared little more than a dried casing, a cracked shell. An empty house.

He felt he had to do something to bring Benfield back to life. "I'm sure that can't be the case, Mr Benfield. Perhaps I could take a look? Wiggle the aerial, something like that?"

When the old man's eyes raised, Daniel jerked backwards in alarm. The look was exactly the same that his father had given as he waved from the car before leaving, that final time. He had been searching, committing a face to memory, but something else too. Pleading.

They stared at one another, each tethered by the other's gaze. Daniel saw his father, himself, William. The faces of all the men he knew were contained in Benfield's peculiar, blank expression.

Harrigan broke the spell. He waved a hand without looking up. "We'll tell the lackies. That's what they're there for." He sounded as though he had just woken from a nap. "Look, there's a few chores I need to do. Drop in on the village before everything closes. Hope you don't mind, Jeremy? No? There's a good sport." He hefted himself upright. "Florrie'll be in touch, I'd expect."

Harrigan waved an airy goodbye to the nurse, before his eyes dropped to her stockinged legs. "Coming, Faint? Unless you want to hang around here and watch some Attenborough with the seniors?"

Daniel retreated from Benfield with his palms outwards in apology.

"Nobody's there," Benfield said as he watched them leave.

~

Harrigan announced that he was ready to drive once again. Daniel tried to block out the return journey with sleep, but the constant lurching of the Range Rover, and the twin aches from his foot and neck, kept him miserably awake.

Just as he settled into a fitful doze, the car rocked to a halt. Daniel squinted from his half-dream to see that a high street had materialised outside the windscreen. This must be the centre of Broughton-in-Furness. Harrigan swung out of the car, rapped his wedding ring on the window, then plodded away when Daniel remained slumped in his seat. Daniel watched in the rear-view mirror as Harrigan's wide shoulders parted the chain curtains of a butchers shop.

He played with the radio, feeling once again like an abandoned child. The first couple of stations played modern pop music. It sounded flat and mangled. On another station, interviewers discussed the growing problem of squatters in some housing estate, the location of which he didn't catch.

He turned to look out of the window. The car sat at the curbside in front of a grocers shop. A woman wearing an apron stood in its doorway. Presumably, she was the shopkeeper. Her tight ringlets of hair made a triangular halo, or the headdress of an ancient Egyptian king. Daniel slumped further into his seat. The woman emerged from the shop and busied herself rearranging the fruit that lay in tilted wooden crates. Daniel looked at his hands and wished he had a mobile phone.

He glanced up. Now the woman was staring openly into the car. What was her problem? She must be a friend of Nic's. In all likelihood, everybody in the village was a friend of Nic's. The woman scowled and shook her head slowly, then stepped backwards into the darkness.

Soon Harrigan returned with a brown-paper package, which he threw onto Daniel's lap. By the time the car hurtled through the iron archway and crunched to a halt in the centre of the forecourt of the Manor, grease and blood had begun to seep from the package and onto Daniel's jeans.

Harrigan bellowed, "Home sweet home!" He craned his neck to look towards the building. "Friend of yours?"

Daniel turned. A man sat on the doorstep of the Manor. No, not a man. A ghost from the past. If Harrigan hadn't already acknowledged it, he would have assumed the vision was a product of his own paranoia.

He choked on words. His seatbelt jammed as Harrigan heaved himself out of the car. Finally, Daniel toppled from his seat onto the forecourt, regained his balance and pushed past Harrigan to put his own body between Harrigan and the ghost.

"Jimmy?" he hissed.

The ghost raised his head, solid and real. It grinned.

"Danny Boy! Good to see you, old pal." Jimmy extended a hand. When Daniel didn't step forward, Jimmy caught at his hand, gripping it tightly to pull himself to his feet with a grunt. "Been sitting there for hours, you bastard. Still, the views around here aren't to be sniffed at."

Ignoring Daniel's boggled stare, Jimmy stepped aside to greet Harrigan. He smoothed back his greasy, chin-length blonde hair, then wiped his hand on his denim thigh. "Jimmy Williams. Pleased to meet you, squire."

Helplessly, Daniel waved his arm from one man to the other. "Jimmy, this is Ian Harrigan. He owns the Manor."

Jimmy affected a polite bow. "Squire's the right word, then. It's a grade-A setup you've got here."

Harrigan turned to look at the Manor as if seeing it for the first time. "Suppose you're right. It shows in the valuation, of course. Could be a tad more up-to-date, but the shell's sound. Anyway, delighted to meet you. Now, that accent. Belfast, I presume?"

"Born and bred. You never told me you had friends up north," Jimmy said, addressing Daniel.

"I'm just the house-sitter."

"Ah. Aah." The second sound extended; he had begun to grasp the situation.

Daniel widened his eyes as a warning: *Say nothing, you fool.* But if he even noticed, Jimmy ignored him.

"Like I say, it's grand to see you, Danny Boy. You're a slippery fish, you are. You'll never know what a faff I've had trying to hunt you down." He pulled at his goatee as he looked from one man to the other with an amused expression. "So, are you fuckers going to invite me inside?"

~

The second time Daniel had seen Jimmy had been from a distance of fifty metres or more, in the half-light of dawn. Jimmy had been instantly recognisable as he emerged from the lab. His blonde hair was half hidden under his black, peaked cap.

Daniel clung to the brick wall of the neighbouring building. He was a shadow among the shadows.

He smiled to himself as he noted the uniform. Of course. Jimmy was a guard. All that self-aggrandisement about his involvement at the lab, and he was just a security guard.

The stillness of the air meant that even at this distance Daniel could hear the click of the door behind Jimmy. Had he used a key? No, there appeared to be a keypad beside the door. Some kind of pass card, perhaps.

The low building that contained the lab looked nondescript. This section of the Shotover industrial estate had been mostly abandoned in favour of a redeveloped science park, half a mile closer to the city centre. The buildings here had been left to decay; the only other one in use carried hoardings advertising refrigeration services. The place was an ideal hiding spot for a project to be kept under wraps.

He ducked back behind the wall as a car pulled into the complex. It must be the first of the lab scientists, though it was only a little after four in the morning. They were certainly dedicated. Jimmy waved at the driver and retrieved a lanyard from around his neck. He passed it before some hidden device beside the gates, which opened automatically. He saluted as the car passed.

Jimmy stepped through the gate. After checking the locks, he set off on foot in the direction of the city. Daniel gave him a headstart, then followed.

When Jimmy reached the outskirts of Oxford he made directly for a bar with a neon sign advertising 'All Night Service'. With a sigh, Daniel chose a bench within sight of the entrance. He pulled his jacket tighter around himself and huddled down.

By the time Jimmy emerged again, sunlight had appeared over the roofs. His walk had become slow and unsteady. Daniel followed, skirting around the first commuters waiting for buses. Jimmy stopped at a doorway between a bicycle shop and a computer repair shop with newspaper-blanked windows. He patted his pockets before producing a bunch of keys. He leant on the door, pushing heavily to force it open and almost toppling onto the pavement in the process.

Daniel waited. He ordered food from nearby takeaways. He watched. He waited.

This routine continued each morning for more than a fortnight. Jimmy's habits were rigid. He visited the same bar every morning after his guard duties ended. Then he slept, or at least failed to emerge from his flat, until late afternoon.

Daniel chose a Friday night to put his plan into action, in the hope that weekend revellers would provide additional camouflage. Jimmy, unwittingly, played his part to perfection. When Daniel, with his hoodie pulled tight around his face, appeared at the doorway to his flat and supported Jimmy as he heaved open the door, Jimmy grunted gratefully. Daniel jammed his foot in the doorway before it slammed shut.

Jimmy had already stumbled up the stairs. By the time Daniel located the bedroom the Irishman was already asleep, face down upon the bed. His phone and lanyard lay on the bedside table. Daniel pocketed both and slipped out of the building, easing open the front door slowly to prevent it from creaking.

~

Before Daniel could accost him, Jimmy insisted that he would be the one to cook. His reedy singing voice carried from the open door of the Manor's kitchen and into the lounge. The lilting melody, some old pop song, sounded ridiculous due to his harsh Belfast accent. He mangled the words: *I can see Claire Lee now Lorraine has gone, now I've got old Bob Stackles in my way...*

Daniel only half-listened as Harrigan gave a dreary lecture about conventions of the hunt. His brandished whisky tumbler magnified the wide pores on his chin. At that moment, Daniel felt that he could not have disliked the man more. Nevertheless, he nodded every so often and managed several hollow chuckles which sounded like weak echoes of Harrigan's belly laughs.

He sunk down into his thoughts. Jimmy must have suspected immediately that it was Daniel who had stolen the machine. Was he enough of an imbecile to have spoken to anybody else about it?

Daniel rose from his seat. Still nodding at Harrigan's anecdotes, he strolled the length of the room. He pretended to admire the view from the window in between furtive glances at the space where the time machine had stood. He saw no trace of the apparatus, not even the faintest of carpet indentations where the ring of panels had been. How much time had passed?

There could be only one explanation for the disappearance of the time machine. Jimmy must have taken it. He must have had access to the Manor, despite his pretence of waiting outside for Daniel and Harrigan. He might have been skulking in the grounds for any amount of time. Daniel felt a wave of relief. So he hadn't imagined the prowler, after all.

Jimmy appeared at the doorway. He wore a flower-patterned apron spattered with golden grease. "Grub's up, lads!"

Harrigan roared with approval. He attempted to raise himself from the sofa twice before he regained his balance.

Jimmy had set all three places at one end of the kitchen table. Harrigan deposited himself into the chair at its head. He spread his arms wide to receive the food that Jimmy placed before him.

"Honest to God, you won't have tasted steak like this before," Jimmy said.

Harrigan had already begun to eat. He spoke between slurps. "Delicious! What's the sauce?"

"Family secret, old pal," Jimmy said. "I'd have to kill you and all that."

Daniel's eyes widened as he noticed Jimmy's sly smile. Might he really stoop to poisoning their food? If he had already taken the time machine, what could be his motive for returning now? To finish them off, perhaps, and therefore cut short the trail of evidence. He looked down at his own plate and then back at Jimmy. But, seeing Jimmy tuck into his own steak, and for lack of options or conviction, he cut himself a small slice.

In a subtle motion unseen by Harrigan, Jimmy held up a flattened hand: *Stop*.

Daniel froze with the meat halfway to his mouth. Horrified, his eyes flicked to watch Harrigan.

Jimmy guffawed, coughing a spray of spittle onto his plate. He turned his raised hand and curled his fingers so that only the middle one still extended.

Daniel mouthed the word, "Bastard."

Harrigan remained oblivious to the exchange. He gestured at each of them in turn with a fork. "So do you two study together?"

Jimmy snickered. "Study? Aye, that's right. Cribbing homework, all that." He frowned at Daniel. "Seriously though, me and Danny Boy go way back. Thick as thieves."

"And what're you studying, again?" Harrigan said. "Faint here did tell me, but my brain's a—you know—sieve."

"Physics," Daniel said.

"Accounting," Jimmy said, at the same time.

Daniel coughed in an attempt to hide the mistake. The fool was going to ruin everything. "Applied sciences, really," he said. "It takes in all sorts of subjects. It's hard to explain."

Harrigan finished his steak. The wooden chair creaked as he leant back with his full and considerable weight. "That's why it's not the sport for me, I suppose. You don't hunt, do you, James?"

"Jimmy. Aye, I hunt. Nothing like stalking a prey. Am I right?"

"Ha!" Harrigan jabbed a finger towards Daniel. "This poor chap wouldn't agree. Found him cowering in the mud this afternoon. Hadn't taken a single shot and promptly lost his rifle!" He pushed a few leaves of rocket around his plate with his fork, eyeing Daniel's half-eaten steak.

"Aye, well, he's not exactly got the killer instinct, this one." Jimmy said. Daniel flinched as a clammy hand closed around his arm. "But give him a few snares and he'll string you up good and proper."

The dinner seemed to last hours. After clearing the plates, Jimmy produced three dusty bottles of red wine—he must already have located the bar—and Daniel watched on as the other two men muttered in a conspiratorial manner. Their giggles—Harrigan's low, a borderline cough, and Jimmy's reedy and weaselly—mingled with the loud hum of the fridge. The whispered conversation washed over and through him as he sunk further into despair. Had Jimmy arrived only to torture him? Despite giving all appearances of being absorbed in Harrigan's impenetrable anecdotes, Jimmy shot a warning look at Daniel whenever he made to rise from his seat. Daniel sat glassy-eyed, only sipping wine occasionally, until the two other men agreed to retire to the lounge.

As Harrigan lumbered across the lobby, Daniel took his opportunity. He blocked Jimmy's path. The misaligned lobby mirrors produced duplicates of them both.

"What do you want with me?" Daniel hissed, barring the lounge doorway with an arm. Over Jimmy's shoulder he saw Harrigan stumble drunkenly into a sofa before apologising to it.

Jimmy smirked. "What do I want? To see my old buddy. To make a new friend." He gestured with a thumb towards their host.

"We're not buddies," Daniel said. "We barely know each other. I never liked you, and I know you feel the same."

"Call me hopeful, then. We have a bond, you and me. Peas in a pod."

As if to illustrate their similarity, Jimmy leant against the door frame, mirroring Daniel's pose. Daniel scowled and pulled his arm away.

"There's nothing here for you," he said.

Jimmy shrugged and spread his arms wide to encompass the contents of the Manor. "So it seems. You crafty dog."

So Jimmy was going to play this game after all. If he insisted on denying any knowledge about the whereabouts of the time machine, then Daniel would have to play along, too.

"I needed time out so I travelled up north," he said. "What's so strange about that?"

"What's strange was the look on your face when you clocked me. I said to myself, 'O Jimmy, ye of little faith, why did you doubt?'"

"I just want a new start." Daniel put his hand on Jimmy's shoulder, then pocketed it. "Harrigan's leaving tomorrow morning. I want you gone too. All right?"

Jimmy smiled. "Like you say. If there's nothing for me here, why would I hang around? Apart from our gentle host's offer of setting me up with one of the local trollops, course."

So that was what they'd been whispering about. Daniel prayed that Harrigan hadn't been referring to Nic.

"Isn't that right, big man?" Jimmy called to Harrigan. "Boys out on the town? All the mice having a good old play while the cat's tucked up in bed in London."

Harrigan raised his glass in salute but then his head fell. Like a sleepwalker, he rose unsteadily to his feet. The glass dropped to the carpet. Daniel felt certain that he couldn't have hated him more.

"Christ, he's out for the count," Jimmy said. He dashed into the room to support the swaying man. "Jesus, Ian. You should consider the Atkins. You're heavy as hell." All the while, he kept his attention fixed on Daniel standing in the doorway.

"Well, let's get this drunken lump some well-deserved kip," Jimmy said. He was struggling for breath. He tilted Harrigan's chin, which now rested upon his chest. "Come on, fella. Up the stairs to Bedfordshire."

Harrigan grunted and leered stupidly.

"Good lad," Jimmy said, patting Harrigan's cheek. "Now that I think of it, I'm ready to turn in, myself."

Daniel watched them stagger three-legged towards the stairs. He slouched into the lobby, chewing his lip.

Jimmy turned on the bottom step. "Oh no you don't." He grinned, despite the discomfort of Harrigan's weight against his shoulder. "You go first, Danny Boy. I insist."

Daniel strode up the stairs two at a time, muttering to himself.

~

He jolted from sleep. The noise came again. It was from within the Manor, close to the door to his room. In moments he was on his feet, still dressed in yesterday's clothes. Moonlight turned the stonework around the window silver. Once again, time had slipped past him. After Jimmy had escorted him into his room he had intended to stay awake, not trusting the Irishman for a second, but he had no memory after he had stretched out upon the bed. He must have fallen into a deep sleep immediately.

He eased open the door, keeping one finger on the latch to silence it. A creak of floorboards echoed from the direction of the landing. He crept along the corridor with one hand trailing along the dado rail, as if it might allow him to move with greater stability. Which bedroom had Jimmy picked for himself? Which had he deposited Harrigan into, for that matter? The Manor had rearranged itself around him again, its rooms reordered at random.

He peered around the corner. A shadow descended the stairs, legs raised high with each step like a jewel thief in a cartoon. Harrigan could never have moved that lightly, even while sober. It must be Jimmy.

The only explanation for the disappearance of the time machine was that Jimmy had dismantled and hidden it after

Daniel had last pressed the trigger. He had been oblivious, in whatever ghostly limbo constituted time travel. Perhaps that in turn explained why Daniel had shifted to another room on his return. The time machine had done its best to restore him to his original position, despite having been pulled into pieces after his departure. That bastard. As far as Jimmy knew, taking apart the machine might have killed him.

But why had Jimmy revealed himself? Daniel had had no clue that he had been hiding in the grounds of the Manor, other than a general sense of unease, easily attributable to paranoia. With the time machine in Jimmy's possession, he might have left the Manor far behind and been untraceable.

Only one answer made any sense. The time machine alone hadn't been enough for Jimmy. Either he didn't understand how to operate it—difficult to imagine, given the simplicity of its controls—or he was too cowardly to use it himself.

He needed Daniel.

There. A weakness. Except that Daniel wasn't willing to be a test subject for Jimmy's benefit. And there was no doubt that coercion would be required for Jimmy to use it himself.

But still, this was more or less what he had hoped for: a chance to observe somebody else using the time machine. Let Jimmy be the guinea pig. And if Daniel, in the heat of the moment, decided to disassemble the machine once Jimmy disappeared, so be it. It would be fascinating to see where Jimmy ended up, and his state of mind when he returned. Science in action. Label the axes.

From his vantage point on the staircase half-landing, he watched Jimmy move into Benfield's study. Daniel frowned, trying to picture the small room with its dust sheet-covered desk and chair. Were there even cupboards in there? Certainly nothing large enough to hold even one of the machine's panels.

Jimmy reappeared a few seconds later. Next, he moved towards the bar, pushing aside its curtain covering. Daniel tiptoed downwards to the lowest stair. He hesitated, resisting the temptation to follow.

When Jimmy emerged once again, Daniel slipped into the study at the last second. He held his breath and perched awkwardly behind the door to avoid disturbing the plastic sheet that covered the armchair. He leant forwards far enough to see into the lobby. Jimmy stood in its centre, turning first one way and then the other. Finally, he headed towards the leisure centre. A whoosh of air accompanied the opening of the plate-glass door.

A minute passed. Daniel fidgeted. Should he follow?

In the lobby he consulted Benfield's grandfather clock and waited another minute. He clucked his tongue.

One minute more and he could no longer bear the tension. He kept to the walls to edge around the lobby, ready to leap into the lounge or kitchen at the first sign of Jimmy's return. He placed a hand on the glass door and winced at its coldness. It had always been warm to the touch before.

The door opened with a sigh. He held it ajar and waited for his eyes to adjust. Moonlight through the conservatory roof illuminated only a small circle of the chequered lino, throwing the rest of the reception into relative gloom.

It was empty. Daniel stifled a nervous laugh. It wasn't as though he had expected to find Jimmy manning the reception desk.

He turned towards the changing rooms and gym, then stopped. He shivered as cool air pulled at his T-shirt. When had it ever been cold in this part of the building? The heating from the swimming pool was usually enough to make the atmosphere tropical.

He turned. Using the reception desk as a shield, he raised himself up to see into the pool.

His breath caught. At the far end of the emptied pool, with the blue tarpaulin crumpled in hillocks at his feet, Jimmy stood before the stacked panels of the time machine.

~

The next morning, Daniel and Jimmy stood side by side on the front doorstep to watch the Range Rover pull away. When it disappeared through the iron gateway, they remained standing together in tense silence.

After discovering Jimmy and the time machine in the emptied pool, Daniel had watched and waited. Jimmy had simply made an inventory of the parts of the machine, tiptoeing around the pile of grey panels without touching them. Afterwards, he had covered the swimming pool once again with the blue tarpaulin. Daniel had snuck away, unseen, before Jimmy re-entered the main building and returned to his bedroom. In the remaining hours Daniel had lain awake. He had stared at the ceiling until the peacocks announced the dawn, then Harrigan and Jimmy rose to rattle kitchenware downstairs. Now his eyes felt puffy and dry.

Finally, he said, "When did you arrive?"

Jimmy smirked. "Does it matter? Before you got back from your would-be killing spree. Wish I could've seen it. Daniel Faint at a duck hunt, what a thought! A bullet in the neck is just what you deserve."

Daniel's fingers went to the wound. It had healed well overnight. It was just a graze after all, as Harrigan's hunter friend had predicted.

"I haven't seen your car," he said.

"I hitched," Jimmy said. "Not as easy as once it was, I can tell you, especially this far north. Pricks. I'm referring to the far-from-generous second-home owners, our absent host excluded." He kicked idly at the boot scraper beside the doorstep. "Ian's a riot. I'll miss the old bugger. But at least we still have his wine cellar, right?"

Lies. Jimmy must have been lurking in the grounds well before Harrigan's arrival, in order to have moved the time machine and restore the furniture to the lounge. Nothing Jimmy said could be trusted.

Abruptly, Jimmy clapped his hands. "Fuck all this. Are you for a swim?" He ducked back inside the Manor.

Daniel's head pounded. If only he could return to a time when he was alone, or at least believed that he was. People complicated everything.

"Jimmy? Stop." His anxiety made his voice louder than necessary, with a note of pleading. In a lower voice he said, "It's just us now. So stop all this."

Jimmy's eyebrows raised.

Daniel felt lightheaded, but he told himself not to lean against the wall. It would show weakness.

"Was it you?" he said. He noticed that his hands were shaking. "I know it was you."

"Was it me?" Jimmy's smile might have appeared genuine, if Daniel didn't know better. "A short question, to the point. But you're going to have to provide me with a bit of context, pal."

Daniel flinched as Jimmy stooped to meet his eyes.

"Christ, you look abysmal," Jimmy said. "Have you looked in the mirror recently? You didn't even look this bad when you were pissed."

Daniel glanced into the portrait mirror that hung on the left wall of the lobby, the one he had moved. It was true, he looked dishevelled and pale. His tousled hair had grown longer than he usually allowed, so that dark curls crept over his forehead, contrasting his bluish-white skin.

His eyes were worse. Could a single sleepless night produce the jagged red streaks from each tear duct to iris?

"You don't know me," Daniel said, "and I already told you to stop this nonsense, all this play-acting. Just tell me. Was it you?"

The smile disappeared. "I might ask you the same question, about all sorts of things. Come on, let's have a shufty at the bugger, how's about that?"

Daniel felt a sudden conviction that if he let Jimmy go now, he might never have the answers he needed. He barred the way to the leisure centre. "How long have you been here?" Any of the shadows lurking around the Manor might have been Jimmy's. On balance, it would be preferable to the alternatives.

Jimmy gave a lopsided grin. "You're a stuck record. Didn't we just have a tender reconciliation only yesterday? Didn't we break bread together—or steak, at least?" He paused, tugging his beard. "Unless... Unless there's a good reason for you being so buzzed. Jesus. You haven't actually used the thing, have you? While I've been here?"

Daniel shook his head. The movement became a shudder. Jimmy was no actor. He genuinely didn't understand what Daniel was talking about. But Jimmy must be guilty of something. Daniel gripped him by the forearm and spun him to face the wall of the lobby. With his free arm he pushed the heavy portrait mirror to one side.

Jimmy gazed at the words written on the wall. He blinked each time the mirror swung to obscure them.

YOU DON'T BELONG HERE.

"Is that how you welcome all your guests?" he said. "It's imaginative, I'll give you that."

Daniel let his arm drop. Nothing made sense. The mirror scraped to stillness.

"What the actual fuck is going on here?" Jimmy said. "Have you lost it? And by 'it', I don't mean your ill-gotten loot, which we both know is right now taking an unscheduled dip in the pool. I mean your godforsaken mind."

Daniel stared at him. He leant heavily against the wall and then slowly slumped to the ground. His words came out only as a whisper.

"I don't know."

EIGHT

Locals trickled into the pub. Each newcomer in turn greeted Georgie the barman, who responded with an easy smile.

Daniel only sipped his drink as Jimmy knocked back a second pint of bitter. The more drunk Jimmy became, the better. He was inconsistent, wild. Sooner or later he would reveal something that Daniel might exploit.

Shifting the time machine from the swimming pool to the lounge had taken them a couple of hours. Daniel could have sworn that the panels had increased in weight. Several times, they had narrowly avoided dropping one. Despite his bravado, Jimmy had handled the apparatus gingerly. It had been he who had insisted that they head to the Cradle before connecting and testing the machine.

"And to think I trusted you," Jimmy muttered. "Your features are deceivingly honest-looking, you know that? You'd never guess you were such an irredeemable turd beneath it all."

"You didn't have to tell me about the time machine in the first place."

Jimmy scowled. "Yeah, I'll know better next time, won't I? Anyway, we're partners now, like we should have been all along."

"We're not partners," Daniel said, unable to hide the anger in his voice. "I know where I'm going. You, you're just a floater."

"All right. Whatever, big man." Jimmy appeared genuinely hurt. "You're the boss. But you'll not find me floating anyplace else, now that I'm here. Which brings me to my next point. My arms are knackered from all this beating around the bush, if you catch my drift. Here's the million dollar question." He pulled at his beard. "I know you've used it."

"That's not a question."

"It bloody well is."

Daniel made Jimmy wait. Then he nodded.

Jimmy clapped his hands in delight. "What's it like? Did it work? It worked, didn't it?"

"Why don't you see for yourself? We could head back to the Manor and test it, right now."

Jimmy's fingers trembled a little as he rapped on the tabletop. "You do it. I'll watch."

"Like I said. I've already used it. It's your turn."

"Come on, you fuckbag. I've waited all this time. I've travelled all this way. Show a little hospitality."

"Well, I'm not the one who needs convincing, am I?" Daniel said. He was beginning to enjoy himself. "Maybe let's stick it back in the pool for safekeeping."

"Until when?"

Daniel noted the panic in Jimmy's voice. "Don't know. Now that I'm here, I fancy taking a proper holiday after all. Time out."

Jimmy puffed his cheeks. "It doesn't suit you, you know, being lord of the manor. Acting as though you have a claim on that fucking machine. Next you'll be telling me you understand how the thing works."

"I don't see that I need to know." But Jimmy had touched a nerve. Maybe it really was unreasonable to expect he might develop the time machine's capabilities, given that he didn't comprehend even its basic principles. "Anyway, don't get all high-and-mighty. You don't understand it either."

Jimmy made an *oh really?* face. He held his empty glass in his right hand and grabbed for Daniel's half-full pint. Beer spilled onto the sticky table.

"There are two options, see," he said, ignoring Daniel's glare. His voice had the tone of a learnt speech. "Relative velocity, or gravity. These glasses here, they're spaceships, right? And look! There's a clock on the wall of each cockpit. When they fly past each other, our spacemen chums look in at each other's window. And each of them sees that the other one's clock is running slower than their own."

Daniel watched, trying not to appear impressed. Second-hand knowledge it may be, but Jimmy at least demonstrated a grasp of the concepts.

"Ever heard of the International Space Station?" Jimmy said.

Daniel shrugged. What did he care about that sort of sci-fi nonsense?

"Then you're missing out," Jimmy continued. "It's only the greatest achievement of our era, you arts-and-craftsy fuckwit. You'd rather watch Grayson Perry wax lyrical about pots on the Culture Show than learn about staggering examples of human triumph over the unsullied expanses of space. Fine. So it's a space station hanging above the Earth like a giant fucking..." The glasses clinked together. "Moth. Except it's a moth filled with astronauts."

"So not like a moth, then."

"Who the fuck cares, Danny Boy. Think up your own analogy. Anyway, the pertinent detail is that, believe it or not, astronauts up in the ISS age more slowly that they would on Earth. Point-oh-oh-seven seconds every six months."

"So the secret to eternal youth is to live on a spaceship."

"That's beside the point. Anyway, that was all just preamble, but it shows that time travel's real and happening all the time. The whole relative velocity thing isn't any use, 'specially if you don't happen to have a spaceship. Which, illustrious and well-funded though they may be, our

Oxfordian triple-science boffins do not own. Did not. So it had to be gravity."

Daniel thought of the gravitational pull that the time machine seemed to exert upon him. He felt it now, even this far from the Manor, trying to draw him back. "So the machine..." He realised that he had no idea how to finish the thought.

"Far as I understand it, it simulates a massive decrease in gravitational force. All those big old grey panels, they're for focussing, like a satellite dish. So when you sit in the middle, they—don't ask me for details, I can't even wire a plug—they create a gravitational field around you. And lickety-split, it's suddenly as though you're farther away from the centre of the Earth. To all intents and purposes, you are."

Jimmy sat back in his chair, apparently satisfied that he had explained the mystery.

"Firstly, that doesn't explain anything, if you don't even know how the panels work," Daniel said. "And secondly, it still sounds impossible."

Jimmy leered. "I didn't say it wasn't impossible. *You* were the one who said you'd tested it and it worked."

Daniel's attention wavered as he noticed a familiar figure at the bar. He recognised the broad back, though it seemed less bent than before. Tosh. The gardener stood upright, both hands flat on the bar, deep in conversation with Georgie the barman. Perhaps the hunched back was a pose he adopted only while at work.

The barman nodded and then, abruptly, Tosh turned around. Daniel slid down further into his seat, trying to hide behind Jimmy. When he raised his eyes, Tosh was still looking in his direction. To Daniel's surprise, the gardener raised a hand in a solemn salute. Stranger still, he flashed a smile. Daniel shuddered and nodded stiffly in response. Tosh knew something, he was certain.

Jimmy, bored by the silence, rose and approached the bar. Daniel watched carefully for any sign of recognition between him and the gardener, but there was no hint. Jimmy stood apart from Tosh, who had now resumed his conversation with the barman, and paid for two more pints with money he had borrowed from Daniel.

Daniel glared at Jimmy's back. He was starting to believe the Irishman's version of events more all the time. Or, at least, events as seen from Jimmy's uninformed perspective. But one aspect still remained unexplained, one that might be vital. Their hostility to each other had thawed a little since they had reconstructed the time machine. He could push his luck a little.

"You never told me how you found me," he said when Jimmy returned.

Foam formed a white moustache over Jimmy's reddish stubble. "Aye. Bet you're shit scared of the others tracking you down. Don't worry, I didn't let on to a soul. And I'm untraceable. SAS style."

"You were in the SAS?"

"Yeah. No. No. But I've got the principles down. Sleeping in dug pits, all that."

"Did you contact the van hire company?"

Jimmy raised a finger to tap his nose. He missed.

Daniel frowned. There had been a dozen weaknesses in his plan. The student temp at the van hire company. His face or gait recognised in CCTV footage from the cameras outside the lab. Fingerprints, DNA processed and identified. A dozen dangling threads that anybody might have pulled at in order to unravel his trail.

He rubbed at his face. When he looked up, he groaned. Even facing away from him at the bar, Daniel recognised the Egyptian-headdress hairstyle of the village grocer. Beside her stood Nic.

"Are these seats free?" the grocer said, pointing at two empty stools at their table. "This place is rammed."

She sat down beside Daniel and pulled Nic onto the remaining seat. Her hand extended towards Jimmy. "Lillian. Nice to meet you."

Jimmy took her hand and bent to kiss it, transferring a dot of foam onto her knuckle. "Jimmy. And I'll raise your 'nice to meet you' to 'charmed'." He smiled at Nic, registered her frosty expression, then turned to Daniel. "I take it you're both already acquainted with Danny here?"

Lillian giggled, wiggling her fingers as she pulled back her hand. "By reputation."

Daniel glanced at Nic. She was concentrating on loosening and refitting a thumb ring.

Jimmy gave a pantomime shudder. "Is it me, or did it just get a shitload colder in here?"

Lillian turned to Daniel. "Thought you'd have dropped into the shop by now. Are you eating? You'll waste away, you will. Unless you've been getting takeaways, which you shouldn't. Different flavours every night, it's not good for the constitution. Just pick one and stick with it, that's what I say."

Daniel frowned. "Look, is that supposed to be some veiled reference—"

"Lil, let's go," Nic said. "He's not worth it." Tears glistened at the corners of her eyes. Perhaps she really had liked him, at first.

"I don't belong here. Is that what you're going to say?" Daniel said and immediately regretted it.

Jimmy stood up, bumping the table with his thighs. "Yikes. You won't go before I buy you lovely ladies a drink, I hope?" He left without taking their orders. Daniel fidgeted as Lillian ushered a surly Nic to retake her place. The three of them sat in silence. When he returned, Jimmy splashed Guinness onto Daniel's knees. The drinks he placed before Nic and Lillian were a murky yellow.

"So, what's doing around here?" Jimmy said, beaming. "What local attractions can I expect to see? Apart from the delightful present company, of course."

Lillian giggled again. "How long are you planning on staying?"

"Oh, you know. A while. Dan and me, we've got business. Old scores to settle."

Nic mumbled something into her drink.

"Speak up," Jimmy said. "Like the fellow with cake in his ears, I'm a trifle deaf."

"I said, that makes two of us," Nic said with a scowl.

Jimmy gave a low whistle. "Look, love. I don't know what Danny's been up to, but you can join the queue. Or the club. The Daniel Faint Grudge Society. This one's a fucker through and through." He leant close and lowered his voice to a stage whisper. "Tell me your woes."

Nic's cheeks reddened and her back straightened. "No, you tell me. How do you two know each other?"

Jimmy indicated his own pint and Daniel's. "We met much as we are now. Drinks, general gaiety. Sweetness and light."

"Leave it," Daniel hissed. He had already become too visible in the village, even without Jimmy blundering around, drawing attention and providing any snoopers with extra information.

"Can't quite pin down why Daniel was there in the first place, mind!" Jimmy continued. "It was a stag party, see, not the natural habitat of the lesser-spotted sourpuss. A long weekend in Bath, a mere three months ago. As you might have intuited from my amenable disposition, I was the obvious choice to be best man. For Tom Bradshaw, this is, a stand-up pal. God alone knows how he imagined Danny here would add to the jollity."

Daniel remembered Jimmy's entrance on the first day of that weekend. He had arrived at the rented apartment late, already steaming drunk, with a mascara-smeared girl half his age. After the girl vanished along with his wallet, Jimmy appealed to the dozen or so men in the group and somehow convinced them that the weekend would be all the more enjoyable if they paid his way. Tom Bradshaw himself had been wary until his spiked drink took effect.

The most meaningful exchange Daniel and Tom had at school was when Daniel had chased him down with a branch in the copse beside the football field. Looking back, it had probably been a displaced response to some run-in with William at home. Tom's invitation to join his stag weekend, fifteen years later, seemed like a delayed punishment. It was as if he wanted to draw attention to Daniel's friendlessness in adulthood.

He had felt absolute scorn for Jimmy that first day, despite his obvious charm. But that had changed once Jimmy had let slip his secrets and, eventually, shown him the video on his phone. The teddy bear disappeared and, in an instant, Daniel found a renewed purpose in his life.

"I'm leaving," Daniel said, struggling to stand, "and so are you."

Jimmy pulled him back into his seat without turning away from Nic and Lillian, who both listened intently.

"Danny takes the 'law of the stag' very seriously," he said. From the side of his mouth he addressed Daniel in a stage whisper. "I won't let on about the seedier goings-on, big man." He grinned. "Anyway. So we're having a fine old time, bumping along from drinking establishment to drinking establishment. The watering holes of Bath are a decent sort, if you can ignore the stink of rotten eggs surrounding the whole place. And of course we're bonding nicely, all dozen or so of us. But Danny's a bit of a withdrawn sort of a chump, so as best man I make a special effort with him."

His hand clamped onto Daniel's shoulder even before he attempted to rise.

"So in the course of the first evening, and then the hungover next morning, and the okay-fellas-let's-do-this-all-again next night out, Danny and me have our chitchats. And, as we've established, I'm an amiable chap and perhaps I say some things that I shouldn't've. Little tidbits, here and there. Gossip. Things I've noticed while going about my daily business. Plans and schemes, pie in the sky, you know."

"We can talk this over back at the Manor," Daniel whispered. The other night, Nic hadn't believed Daniel's explanation about the time machine, which was just as well. It was better that she thought he was a nutcase than her suspecting that he had been telling the truth. The last thing he needed now was for Jimmy to reinforce the idea in her mind.

"No, how about let's talk it over right here." Jimmy rose, holding his pint aloft. "In fact, I'll put it bluntly. You stole from me, friend. Not materially, I grant you. But you stole my grand plan. And then you went and stole—"

The other glasses crashed to the ground as Daniel upended the table. Nic and Lillian jumped backwards as he sprang towards Jimmy. His fist crackled as it made contact with Jimmy's bristly chin.

~

"If I'd known you felt so strongly about it, I wouldn't have laboured the point," Jimmy said. He rubbed his jaw and made a series of exploratory open-mouthed vowel sounds.

Daniel held open the gate that opened onto the dark expanse of the golf course. Jimmy flinched as he passed, as if expecting Daniel to hit him again.

"You've a better left hook than I'd have expected, too," Jimmy said. "Yet another of your hidden qualities."

"I should have thumped you sooner," Daniel said. The episode had left him lightheaded, having glimpsed a new approach to defining relationships. Perhaps violence was the only way to keep Jimmy in check. Perhaps that was the only way to deal with anybody who represented an obstacle. "Do you realise the damage you've done? I was struggling to stay incognito before, but now, with you here..." He puffed out his cheeks.

"The damage *I've* done? That's fucking rich," Jimmy said. "What about the damage you did to me? You think I could carry on as usual, do you, back down in Oxford? That was a tasty little job I had, I'll have you know. But you did me out of it when you waltzed into the lab masquerading as me, using my fucking credentials. I'd say that entitles me to compensation. And that's without even mentioning all the other stuff. You nasty bastard."

Daniel thought of that final day in Oxford, watching the door to Jimmy's flat, checking him in and out, praying that he wouldn't notice the missing lanyard and phone until too late. Later, as darkness fell, he sat in the van parked around the corner from the lab, trying to summon the courage to set the plan in motion, to pull the trigger.

Police? I'd like to report some suspicious behaviour. I keep seeing young girls going in and out of my neighbour's building, at odd hours. The two that just went in there, they look... well, they look dreadful. Williams. Jimmy Williams. I don't know him, he's pretty evasive. 148a Cowley Road. He's in there right now. Please hurry.

Once he had gone that far, there could be no going back. He pulled the black cap further over his eyes as he left the van. He swiped the lanyard. He entered the lab.

Each aspect of the plan had been necessary and considered. Jimmy had to be prevented from entering the lab, so Daniel had given the police just enough of a story for them to hold him for a few hours.

At the end of the fairway the Old Man of Coniston merged absolutely into the darkness, as if it had been plucked from the horizon. Daniel shuddered at the thought of something so large going missing. He pulled his jacket tighter around himself.

"Aye, well. Fuck it." Jimmy span slowly on the spot, grinding a heel into the damp grass. Tosh wouldn't be pleased. Jimmy reached inside his coat to produce a half-full bottle that glinted rust-coloured in the moonlight.

Daniel stopped dead. "Did you steal that from behind the bar?"

"You're the master thief around here, not me."

Daniel clapped a hand over his eyes. "I don't believe this. Do you have the faintest idea of what 'keeping a low profile' means? And you seriously expect me to make you a partner in this whole business?"

Jimmy pirouetted closer and bent to peer beneath Daniel's shielding hand. "Aha! So you're coming around to the idea!"

Daniel sighed.

"So what's the big idea, anyway?" Jimmy continued. He seemed satisfied that the argument was over. He swigged from the bottle noisily. "If the machine works, I mean, and I presume it does. Stick in on eBay? What category would you even list it under?"

"We can't sell it, you cretin. It's stolen goods."

"What's the use of it if we can't sell it?" Jimmy said. "It's worth a fortune. Isn't it?"

"I just need to learn enough about it. Change a few aspects, refine the control mechanism." Feigning expertise was the secret to keeping the upper hand. "Mostly aesthetic, nothing major. But enough to present it as a half-plausible new development."

Jimmy snorted. "So you're expecting people to believe that you built this thing at exactly the same precise moment that a bunch of more plausible fuckwits built one down south? You're not exactly a renowned scientist. Did you even see those bespectacled twats at the lab? Now *that's* a crowd of Oxford-educated virgins people'd believe might build this kind of thing."

During the break-in at the lab, Daniel had seen the desktops full of anime plushies, the dartboard with a pristine treble-twenty. Even empty and in half-light the lab had looked more like a university common-room than a serious workplace.

"Jimmy, you talk so much that half the time I don't think even you're listening to what you're saying," Daniel said. "It's just like you told me, three months ago. Think of all that seed money the investors put into the project over the years. It would have dried up, evaporated, as soon as the machine disappeared."

Jimmy's expression darkened. "Aye. Fair point. But they were stinking rich, those investors. The boffins sure were wary of their wealthy overlords. Must have been desperate, taking money from crooks like that. They weren't exactly you might call 'angel' investors, at least judging by the gents they used as enforcers."

"'Enforcers'?"

"Didn't I mention them before? They're some serious fuckers. You wouldn't want to get on the wrong side of them. I'm not scared of many folks, but..." Jimmy pulled back the collar of his shirt to reveal wide, pale continents of bruises on his shoulder. "That's another injustice I can chalk up to you. I gave them the slip, but there's another reason why I won't be hurrying back to the dreaming spires of Oxford. You get me?"

So there could be no way of keeping Jimmy at arm's length, after all. Now he was as invested in the time machine as Daniel himself. Instead, he would have to mould Jimmy into somebody useful to him.

"Don't you see, then?" Daniel said, "It's imperative that we don't draw attention to ourselves."

Jimmy nodded. Daniel almost felt sorry for him. He was like an enthusiastic dog who understood that he had torn up a sofa. After a few moments, Jimmy brightened. "But it looks like the research group's disbanded. The lab's been gutted, bare bricks. Looks like the backdrop to a Def Leppard video."

"Makes sense. All the available money would have been pumped into the time machine—*one* time machine, singular. It'd take years to raise enough to start again, with new investors who'd require at least a proof of concept before they'd stump up cash. Without cashflow, the research team are nobodies."

"So it's just the first lot of money-men and their pals that we should worry about."

"Right. And I'm positive they can't follow my trail. At least, I was."

Jimmy raised both hands in a defensive posture. "Don't look at me. Like I said. SAS-style."

They trudged the length of the golf course. After a minute, Jimmy said, "Jesus. All the same, I can't deny you took the ball and you fucking ran with it." He kicked idly at the grass. "No idea how you figured out so much about the time machine, just from what I told you at the stag. I only gave you the teensiest hints."

Daniel snorted. "You shot your mouth off the whole time. And it was clear that you were never going to do anything about it. You're passive, Jimmy. You watch from the sidelines." He tailed off, peering at the copse. Not for the first time, he thought he saw movement within the clump of trees, something shifting from trunk to trunk. He narrowed his eyes and slowed his pace. But the harder he stared, the less certain he became that he had seen anything.

"All right, guilty as charged." Jimmy held up both hands. "But I'm not nearly as guilty as you. You're a regular Raffles now, and the stakes are higher with it being a hush-hush project. When they finally come after you, it'll not be the coppers knocking politely on your door, you get me?"

"I get you."

"So we're partners after all. I know what you know, Danny Boy. We're in this together."

"So it seems."

They reached the door of the Manor. Instinctively, Daniel glanced at the dark patch beneath the monkey puzzle before scrabbling to unlock the door.

NINE

Jimmy held up the plastic handle. "It looks like something from a Fisher Price toy. I was expecting more settings. Dials."

"We'll need all that," Daniel said. "Without precision, it's just a curiosity. Nobody in their right mind..." He clamped his mouth shut, hoping that Jimmy wouldn't complete the thought. It wouldn't do to put Jimmy off the idea of using the machine.

"So there's no telling where you'll end up? I mean when."

Daniel squeezed the trigger and Jimmy winced. Daniel laughed and pointed at the other, unconnected end of the cable.

"Somewhere between an hour and a couple of days. But I've been thinking about it. I daren't pull this thing apart—" Daniel waved the trigger handle. "—but there must be a way of rigging it up to other controls. We can't trust just pulling it willy-nilly each time. I'm thinking of some sort of motorised pump, computer-controlled, squeezing this thing to an exact degree. Of course, eventually it needs to be even more accurate than that. But first things first."

Jimmy's eyes had glazed. "And it's been just you using it, so far?"

Daniel nodded. Better not to mention the tests with the clay figurines. If Jimmy hadn't already thought of demonstrating the machine using something inanimate, he wasn't about to prompt him.

"Has anyone seen you do it?" Jimmy said.

That was a more difficult question to answer. Daniel hesitated, then said, "No."

Jimmy pulled at his beard. "I wonder if there's a flash. Or whether you go all speckly, beam-me-up-Scotty, or just disappear in a pop. C'mon Dan, show me, will you?"

Daniel stepped aside to give Jimmy an unobstructed view of the time machine. "Seeing as we're partners now, I think it's only right that you have a go yourself."

Jimmy's eyes flicked to the central tube. "To tell the truth, Danny, I'm not a great traveller. I'm all right when I'm driving but anything where I'm not in control, I'm sick as a dog. You know? Can't even take the train to see my ma, these days. No, it's not for me. You knock yourself out though."

Daniel sighed, affecting nonchalance. It would take effort to get Jimmy into the machine, but it was the only way he could observe its powers, its possibilities. Testing it again on himself might only cause further disorientation.

"Fine," he said. "But I'm not using it either."

Jimmy reached forwards, then looked hurt and disappointed as Daniel brushed away his hand.

"Look," Jimmy said, "I see what's eating you. I'm not blind. You think that if you get into that machine and—pop—disappear in a puff of smoke, or whatever, I'll—"

"You'll pack up the machine and head to the hills." Daniel frowned. It still bothered him; hadn't Jimmy done just that, before Daniel returned after last using the time machine? The more time they spent together, the less certain Daniel became.

Jimmy chewed his lip. "Course, I might worry that you might do the same thing. I could wake up here with you long gone, and I'd be right back where I started, months later with the trail gone cold. Old man Harrigan wondering why the hell I'm still sitting on his sofa."

"It's quite the puzzle, isn't it?" Daniel coiled up the trigger cable, then hung the loop from the wall of the slatted tube.

"So we won't use it," Jimmy said. Daniel noted the relief in his voice.

"That does seem the only conclusion."

Jimmy exhaled. "Jesus. I'm not great with tension, you know that? And what we've done here is crank up the tension big time. You know what we should do? We should talk about the future. And I don't mean the *kazaam*-jumping-instantly-to-the-future kind of future, either."

"No," Daniel said. "More like the work-your-arse-off kind."

Jimmy flopped onto the sofa. "So. Spit it out, then. What's this master plan of yours? Show me the money."

Daniel paced back and forth, making him wait. Talking things through might well cause him problems later, yet he felt desperate to unburden himself. His new idea—the master plan—still felt embryonic. Even worse, he was beginning to mistrust his own perspective. Perhaps a sounding board was exactly what he required.

He settled into the sofa opposite. He steepled his fingers in a caricature of a lecturer.

"Cryogenics," he said. "Well, sort of. Same idea."

Jimmy squinted at him. "Like Walt Disney freezing his head, ready to be implanted on a robotic body someday?"

"Exactly," Daniel said. "Except simpler. And less overtly like the plan of a Bond villain."

"Well, that's debatable." Jimmy's forehead creased in thought. "So, instead of freezing yourself in dry ice, you pop yourself into the machine and wake up when the robot body's finished and ready to go."

Daniel shrugged.

Jimmy's hands moved as if he was turning over the plan made solid. "Nah, I still don't get it. So we've got the power to time-travel into the future. A world of fucking possibilities. Watch World Cup twenty-twenty-two. Shag your mate's great-granddaughter. And you're talking about just having a nap for the good of your health. Is that the best we can do?"

"Think about it. We—I—stole it, Jimmy. We're on the run. It's not like we can set up a time-travel estate agent in Regent Street, or even sell the machine to Google. We have no choice but to keep it under the radar."

Jimmy's hands settled on his lap. "Okay. All right. But the first time we showed it to somebody, offered them a one-way ticket to the twenty-third century... Then it would be *above* the radar, wouldn't it? On the radar. Whatever."

"Think about it. Who is this hypothetical customer?"

"I don't know. Someone with pots of cash. Clint Eastwood. Richard Branson." Jimmy's eyes glistened. "Aha! So we only show it to the super-rich, right? Charge them an arm and a leg, and they'd never tell a soul, because they're secretive bastards anyway?"

Daniel nodded. "It'd still be risky. There aren't many people who wouldn't fear the authorities bearing down on them. You need to narrow it down. Not just super-rich, but also old, ill. Terminally ill. There's your target demographic."

"A billionaire with a tumour. And he wouldn't let on, because..."

"Because he's desperate."

"So we shoot him into the future, far enough to hope that there'll be a cure for his particular malaise." Jimmy lapsed into silence for several moments. "He'll be sceptical. I mean they will be, all these hypothetical cash cows. It's not like we can give them any guarantees. No directions to the nearest cancer-cure centre, or robot body shop, or whatever. We wouldn't even know if the world still exists, or whether we end up blowing it up in World War Three, or whether the whole population lives in the fucking Big Brother house."

Daniel smiled. For all his bluster, Jimmy was still naive. "Don't you see? It doesn't matter. These people—this theoretical demographic—they've got nothing to lose, because they're already on their way out. They'll keep a secret, if it secures even the faintest chance of them extending their lives. Their desperation means they'll do it. I swear they'll do it. And no amount of money could prevent them from doing it."

Jimmy pondered for a minute, then leapt to his feet. "Danny Boy, you're a fucking genius. Psychotic too, quite possibly. But we'll get along famously. So where do I come in?"

It was a good question. Daniel clicked his tongue in thought.

~

It would take more time to wear Jimmy down and to encourage him to use the machine.

The red ball thumped into Daniel's own, knocking it away to spin across the length of the lawn.

Jimmy whooped. He had retrieved his plastic beaker of wine even before the ball came to a halt. "And that, my friend, is how you play fucking croquet."

Daniel crossed the lawn to stand behind the deflected black ball. His other, blue, ball lay at the corner of the lawn diagonally opposite. There could be no way of using his second ball to reach a position closer to the final hoop.

Just as in the croquet game, he and Jimmy had been manoeuvring themselves into position all afternoon. While the tone of their conversations had been light, strong currents pushed underneath.

The croquet mallet, a childlike replica of a real tool, dangled from Daniel's hand. He swung it between his legs to simulate the angle of impact.

"Hey, Danny Boy?" Jimmy said.

"I'm concentrating."

"Sure. Soz."

Daniel sensed Jimmy's impatience as he rocked the mallet back and forth, still unwilling to commit it to the ball.

"Here's a question," Jimmy said. "How far would you go?"

"I'm trying to concentrate."

"Ah, still in denial, are you? Face it, the game's over. You're not coming back from this."

Daniel sighed and looked up, still gripping the mallet tight. "How far would I go with what?"

"In the fucking time machine, of course. What do you think I'm thinking about? You say you've used it, but you haven't really. Not properly. Not life-changingly. We're talking about sending poor rich bastards into the far distant future. Are you telling me you haven't thought about doing the same thing yourself?"

Daniel frowned. There were certainly clear reasons why he wouldn't do so, but at this moment they eluded him. He shook his head. "Too risky. Like you said. World War Three might have broken out."

Jimmy considered this. "Yeah, but World War Three could start tomorrow, too."

"Look. Any catastrophe could happen, at any time. Every day you gamble that you'll still be alive at the end of it. Why increase the chance? I choose to live in the here and now." His voice caught.

"Yeah." Jimmy tipped his beaker horizontal so that wine sprayed from its edges as he drank. He wiped red rivulets from his beard. "Sometimes I wonder, though. Whether the here and now is all that much cop."

Daniel chewed his cheek. He had boiled down his 'here and now' to just three constituent elements: the time machine, the Manor and, now, Jimmy. All recently acquired, all stolen, to differing degrees. Was that really all that he had? For most of his life, he had felt free to burn bridges. After he had lost William he had barely noticed the further loss of his mother, then the gradual shedding of friends. Even abandoning his possessions, when he had fled with the time machine, had felt only cleansing, a jettisoning of weight.

"I don't want to sound like a wet blanket," Jimmy continued, "but I'm tired of this shit, Dan. The twenty-first century ended early, when John Peel died. Now it's all autotune and social media and loyalty cards."

"What makes you think that the future'll be any different?" The wine had begun to work its way into Daniel's system. The croquet mallet became a loose pendulum, his pulse a loud ticking.

"Like you said. A gamble. But maybe I like the odds, you know?"

"But you're still afraid of the risk," Daniel said, "and if we're going to do this thing together, we need to play safe. Plan."

"You calling me a coward?" Jimmy said, affecting bravado. Then he crumpled. "But, yeah. Afraid, maybe a bit."

Daniel returned his attention to the croquet game. The wine gave him courage. He swung and hit the ball cleanly and it scooted away. It rocked and came to rest touching the red ball.

Jimmy slow-handclapped. He tossed his empty beaker into a bush and ducked from side to side, surveying the state of the game. "Anyway," he said in a thoughtful tone, "don't you go making out that you're perfect. You're no Bond villain yourself, despite this new lair of yours. Want to know how I found you?"

Daniel discovered that he was suddenly unable to speak.

Jimmy gave a broad smile. "Jesus, you look petrified. Don't panic, nobody'll follow me. Whoever it is that's after you, they don't possess my charm."

"You talked to Mrs Gent."

"Talked to, flattered, borderline groped. She's all right, for a woman in her fifties. If she'd been my landlady, I'd have lived rent-free."

"So she let you into the flat? But it was empty." He had scoured his flat in the weeks before the theft. The local charity shops had bulged with his clothes and possessions.

"Aye, and she was flabbergasted, poor cow, weeping and carrying on. Thought maybe she saw you as a surrogate son, but no. It was just the money." Jimmy bent low to peer at the two croquet balls. They touched, just.

"I don't understand. She didn't know a thing. So how did you trace me?"

Jimmy raised himself up again and stood with his hands on his hips. "I'd like to say it was some fancy-schmancy detective work. But not really. Sure, the flat was empty, but you can't blame me for rummaging all the same. Looks like you had a blind spot. Hey presto, this was taped to the back of your cutlery drawer."

From his pocket he pulled a small business card. Daniel leant forwards. Some tradesman's calling card, difficult to make out due to a sellotape strip that obscured the print. He frowned. Jimmy flipped the card over. On the rear, in his own handwriting, Daniel saw a string of letters and digits.

"Shit," he said. His memory had never been good. He must have noted down his Gmail password when he set it up, years ago.

"Shit indeed. I had your email address already, of course, from Tom's stag. Logged in, tapped in this gobbledegook, Bob's your fucking uncle. Read the whole chain of emails about the house-sitting gig. All your passwords in one place! I do despair. You should be grateful I didn't hack your bank account too."

Daniel gulped. Jimmy didn't need to point out that, if it hadn't been for his intervention, the password would have remained in the flat for somebody else to find. He had Jimmy to thank for the enforcers not being on his trail.

Jimmy picked up his mallet and approached the two touching balls. He placed one foot on the red.

"Hey," Daniel said. Suddenly, injustice within the croquet game seemed too much to bear. "That's the wrong one. You have to play the yellow ball next."

Jimmy grinned. The mallet swooped down to collide with the red ball trapped beneath his foot. The energy from the impact transferred directly to the black, startling it into abrupt motion. It zipped away, shooting off the lawn and into the dark depths of the hedge.

~

Daniel gagged as his head thumped against something. He heard a shrill wail that, at first, he thought must be the peacocks. Then, blearily recognising that he was no longer in his bedroom beside the monkey puzzle, he discovered that the sound came from within his own skull.

His head rose and dropped again and his nose pressed against a rough surface. He seemed to be facing downwards with his body hinged at the stomach, uncomfortably straddling something. The wound on his neck throbbed. He opened his eyes, his dry lids scraping painfully against his eyeballs. He felt a pang of terror that he had gone blind, until a sliver of light appeared below him.

The rough object beneath him undulated. His fingers fumbled clumsily for purchase. He imagined the thing as a rock encrusted with barnacles. No, less rough than that; the coarse sensation came more from his fingertips that prickled as though wasp-stung.

His mouth opened but only a retching sound emerged.

The rock spoke in a low whisper. "Easy, Danny Boy. Easy."

The voice revived him a little. Something swung past; he recognised the carved wooden post at the head of the Manor's staircase. He had seen it often, but only now noticed that its top was the shape of an acorn. A tiny, carved mouse sat at the top of the banister, its nose touching the acorn as if inhaling its scent. Daniel smiled stupidly. He reached out to pat the mouse but his hand flapped loosely, clapping Jimmy on the back.

Jimmy.

As the Jimmy-rock began to descend the stairs, Daniel tried to recall the previous evening. Following the game of croquet, and with neither one of them willing to volunteer to test the time machine, Jimmy had insisted on cooking up a meal using leftovers from the fridge. Quite which meals the leftovers had been left over from, Daniel had been at a loss to explain. It was only once the food had been served up that he had discovered that he was famished. When had he last eaten before that? He had wolfed down the fried vegetables and fishcakes, tolerated Jimmy's constant chatter, drunk a great deal of the—

The wine.

Jimmy had insisted that the bitter taste had been due to the bottle being slightly corked. Nothing to worry about, he had said, and neither of them were aficionados enough to really mind. Daniel might not have even noticed if not for the slight cloudiness as the wine settled in his glass.

He was a fool for having trusted Jimmy at all, for letting him set foot in the Manor. And as for showing him the time machine, even allowing him to help in its construction... If had the strength to lift his hand, he would have slapped himself in the face.

As they reached the foot of the staircase, Jimmy grunted and resettled Daniel's prone body on his shoulder. Daniel's arm thumped against the door frame as he was manoeuvred into the lounge. He let out a guttural moan.

Jimmy leant against the light switch. Daniel hissed as the room exploded into brightness. The wail that bounced around within his head became louder, shriller. He felt himself manhandled and his body sagged backwards. Jimmy's sweating face hung inches from his own as he lowered Daniel to the floor. Sharp surfaces dug at Daniel's legs. He realised that he was being lowered into the slatted tube. The rim either side of the curved doorway scratched at his skin.

"You're fucking heavy for a skinny guy," Jimmy said.

Daniel simply stared upwards, unable to stop his body from slumping against the rear wall of the tube. He tried to form words.

"Ah, don't go giving me puppy-dog eyes," Jimmy said, shaking his head. "You can't blame me for taking the upper hand. I just want to see the bastard working, Danny Boy. Sure, you can't hold that against me. You'll be right as rain in the morning. Or whenever it is that you show up."

Daniel watched in horror as Jimmy inspected the trigger handle. "You never did tell me how far ahead this contraption'll take you. So I just pull this, and away you go?" He gave a high-pitched giggle. "Seems like I should make a speech, or crack a champagne bottle against you, or something. But nothing's springing to mind, so I suppose this is goodbye for now. See you when I see you." He raised the hand that held the trigger, posing in a mock salute.

There was no telling how far Jimmy would push the trigger. No telling whether he'd leave the time machine intact after Daniel disappeared. Despite Daniel's paralysis, a shudder ran through his body.

He concentrated on the shiver, using it to identify the location of his drifting limbs. His mouth contorted with concentration. With a shout, he flailed his right arm upwards to bat weakly against the cable still looped over the rim of the slatted tube. Jimmy watched on, bemused, at the zombie-like motion. His expression turned to panic as he scrabbled to grip the cable and missed. Daniel's wild, wandering arm yanked the trigger handle from Jimmy's grasp. It clattered against the rim of the tube before falling to the floor within.

Jimmy stood as paralysed as Daniel had been, torn between retrieving the trigger and escaping the ring of grey panels.

Daniel leered upwards, watching Jimmy as he leant into the tube, scrabbling to grasp the trigger handle. Daniel swatted at the plastic object, moving it closer to himself.

"Don't you fucking dare," Jimmy whispered.

Unable to prise the trigger handle from the carpet, Daniel hefted one heavy foot up against it. With his foot acting as a backstop he jabbed at the trigger with a numb index finger. The contoured grip slipped into its plastic housing.

Jimmy was still within the ring of panels, too.

The hum of the machine grew. Dimly, Daniel wondered whether it would be able to transport both he and Jimmy together.

If Jimmy shouted something, Daniel didn't hear it due to the popping of his ears.

TEN

Daniel's body swayed a little as he rose from bed. He recovered his balance, leaning against the wardrobe and disturbing the suit that swung from a hanger hooked onto its handle.

He was alive, safe.

But.

Jimmy?

Jimmy.

The Manor had become lighter. He paused in the corridor outside his bedroom, taking several seconds to pinpoint the differences. The curtains of the windows along the corridor and at the head of the staircase had been opened. Sunlight turned the carpets a rich peach colour.

He stumbled to Jimmy's bedroom.

The only sign that the room had once been inhabited was an indentation at the foot of the neatly-made bed.

Momentarily weak, Daniel sat in this dip, which reshaped to accommodate him.

Somehow, Jimmy had won.

Jimmy must have escaped from the clutches of the time machine before it had kicked in, leaving Daniel to hurtle alone into the future. The fact that he had woken in bed rather than within the slatted tube proved that Jimmy had disconnected the time machine, prior to his return. Both Jimmy and the time machine would be long gone now.

He felt a tinge of relief along with the frustration. Life without the time machine would be simpler. If there really could be no going back, perhaps he might find other routes onwards and upwards.

He slunk down the stairs. He would leave the Manor today. Sod the Harrigans and their security.

His stomach growled with hunger. He walked towards the kitchen, then stopped mid-stride at the foot of the stairs.

Through the doorway to the lounge he saw the time machine, waiting.

He stared at it.

Abruptly, a phone rang from behind him. It was coming from Benfield's study. He remained frozen, caught between the equal and opposite pulls of the time machine and this new emergency.

It might be Jimmy on the phone, making his play. If so, it would be better to let him to reveal his hand.

In the study he pulled aside the dustsheet to lift the phone. He listened without speaking. From the tinny speaker he heard distant mumbles, more like cattle than a human voice.

After ten seconds his resolve broke. "I know it's you."

"You know?" It wasn't Jimmy's voice. It was tired and faint. It sounded like his father when he finally left. *Son, I'm not coming back. You know that. There are two men of the house now, you and William. Look after your mum. And each other.*

"Who is this?" Daniel said.

"You said you knew."

Had it been Daniel who had driven his father away? Nobody had ever accused him directly. His father had never been the type to discuss feelings or motivations. And his mother, afterwards, wasn't the type to discuss his father.

He should put down the phone. But he was afraid of returning to the time machine.

"I was wrong," he said. "I don't know who you are. I don't live here."

"You're the house-sitter."

In the next moments, the rumble of cattle became recognisably human; several voices, followed by a melody. Sounds from a TV. Of course. Who else had he expected to ring this number?

"Mr Benfield," he said. "I'm sitting in your study."

The voice replied quickly, eagerly. "My notes are in there."

"They are." Daniel placed a hand on the desk drawer that contained Benfield's folder. He thought again of asking about the scribbled shorthand, but he was so tired. "Look, Florence isn't here. Your son-in-law, either. I can't help you."

Clicks came from the receiver. It might have been a fault in the line, or Benfield tapping on the phone at his end. "I'm lost. These people. I need to get out. Just for a time. Sort my affairs. I can't even get my shows and my books are missing. You know that. Daniel. I'm lost."

Daniel shuddered, partly due to unexpected sympathy, and partly due to the fact that the old man remembered his name.

"I can't help you," he said again, and replaced the handset.

~

He climbed the low slope of the golf course. The Old Man of Coniston glowed. Shadows of skidding clouds gave it the appearance of being covered with a blanket lightly disturbed by the breeze.

It was good to breathe. He ought to celebrate. For the first time in a week, he felt like eating something fresh.

The vague sense of horror of Benfield's phone call had faded. Somehow, things had worked out. He possessed the time machine, still. Jimmy had gone. As he took the path from the golf course towards Broughton-in-Furness he whistled a tune from his childhood. *Ee-I-Addio.* In the garden of a white cottage a shrunken old woman turned from pegging out her washing and watched him pass. Daniel waved and she raised a hand. Her head tilted to one side, a wordless question. He looked away, his enthusiasm wilting under her scrutiny.

A lingering sense of embarrassment hung over him as he entered the butcher's shop. The butcher broke off a conversation with a customer to give Daniel his immediate and full attention. In his awkwardness Daniel rubbed at his neck. He noticed that he felt no trace of the bullet wound. After he passed sausages and bacon over the counter, the butcher pressed coins into Daniel's palm, combining the action with a clumsy, damp handshake. As Daniel left the shop he became entangled in the chains that hung in the doorway.

His pace slowed as he approached the grocers. He took a breath and stepped inside, adopting as neutral an attitude as he could muster.

Lillian stood in the far corner of the shop, reaching upwards to push packets of crackers onto a high shelf. She turned and froze. Daniel gave a tight smile, remembering her shouted accusations as he and Jimmy had left the Cradle. Jimmy's nose had been streaming blood, Daniel had still snarled insults at him.

He busied himself putting items into a basket, selecting tins and packets almost at random in his hurry to leave.

When he glanced up he found that Lillian hadn't moved from the far corner. She smiled lopsidedly and indicated the crate of cracker packets. "Give a girl a hand?"

Daniel placed his basket onto the counter and moved, cautiously, to stand beside her. He half-expected her to lash out. He took the packet from the box and, without much effort required, set it onto the high shelf. He felt her eyes on him as he stacked the remaining packets.

Lillian moved behind the counter. She surveyed his filled basket. "Is this everything?"

He nodded.

"That's a lot of tins. They're not good for you. I probably shouldn't say that, seeing as I sell them! But you know what I mean. Everything in moderation."

Daniel felt he must be caught in some kind of trap. "It's okay," he said, glancing at the door. "I'm in a hurry."

"Of course you are." Lillian's gaze lowered again. She bagged the items. Her hands moved carefully as if she was trying to avoid disturbing the paper bags. When she finished she slid away from the counter and through the open front door. Daniel watched on, bewildered, as she returned with a handful of apples and two large, ripe ears of sweetcorn. She placed them into the bag, once again giving the same lopsided, apologetic smile. Daniel paid and left, blinking due to confusion and the low, dazzling sun.

The extra items made one of the paper bags far heavier than the other. He stopped at one of the benches in the village square to redistribute their contents.

"Daniel?"

He groaned as he saw Nic approaching.

"What are you doing here?" she said. Daniel imagined a silent addendum: *You don't belong here.*

Nic now wore her hair loose rather than in pigtails. She looked far more her age. Her heels clacked on the stone flagstones.

"I'm just leaving." He rose to his feet but Nic blocked his way. She reached out a hand, awkwardly tapping against his elbow.

"Look," he said, pushing her away, "Don't start laying into me again. I'm sorry. I'm sorry I was so—"

"So what, Daniel?"

He felt he would say anything to make her leave. "Just... so. I've not been myself. But I'm leaving now. You don't have to worry about seeing me again. Okay?" He felt tired, suddenly. Tired of the network of busybodies that had arisen around him in the village. The net.

Nic still refused to step away. "You're leaving?"

"That's what I said."

"*Leaving* leaving? Today?"

Again, Daniel sensed a silent phrase that ought to be added. This time, the phrase was '...of all days'. He pushed past her.

"No. Daniel," Nic said. "You're coming with me. This is important. You need this."

He wavered, nonplussed.

Two villagers that Daniel vaguely recognised as Cradle regulars appeared at the corner of the square. Like Nic, they wore formal outfits. The couple walked directly to one of the cars parked at the edge of the square.

"We're all going," Nic said, indicating the newcomers. "But we'll head by the Manor first. You can't go dressed like that."

~

The only explanation was that this was a nightmare. Conforming to his role of dreamer, Daniel allowed himself to be pushed and pulled, handled like a puppet with cut strings. Nic stood guard outside his Manor bedroom until he emerged dressed in the dark suit that hung from the wardrobe door. It had been there when he woke, he recalled. Ready and waiting. Nic smoothed his hair and retied his tie.

The car journey must have lasted forty minutes but passed in a blur. Daniel watched for glimpses of the Old Man between the grey buildings of the villages that they swept through. Mist hung just above head height, lowering and flattening the sky. The driver of the car said nothing. His wife, who sat in the passenger seat, cast wistful smiles into the back of the car. Nic's hand stroked the back of Daniel's. She spoke occasionally, but he tuned out her words.

With each passing minute his body slackened a little more. When the car pulled to a stop he tried and failed to lift himself from the seat. Finally, he allowed Nic to support him as a gathering crowd made its way from the car park to a flat, red-brick building. Onto its functional nineteen-sixties shell had been added a modern, smoked-glass foyer, giving it the look of a municipal leisure centre.

Inside, air conditioning made a sweet taste on his tongue. Nic guided him to the front row of canvas-seated chairs that reminded him of the ones in the assembly hall of his secondary school. He picked his way through shuffling and apologies. Faces familiar from the village filled the rows behind him. Few people met his eye.

The framed wall posters reinforced the assembly-hall atmosphere. His school had favoured motivational slogans, which were held dear and repeated by William, but were mocked by Daniel. These ones were soft-focus, stock-photo images captioned with italicised Bible quotes that were too small to be totally legible. He stared at the pictures. A penguin and chick. A woman staring pensively at the sky. A man with his arms wrapped around his knees.

Nic pressed a tissue into his hand. He worked it between his fingers. Why couldn't he wake up?

Reluctantly, he allowed his attention to shift to the front of the hall. Beside a metal lectern like a music stand, he saw the snub end of a beechwood coffin. His temples prickled. Sweat dampened the armpits of his fresh shirt.

A soberly-dressed official appeared beside the coffin. He placed his left hand upon it. The fingers of his right hand ran through his white hair. He patted the surface of the coffin lightly, twice. The aim of his beatific smile shifted around the assembled crowd, lingering longest on Daniel. Daniel fidgeted.

The man spoke. Despite the secular tone of the ceremony, his mannerisms were overtly those of a vicar. Daniel phased out the words. His gaze fixed on the coffin.

Soon he became aware that the people around him had risen from their seats. He stood, too, with Nic's help. A Buzzcocks song played from hidden speakers, eliciting a murmur of polite surprise from the crowd. The coffin slid away on silently spinning rollers. The song was playing at far too low a volume. And it should have been a religious ceremony, too, with drama and hysteria.

Outside, a few of the villagers summoned the courage to approach Daniel. They placed their hands on his arm or his shoulder. He shied away, and they left him be.

A man with sleepy, bright eyes approached. He was wearing a grey suit, but Daniel imagined red checks. He flinched as the man extended both of his hands.

"You shot me," Daniel said simply, without blame.

The man—Covell, wasn't that his absurd name?—gave a hollow chuckle. "That's how we met," he explained to the woman standing beside him. He clasped both of Daniel's hands in his own. His grip suggested an abundance of confidence. What right did he have to be here?

"Ian and Florence send their regards," Covell said. "They're so terribly sorry for your loss."

Daniel glanced up at the too-bright sun. Specks danced at the corners of his vision. He thought of Florence Harrigan's constellation of golden freckles.

"My loss," he repeated.

"Yes. I wish I could have met him. Ian spoke highly of him. Said you'd all had a ball together. It's a rotten shame. You must be devastated, especially given the circumstances."

Covell's eyes sought Daniel's. Daniel kept staring at the sun, enjoying the tickling prickle of light. He felt Covell press something into his palm. He looked down to see a business card. *Covell Jones. Psychologist & therapist.* A string of initials.

"Let me know if you feel like talking," Covell said. His bright eyes watched Daniel's hand until the card had been transferred to his trouser pocket.

Daniel opened his mouth to speak.

His legs buckled.

~

His hands shook as he rifled through the contents of the recycling bin in the corner of the tiny kitchen of Nic's flat. He could hear Nic speaking to somebody at the front door. A few words kept being repeated. *Tragedy. Future.*

Except Daniel felt no sense of tragedy. He had wanted rid of Jimmy. He had wanted to secure his own future.

Soon Nic would notice his absence and go knocking on the bathroom door. Since his collapse at the funeral parlour she had treated him like something impossibly fragile. He pushed his hands deeper into the bin, shifting aside plastic wrappers and cardboard packaging. Finally, he found what he wanted. He spread the two editions of the Westmorland Gazette onto the melamine table.

The first newspaper, dated the previous week, contained nothing of use. He flicked through the pages of the newer edition.

There. Page six, less than an eighth of a sheet.

CLIMBER'S DEATH SHOCKS COMMUNITY

He gripped the table for support and tried to focus on the smaller text below the headline.

18 July: Tourist James Williams fell to his death during a solo climbing expedition in the Great Langdale area. Mr Williams, an experienced climber, attempted to navigate 'Jack's Rake', a well-known Grade 1 scramble traversing the Pavey Ark fell. His body was subsequently recovered from Stickle Tarn, directly below the ridge.

Mr Williams had been residing in the area with another holidaymaker, Daniel Faint. The Cumbrian fell-walking community have expressed deep regret over the incident and some locals have since petitioned for signage to be placed close to the approach to Jack's Rake, warning climbers of the dangers of the ridge.

Following a coroner's verdict of accidental death, James Williams' funeral will be held in Ambleside on Thursday.

The article contained no explanation as to why Jimmy would be buried in Cumbria. Daniel struggled to recall whether he might have seen any of Jimmy's family at the funeral. Perhaps he had been as alone as Daniel was. The photo accompanying the article showed a much younger Jimmy. The image had been inexpertly cropped. Jimmy's raised arm had been truncated where it met another person's shoulders.

He realised that the murmur of voices had stopped. With a start, he saw that Nic now stood at the head of the kitchen table. She had changed into a moss-green, ragged jumper that swamped her upper body. Her feet were bare.

She slid the newspaper towards her and folded it neatly, twice. "There's no need for you to keep seeing that. You mustn't dwell."

Daniel's breathing came in short bursts. "I don't—"

Remember.

Nic waited for a couple of seconds before she spoke. "I don't understand either. He was a good man."

She moved around the table. Daniel edged away. The air seemed thick so that he now had to struggle for each breath.

"I need to be on my own," he said.

"No, you don't. Not after this. He was like another brother to you."

Daniel's head jerked up. *Another* brother. What did she know about William?

"You can't run away from all this," Nic continued. "It's already happened." She had changed, subtly. She seemed to have abandoned the pretence of being younger. The creases at the corners of her eyes were now free of makeup. "And don't leave town. You're not thinking straight."

Daniel almost laughed at the understatement.

Nic leant across the table. He flinched as she took his hands, expecting anger or a come-on, some emotional extreme to rattle him from his numbness. But her fingers only pressed lightly upon his palms as a mother might pretend to heal a child's bruise.

She whispered, "I want you to know that nobody else knows."

Daniel gulped noisily. A sensation of hopelessness, of being cornered, rose up again within him. Nic knew something about Jimmy's death, about Daniel's involvement, but for some reason she condoned his actions.

Nic smiled and tucked the folded newspaper under her arm.

Nothing could be gained from letting Nic get her claws further into him.

"I have to go," he said.

To his surprise, Nic nodded in response. She touched his elbow lightly as he began to move away, feeling lightheaded in his nearness to freedom. "Daniel? I won't let on, I promise. It's your secret. It's not for me to ruin things for you. And you and I, our night together, none of that matters now. I'm happier now, and so are you."

Daniel stared at her open-mouthed.

"Was I..." he began. *Was I with Jimmy when he died? Was I responsible somehow?* He found that he couldn't complete the question. And despite his lack of memory, he already knew the answer. So he said, "I was there on the mountain."

Nic nodded again. Tears glistened at the corners of her eyes.

He felt her eyes on him as he stumbled out of the room and down the stone steps that led from her flat to the village square.

The world outside felt as artificial and hollowed-out as a stage set. The mist had risen to reveal a too-blue sky. The day, frozen until he had left the flat, eased into activity. Ambient sounds cranked up like a wound record player. A cat and pedestrian appeared from stage right. Which part was Daniel himself to play, today?

He closed his eyes. When he opened them, the world had become real again.

What had happened, really? The few details contained in the newspaper report seemed suspect. Jimmy, an 'experienced climber'? Come off it.

He and Jimmy had entered the time machine eleven days ago. Evidently, they had reappeared several days before Daniel awoke in his bed. Why couldn't he remember?

Of course.

The drugged drink. He could recall only snapshot images as he operated the time machine with a sledgehammer-heavy hand. When he had awoken he had assumed that the jump into the future had nullified the effects of the drug. But no, its chemical trace must have left him blank-minded, with the arms of the drug wrapped around him, when he and Jimmy had reappeared in the future.

The last he remembered of Jimmy was his frozen, horrified expression when he had realised that he was inside the time machine. Daniel had hated him, then, pure and clean.

Bile rose in his throat.

Could he really have killed him?

~

Shadows of spindly trees zebra-striped the path. If Daniel squinted and let his vision blur, the stripes appeared to retreat away from him as he approached. It was an optical illusion he had discovered in childhood, sleepily watching the road ahead as his mother drove the car into darkness. They had often visited relatives, after his father had left, returning to the house late at night. Daniel would lean forwards from the back seat, forcing his eyes to focus, monitoring the white markings and roadside ghosts, stealing glances at his mother's taut neck. William would always be asleep beside him, exhausted from the attentions of uncles and aunts, the newly-invented games with cousins. When they arrived home their mother would carry William from the car, and William would pretend to sleep through it.

Dust clumped upon Daniel's shoes as he shuffled along the path towards the Manor. He could almost sleep right here, whilst walking.

A sound made him turn. His hands found a dry-stone wall and he leant on it, grateful for the support. The sight of his unfamiliar grey suit surprised him: *Whose arms are these?*

On the other side of the wall, in a neatly-mown cottage garden, a young boy skipped in circles around the metal pole of a washing line. He wore a navy-blue school jumper and shorts. Give him a cap and he could have been from the fifties. Grass stains marked both of his knees. He whistled a tune. Daniel frowned. *Ee-I-Addio.*

"Hey," Daniel said. He beckoned with a heavy hand. "Come over here."

The boy seemed doubtful. He faced Daniel without stepping forwards. His hairstyle, a slightly off-kilter bowl cut, reminded Daniel of his own at that age. His mother had done it herself, spreading hairs around the kitchen floor. He suffered jibes in the playground.

Yet this child had no idea how ridiculous he looked. Naivety granted him confidence.

"That song," Daniel said. "It's 'The Farmer's in His Den'. Right?"

The boy shrugged. He glanced back at the pole as if it required his continued attention.

"Let me tell you something," Daniel said, adopting the tone of a teacher; it's what the boy would understand. "It doesn't work like that. Not in real life. The farmer wants a wife, and hey presto, one comes forth from a ring of admirers?" He snorted a laugh. "And she wants a dog and the dog wants a bone and the whole thing's too damn easy." He thought of the shocked reactions of all the women whose behaviour he had misinterpreted. Offers of dates turned down in disbelief. Laughter at a spontaneous, and heartfelt, proposal of marriage. William's commiserations, still with one arm around Lorna's slim shoulders. *The dog wants a bone.*

The boy took a step backwards. Daniel raised a hand to fix him in place.

"I was your age once. Hard to believe. Grass stains and conker bruises. The hickeys and cauliflower BCG scars are all to come. After that, everything opens out. Vast, like the sea. No structure, just—" He spread his arms wide to encompass all of the unfairnesses of adult life. "—weight. Heavy weight, dragging you under."

An elderly woman emerged from the cottage. Daniel recognised her as the one who had greeted him on his way to the village, before the funeral. Could that really have been only this morning? She placed a protective hand on the boy's shoulder. The boy snuck up against her legs.

"He doesn't get it," Daniel said to her. "People say life's hard, and it's true. But life's no problem. It's digital, on or off. Predictable in all sorts of ways, that's what science shows us. It's *people* that are hard. They're bacteria, infecting life."

An image formed in his head, some half-remembered scene from a National Geographic quasi-documentary claiming to predict the future. It was a vision of Westminster, after some apocalypse, after avian flu or some other pandemic. Its spires punctured a canopy of leaves. Life after humans would be serene, eerie and beautiful.

"I'm telling you," he continued, "if you could only look at the whole thing under a microscope. It's all filthy."

The woman's smile hardened. Her legs now obscured the boy entirely. She started to move but Daniel raised his hand again. This time it was a surrender.

"Onwards and upwards," he said.

~

When Daniel and William were ten years old, Daniel pushed his twin into a wasp's nest.

Hills rose from the fields directly behind their home. At the end of their cul-de-sac, a path, then a rough track, led into the woods. In the long weeks of the summer holiday Daniel took this route daily, heaving his bike over the low stile, then pelting up and down the forest trails until his anger dissipated through the open pores of his skin. Hardened shale heaps made ideal stunt arenas for his battered BMX. He shouted and deformed the ground.

William rarely joined him, preferring to read. Piles of science fiction novels made a cityscape of otherworldly towers in his bedroom.

But on this day, he did.

Was it actually the same day their father left the house for the final time? Or was that simply a conflation of events, a trick of the memory? Daniel and William headed to the hills together at the insistence of their mother, that much Daniel remembered. Her ability to entertain them must have met its limit.

Daniel lifted both bikes over the stile. His arms, while just as slender and wiry as William's, had become stronger these last few months. He resented William's ammunition of knowledge gained from school and books, so he took this opportunity to demonstrate his worth. It was the same compulsion that made him lead William to the wasp's nest at the foot of the largest shale heap. It hung half-protruding from a thick bush, ribbed and grey. The two boys sat on the shale slope, legs tucked between their arms, bikes dumped onto the ground before them.

"That's where they have sex," Daniel said, pointing at the nest. "They fly back to the hive and they have sex." He watched his brother out of the corner of his eye. William had pulled an action figure from his pocket, some Doctor Who monster. He manipulated its long, drooping arms, looking at it rather than at the nest. "Hey. We're too old for toys."

"They're not having sex," William said without looking up.

"Reproduction, then. Smartarse."

William shook his head. "It's late summer and the nest's already been set up. There are queens in there, and drones, but they'll go somewhere else to mate. Same as bees."

Daniel relished the cool rage he felt building within him. His ragged, uncut nails nipped at his palms. *Don't think directly about what your body is about to do.*

When he thumped William between the shoulder blades his brother was caught by surprise. He staggered forwards from his seated position. Both his hands went out in an attempt to steady himself but his left jarred against the frame of his abandoned bike. The wheel spokes jangled. With slow inevitability, William toppled headfirst into the thicket.

Daniel watched with interest as his brother flailed to right himself within the bush. Wasps, alerted to the emerging opportunity, dived inwards.

Neither boy called out.

Later, their mother settled William into a bed padded with towels, in the hope of leaving his dressings undisturbed. Inflamed lumps had made red constellations along his arms and back. She joined Daniel on the landing, where he had watched through the door-crack.

"He says that he fell," she said. "But I need to know, Daniel. Was it you?"

Daniel found that he was able to hold both of the possibilities in his mind at once. He did it. He didn't do it.

"I'm tired," he said.

"Daniel. Tell me the truth." His mother's new role as sole parent turned her stern voice pleading.

Daniel placed the fingers of his left hand around his right fist. Could he make them stretch all the way around?

"I hate William," he said.

~

Daniel kept his distance from the copse, taking a less direct route to the Manor by tracing the curve of the longest fairway.

He thought of what Nic had said. *I won't let on, I promise. It's not for me to ruin things for you.*

She knew what had happened to Jimmy, and she had made herself complicit, somehow. If Daniel had been involved in a crime, it would be discovered. And then there was the issue of somebody travelling up from Oxford, following the trail of the time machine. Daniel's name had been included in the newspaper report, pinpointing his location to Cumbria, linking him to Jimmy. The Westmorland Gazette may only be a local paper, but what did 'local' even mean, these days? The story might easily have been shared on the internet.

A speck on the horizon grew to become Tosh, pushing a wheelbarrow. He was an obstacle stopping Daniel from reaching the Manor. Daniel attempted to pass without speaking to him.

"Mr Faint?"

How had Daniel ever feared him? Now that the magnitude of his problems had become greater, the gardener appeared harmless. "Afternoon, Tosh."

Tosh bobbed as a blotch in the corner of his vision.

"I just wanted to say—"

"Thank you, Tosh. It's awful, of course. It's been a long day and I don't much want to think about Jimmy right now." He turned to face the gardener and attempted a dismissive gesture.

Tosh kneaded his hands. "That's not what I meant. I just wanted to say—" His voice dropped to a whisper. "—it's all taken care of."

Daniel froze. The gardener's back seemed to bend further under his gaze.

"She was awful persuasive, Mr Faint. Like one of them off the TV, screwing over politicians and the like."

Where had all this 'Mr Faint' business come from? Tosh had barely acknowledged him in the past, let alone called him by name.

"Slow down," Daniel said. "Who was? Who are you talking about?"

"The reporter, of course. Showed up just the day before yesterday. Notebook in hand. She suggested all that stuff about warning folks about the Rake, about the route up Pavey Ark, blah-di-blah. Your name kept coming up, all commiserations and all. I twigged about her trick before I said the wrong thing, mind."

"What would have been 'the wrong thing'?"

Tosh glanced both ways. "About you and young Jimmy being up on Jack's Rake together. But you'll not see a hint of that in the papers, thanks to yours truly."

"My name was still printed, though." He thought of the 'enforcers' that had beaten Jimmy. They could be scouring the country for the merest hint of the location of the time machine. It wouldn't take them long to locate the Manor.

Tosh blanched. "I'm sorry, Mr Faint. I am." He glanced at the ground, then at Daniel's shoes. "Then there was the police, too. I didn't know what to say. They kept asking where you was. Got me all mixed up." When he looked up, his face glowed. "But I cleaned the muck off of your hiking boots, mind, those ones of Mr H's. Not a trace."

A chill crept up Daniel's spine. The truth now seemed within his grasp. "So you're saying I was definitely there. You're saying I was climbing with Jimmy when he died."

Tosh frowned. He shook his head slowly, as if testing an unfamiliar motion. "Is this a test? No, Mr Faint. You weren't there. And there's nobody that can say you were."

Daniel rubbed at his forehead. When he spoke, his voice sounded hollow and unlike his own. "What about Nic, in the village? What does she know?"

Tosh only frowned. He didn't know anything about that.

"Never mind," Daniel said. "But tell me this, Tosh. Why do *you* care about my name being printed in the paper?"

"Not me, Mr Faint. It's you who cares."

Daniel searched Tosh's expression for malevolence but found none. What did he want, in exchange for his silence? The gardener fiddled with a strip of loose rubber on the handle of the wheelbarrow. A rake and spade shifted inside, clanking against the rusted metal.

"Tosh. Tosh, look at me." Daniel felt no surprise in his newfound calm confidence. If he had murdered Jimmy, he might be capable of anything. "Are you trying to threaten me?"

The gardener's eyes widened. "No! I'm just—you said..." His voice trailed off.

That same cool rage again. Everybody seemed to possess information about him. Everybody but himself. He felt himself pulled in opposite directions. "I said what?"

"That I should tell folks that you'd been here at the Manor all day, that day."

"And now you're thinking of extorting me, is that it?"

"Extort? No, I just wanted to let you know..." Tosh cast from side to side, unable to express himself.

Daniel took a deep, shuddering breath. "Fine, so you've let me know. Thanks so much, Tosh. I'll be on my way."

The gardener gulped, visibly relieved. He hefted the wheelbarrow and turned to leave.

He couldn't be trusted. He couldn't be left free to ruin plans.

Daniel saw William cartwheel into the wasp's nest. It had taken just one push to end an unwanted conversation.

In one fluid move, he pulled the spade from the wheelbarrow, then swung it in a wide arc. It made contact with the back of the gardener's head with a dull thud. Tosh fell to the ground without even registering surprise.

There could be no going back.

Daniel took a lungful of air at the edge of the copse before dragging Tosh's body into its dark centre.

~

He passed through the house like a lonely ghost.

Peacocks peered through every window. Their thin beaks were warped into hooks by glass that, over time, had flowed downwards to settle thicker at the bottom of each frame. Daniel's own weight seemed to redistribute too. His mass flowed to his feet, making them leaden and his head light. In Florence's workshop he lifted and examined each sculpture in turn, seeing himself in their bulbous heads and thin-thick-thin arms. There were more of them than he remembered, crowding the walls.

The depression in Jimmy's bed had already flattened without trace.

In his own bedroom, Daniel discovered Florence's beige stockings peeping from beneath the bed. They must have fallen there as she had packed her suitcase to lie, all this time, just below his own sleeping body.

The house hummed with the vibrations of other ghosts.

But the time machine hummed louder.

~

A killer. He was a killer.

But he had already made that transition, hadn't he? He'd murdered Jimmy—whether he remembered it or not—and now he'd disposed of Tosh, too.

For what?

For safety. For the time machine. For the future.

He glanced down. The left arm of his funeral suit gaped open in a wide tear. A streak of mud smeared his shirt from collar to waist, neatly bisecting him.

For the second time that day, he felt his knees buckling. His limbs ached from the exertion of burying Tosh's body. The soil within the copse had been hard, resisting his attempts to puncture it with the spade. The tree trunks had grown barbs to pull at his hair and clothes.

He must leave. Find another van, somehow, pack up the time machine and be on his way.

But where?

Just away.

He pulled off the destroyed suit, then dressed in his faded jeans and a white T-shirt, and returned downstairs.

A sound from outside startled him. Wheels squealing on tarmac.

So much for Tosh's reassurances. He deserved what he got.

In Benfield's study, Daniel stumbled towards the window overlooking the forecourt. A police car had parked up directly outside the building. Daniel laughed. Compared to the prospect of 'enforcers' tracking him, the threat of the police seemed trivial.

Except he was guilty of Jimmy's murder, somehow. Getting himself tangled in the legal system might save him from the enforcers, but he would never see the time machine again. He would never be free.

A familiar silver car appeared through the iron archway. As two uniformed officers emerged from the police car, Florence jumped out of the MG. She raised both hands in a flattened-palms signal. Daniel couldn't hear her voice but her body language was easy to read: *Slowly, slowly. He's in there.*

He thought of Covell's comment at the funeral: *Ian and Florence send their regards. They're so terribly sorry for your loss.* More lies. The entire population of the village had conspired against him, keeping him within their clutches ready for the Harrigans' return. Perhaps Florence, cold and supercilious even in these circumstances, had insisted on being the one to bring him to justice. Now she would wait for Benfield to die, then make the Manor a tourist attraction. *See where the Pavey Ark murderer hatched his plans. See the exact point where he held his last stand. See his bloodstain on the wall.*

Florence turned to face the Manor. Daniel's eyes met hers for a fraction of a second. He dived behind the curtain.

The front door swung open before he could reach the lobby to pull the deadlock. He ducked back, retreating into the shadows.

"Daniel?" Florence's voice called.

He spun on his heel, took the first couple of stairs, then dropped down again. There was no guarantee he could leave via the rusted fire escapes on the upper floor; he might easily find himself trapped up there. Instead, he lunged towards the leisure centre. At the last second he saw a ghostly silhouette—one of the policeman—through the plate glass door.

They were everywhere.

His body sagged. He was so tired.

The time machine exerted its gravitational pull, altering his orbit. In the lounge the air was still, a comforting inertia. The grey panels of the time machine gave no hint of reflection even in direct light. Even Daniel's shadow appeared blurred at the edges.

"Daniel! Where are you?" Florence's voice came from the lobby. "I know you're here, I saw you at the window."

Daniel's fingers stroked the nearest grey panel as he entered the circle. The time machine hummed without humming, pulsed without pulsing.

He held two contradictory impulses in his mind at once.

Rest.

And run away.

He settled his body into the slatted tube. The trigger handle fit itself snugly around his fingers.

This was what the machine wanted, that was the main thing. But it was also his only remaining course of action. The Manor was surrounded. The time machine would be seized, regardless of what he did next.

So.

Travelling forwards in time might give him an advantage, however slim. With nobody able to predict when he would return, he would have the element of surprise. He would have to trust himself to find a way to escape, whenever and wherever he reappeared.

Florence appeared at the lounge doorway. Her hair had come free of its clip and swung wildly at one side. Daniel interpreted the expression in her wide eyes as glee.

They faced each other without speaking. Florence looked at the ring of panels that surrounded him. It tightened its embrace.

Daniel smiled and raised his trigger hand to wave.

He squeezed the trigger with more pressure than he intended. He stared stupidly as its spring mechanism snapped and sailed across the room.

ELEVEN

Daniel's ears popped. He retched. His limbs felt displaced and his fingers cramped in confusion. A rich, dank smell stung his nostrils.

At first he thought that it was night-time, mistaking the dark flakes before him for a wall in shade. Gradually, he realised that his hands pressed into this solid darkness and that his bare arms were visible before him. He curled his fingers into something damp. The weight of his body pulled him towards it.

Slowly, he reoriented himself. His head hung heavy. Downwards. He pushed with his hands to raise his body. Upwards.

His arms gave way and he rolled onto his back. Above him, patches of blue sky reshaped with the swaying of branches and leaves. He became aware of tall, straight trunks surrounding him. Damp bark shavings stuck to his neck. The trees sighed as they shifted. A lilting birdsong became the call of a human voice.

Where was he?

Slowly, he pulled himself into a sitting position. He wrapped his arms around his knees for balance and comfort. He turned in each direction to see knives of daylight penetrating the dense woodland.

The copse.

It had brought him back here. Somehow, the time machine understood what he had done to Tosh.

His stomach complained as he struggled to his feet. Dimly, he recognised that a voice still called from outside the ring of trees. Not within the copse, though. Nothing living dared enter.

"Daniel?"

Tosh's body must be somewhere around here. Daniel felt a chill as the thought occurred to him that the time machine might have brought him to the exact spot where he had buried him. Was he standing directly above the body, right now? He leapt to one side. His limbs felt taut and strange.

"Daniel? Did you find it?"

Bile rose up in his throat. At first he had taken the voice to be that of the time machine itself, encouraging him to locate the body. But no. The voice was real, coming from beyond the copse and outside his own head.

The voice was male and vaguely familiar. One more person complicit in his crimes. As Daniel backed away from it, his spine jarred against a tree trunk. He fell and scrambled backwards on his hands and feet until he had delivered himself from the dark woods to lie spreadeagled on the fairway. He saw the Old Man in the distance, sparkling golden like a promised land.

A figure appeared, a spindly shadow against the shining fell.

"Good God. You're filthy," the man said.

Daniel looked down to see the soil marks streaked across his white T-shirt. The man's hands reached beneath him, tugging at his elbows. Daniel shielded his eyes against the light.

"What happened?" the man said, echoing Daniel's thoughts. "Was it in there?"

His mind crowded with questions. He abandoned them all. "I couldn't find him," he said.

"Him." The man paused, then laughed.

Now standing, Daniel swung his body around so that he stood between the man and the fell. The intensity of light lessened. He saw a face. Oblique, sleepy eyes above a red checked shirt.

"Covell Jones," Daniel said.

The face wrinkled in concern.

You shot me. Daniel stifled the accusation. How did Covell fit in to all this? He stood still as Covell brushed dirt from his arms and back.

"What time is it?" Daniel said.

Covell paused, still bent before him, and consulted his watch. "Quarter past."

"And." Daniel brought both hands to his face, balled into fists. He rubbed at his eyes, feeling damp soil transfer to his cheeks. "And what's the date?"

Covell rose stiffly. "The date? It's the eighteenth."

"Of."

"September."

Daniel felt tears sting his eyes. What date had it been, when he had entered the time machine? July the somethingth? He shuddered and thought of the broken spring of the time machine's trigger handle, the treacly pressure becoming suddenly yielding. He had travelled further than he had wanted.

But what did the timescale matter? He was free. Just as he had planned. The police had entered the Manor. He had escaped via the time machine. And here he was, now. Free.

What about the machine itself? Surely, once he had disappeared, the police would have confiscated it.

No. Its hum still echoed in his head. He felt an overriding instinct that, not only had the time machine brought him here, safely, to the copse, it was nearby, watching.

He had to know. If, by some miracle, it was still here, he had to retrieve it. Abandoning the time machine would be like abandoning a family member. Like he abandoned William.

Pushing past Covell, he strode towards the Manor. He stumbled as though his legs had telescoped in length. Beyond the copse he saw an abandoned golf bag. He veered away from it. If there were visitors prowling the grounds, he didn't want to encounter them.

He lumbered to the driveway and through the iron archway, then paused at the door to the building. Through the window he saw that the plastic wrapping had been removed from the desk in Benfield's study. The glow of a standing lamp merged with the flickers of a fire in the hearth.

The front door opened at a push. Inside, the golden flowers and red velveteen wallpaper had been replaced by cool blue from floor to ceiling. The plate-glass door to the swimming pool had become oak. Large, bottom-heavy vases framed the doorway to the lounge. This door had changed too. It was made of brushed steel, incongruously industrial in style. He saw a discreet digital keypad below its handle. So the time machine must still be in there. The police mustn't have linked it to his crimes. But that didn't explain the added security.

Covell caught up with him and put a hand on his shoulder.

"Get off," Daniel said. His voice sounded distant and not recognisably his own. He twisted in Covell's grip. "You shot me."

Covell's smile appeared and evaporated in seconds. Daniel noticed flecks of grey in the stubble on his chin.

"I did, I did," Covell said. "Are you going to tell me that it's the old war wound putting you off? That's a bit of a low blow."

Daniel grinned stupidly, recognising that this was some sort of joke.

"You don't look well, Daniel."

Weakly, Daniel waved a heavy arm to indicate the changed décor. "I like what they've done with the place."

Covell noticed him looking at the brushed-steel door to the lounge.

"You need to rest," he said. "Then eat. But you'll enjoy it more if you catch forty winks first. Okay?"

No. He had to get the machine. Steal a van. Escape. The original plan still felt within his grasp.

The time machine, crouching behind the steel door, sighed reassurance. At least it was nearby. His only friend.

But it was true, he was exhausted. His head pounded and his ears still popped intermittently. His stomach growled.

"Okay," Daniel said.

He allowed Covell to lead him like a child, away from the steel door and up the stairs.

~

Daniel stumbled through sleep, waking often. He gripped the sheets, disoriented by his surroundings. The room had changed, not only in décor but even the arrangement of its window and eaves. The shrill call of the peacocks subsided. It had turned dark outside.

He heard a voice. Distant, but also ringing within his head. Something in its urgency alerted him. When he stood up, his legs were thick, heavy trunks. He still wore his jeans and stained white T-shirt. He pulled himself to the doorway and onto the landing, encountering it from an unexpected angle. Once again, the Manor had rearranged itself around him. His bare toes pushed into a thick carpet.

The muted voice came from somewhere downstairs. Too high to be Covell's.

It took his full concentration to creep down the stairs. The lobby seemed smaller than he remembered. A folded partition now obscured the bar. The steel door to the lounge was shut tight. Daniel tried the handle but it remained fixed in place, without even rattling. His fingertips grazed the cold keypad beneath the handle. *Let me in.*

The voice resumed, little more than a whisper. It came from behind him. The door to Benfield's study was slightly ajar.

He recognised the voice at last. Florence Harrigan. What must she be thinking, finding Daniel back in the Manor? How long had it been since he had left? Long enough for her to redecorate the place. Perhaps he had become a distant memory, until today.

He heard the floorboards creak, as if Florence paced back and forth inside the room. Her whispered voice tailed off, but her occasional interjections suggested that she was listening to another person. She must be on the phone.

Daniel crept to the door to peer through the thin gap.

Florence sat at the desk with her back to him. She held the receiver of the old rotary phone in her hand. The computer had been replaced by a tall vase of sunflowers. He saw the edge of a pinboard fixed to the wall behind the desk. On it, he recognised diagrams from Benfield's notes. Had the old man returned to the Manor?

He pressed himself against the wall, straining to hear the tinny voice that came from the phone receiver. From this angle he saw that what he had taken to be a desk was, in fact, a workbench. A series of clay figures, Florence's sculptures, had been arranged upon it. They stood in line as if plodding from left to right. Each successive one rose further from its haunches, an abstracted illustration of man's evolution from apes.

"It's exactly like he said it would be," Florence said into the phone, "I can't understand—I *never* understood—but it's exactly like he said."

He? Covell?

The tinny, wordless voice began again. Florence heaved up a sob. "I know."

Another pause. "Don't start that. You know I will. They're already on their way. I just wish—"

This time the voice at the other end of the line spoke slowly, deliberately. Even without understanding the words Daniel could tell that it was a series of instructions.

"All right." Florence sighed. "I'll call you when it's... I'll call you later." She hung up.

Daniel pushed open the door. The pinboard took up the entire wall opposite the fireplace. As well as the diagrams taken from Benfield's files, somebody had pinned pages of scrawled handwriting. Additional notes had been added in green ink. Shelves on the opposite wall overflowed with sculptures. Florence's style had become more assured.

Most of the figures were less grotesque than before, more recognisably human.

It took Florence a few seconds to notice his intrusion. She turned and stared at him. Flecks of mascara had lodged in the lines at the corners of her eyes.

"Get out," she said. It was a pleading tone, rather than commanding.

"I will," Daniel said. "But answer me just one question. When did you last see me?"

Florence turned to face the window. The golden light no longer shone upon the Old Man, leaving the fell drab and sluglike. Florence's right hand still rested on the phone.

"I won't say it again," she said, without turning. "You need to get out."

"Not until you help me." He realised, standing in the doorway like this, that his back was exposed to anyone who might enter the lobby. "Is Harrigan here? Your husband?"

Florence didn't answer. Her body shook. Fear? She must know everything. Jimmy and Tosh.

"Please," she said. Her free hand pulled at her hair, making it wild. She turned and rose from the chair. Her green-striped vest emphasised a new, low bulge to her belly. Daniel stared, fascinated, at it. Her pregnancy explained the fear, then, and illustrated just how far he'd travelled forwards in time. Florence paused, unable or unwilling to finish her appeal.

"I don't want to frighten you," he said. "All I want is the time machine. Tell me the code to the door, and I promise I'll leave you alone. I won't hurt you."

"Why would you hurt me?" Her hands went to her belly.

"I just said I won't. I'll leave, as soon as I have the machine. You'll never see me again."

Florence wavered, clearly unsure whether to trust him. How could he make her believe what he said? Perhaps he ought to have threatened violence after all.

Finally Florence said, "I've called them. They're coming."

The police.

Or.

Involuntarily, Daniel turned to look at the brushed-steel door. The police had already had their chance. They could have taken the time machine as soon as he had disappeared into it. Was the locked keypad designed to keep people out, or to keep the machine in?

"What have you done?" he demanded.

Florence lifted the phone receiver and held it to her chest as if protecting it. She shook her head and pressed her lips tight together.

Daniel leapt from the room to the lounge door, pulling at the handle in vain. "What happened in there? Tell me how to get in!"

The doorbell rang. Daniel wheeled around. They both stared at the front door.

"Who's out there?" he whispered.

"It's the doctor."

Daniel's entire body became icily cold. A doctor. The lab. The enforcers. Far worse than the police.

In desperation, he changed his tone. "I'm sorry. Florence. I'm sorry. I'm fine, I promise. I don't need to see a doctor."

Florence looked from him to the front door and back again.

"Don't," he said in a weak voice as she dashed forwards to pull open the door.

Two people stood framed in the doorway. The first, a small, bald man wearing large spectacles and a dark suit, peered at Daniel with undisguised interest. This must be the doctor. A heavyset, square-jawed man in a Reebok tracksuit stood alongside, dwarfing him. This could only be one of the enforcers that Jimmy had described.

"No," Daniel said, suddenly unsure what he was protesting against. The heaviness in his legs returned.

He whirled around. Covell appeared from the kitchen, presumably also summoned by the doorbell. So Daniel had been right; Covell was as involved as Florence.

Covell stood beside Florence and squeezed her arm gently. Something in the gesture suggested that he was in charge. Florence stared at the carpet. She nodded slowly.

Daniel cast around for an exit. He yelped as the tracksuited man stepped forwards and pinned his arms, fixing him to the spot.

The bald doctor watched on, offering only a wistful smile. He retrieved a printout from a plastic wallet, then turned to Covell. "I'm sorry that we were a little delayed. May I begin?"

Covell gave a curt nod. Why was his permission being sought?

Of course.

Covell. Daniel was a fool for not recognising that this man had been the common denominator in every recent event. He had been in the background throughout. Calculating, waiting, reporting to the only people that Daniel ought to have feared all along. This was not a police matter. His pursuers, all along, had been interested in the time machine, not Daniel Faint. Covell was no enforcer, but he must represent the real power, the money. What had Jimmy called them? Angel investors. Daniel almost laughed at the phrase.

The doctor glanced at Covell for approval before speaking. "I have a number of questions for you to answer, Daniel."

Daniel writhed, held immobile in the enforcer's tight grip. He glared at Covell.

The doctor continued, unruffled. "What is your full name?"

"Daniel Miles Faint."

"Good. And where are you?"

"The Manor. Cumbria. Broughton-in-Furness. Let me go."

"And who am I?"

"The doctor," Daniel said.

The doctor waited patiently.

Daniel resented giving him any satisfaction. "I'm sorry. I seem to have forgotten your name."

The doctor turned to Florence. "Has he been exposed at all?"

Florence shook her head in silence.

"Good." He addressed Daniel again. "Tell me. What is today's date?"

Daniel struggled to remember what date Covell had told him, out on the golf course. "I never know what day it is," he said. "Anyone can tell you that."

"The month, then."

"September." He felt a rush of pride at remembering the fact.

"And the year?"

Daniel gave a theatrical sigh. "Julian calendar, or Gregorian?"

"Gregorian, please. Daniel, stay calm."

Daniel glanced around, as if a clue might present itself at any moment. He hadn't considered that this might not be the same year, but why would the doctor ask the question otherwise? He thought again of the changed décor of the Manor. "Twenty-seventeen."

Out of the corner of his eye, he saw Covell's mouth tighten. The doctor simply nodded.

"Wait," Daniel said. "What does that nod mean?"

"One final question. A topical one, if you will indulge me. One moment." The doctor crossed the lobby to stand beside Covell. Together, they consulted a list fixed to the clipboard. Covell pointed with a finger and the doctor nodded. "Two days ago, hostilities boiled over in a particular European nation to become outright war. Can you tell me which country?"

Daniel let his head hang down for a moment. It felt good not to have to brace against its weight. "How should I know?"

"How should you know?" The doctor's patience was excruciating.

"I wasn't here."

"You were away? Where?"

Daniel couldn't bear the charade any longer. "I don't know! I don't know, all right? I wasn't anywhere! I don't remember! I don't know!"

Covell, standing beside Florence, said, "I'm sorry, Daniel."

"*You're* sorry?" For want of any other idea, Daniel clung onto the only question easily answered. "So tell me. I know I flunked the test. What year is it, then?"

"Twenty-twenty," Covell said, almost apologetically.

Daniel stared, dumbfounded.

He had travelled four whole years into the future.

Covell looked down at his fingers which now fretted and intertwined. "I'm sorry," he said again. "This is the right thing to do."

Daniel struggled against the tight grip of the enforcer. "To do? What are you talking about? And what the hell are you, anyway, Covell? A psychologist, or an... an angel?" He relished Covell's confusion, then lapsed into sullen silence.

For a few seconds, they all stood fixed in a peculiar tableau. Daniel stared at Florence until she met his eyes. Her chin trembled.

Covell turned to the metal door of the lounge. His taps on the keypad produced four beeps, then he pressed with his full weight to open it. The enforcer pushed forwards with Daniel trapped in his grip.

The air was thick inside the dark room. The sofas had disappeared, but the décor remained the same as when Daniel had last entered. The time machine still occupied the far end. Its quiet hum seemed less welcoming now and contained a low warning note. Perhaps it, too, was a victim here.

It had changed. The grey panels were now fixed in position, with bands of metal acting as permanent restraints. A waist-height, flat-topped podium had been installed outside the ring of panels. Daniel thought of the official who had presided over Jimmy's funeral, standing behind a lectern just like this one.

The slatted tube had been pulled apart, exploded as in a technical diagram. In the centre of its expanded ring stood a steel chair with a black, faux-leather cushion. It looked like a dentist's chair. Loose black strips hung from its armrests.

Daniel heard a groan. It came from somewhere deep within his own body.

He understood.

With the Oxford lab now abandoned, it was Daniel who would act as guinea pig, testing the time machine on the scientists' behalf. They must have realised the danger, the full extent of the machine's capabilities, just as he had.

No, not a guinea pig. A monkey, like the unfortunate animal thrown into space before rockets were entrusted to carry a human. A convenient method of calibration, with low risk.

Perhaps they had even allowed him to steal the time machine in the first place, letting him create his own snare. And now he would be propelled further and further into the future, but always back into their clutches. An image appeared in his mind, a toy that William had owned as a child. A small ball, attached by an elastic thread to a wooden paddle. Always escaping, always returning.

He pulled and pushed against the enforcer, but his body had become weak and flimsy. The enforcer pressed him into the black chair and secured the fabric bands around his forearms. Daniel stifled a giggle at the sudden fancy that he was a king in his throne, and these people were all his subjects.

Covell and Florence stayed close to the doorway. Covell gripped Florence's arm. What threats had he made to her? The thought that she had been involved with the time machine's investors since the beginning was difficult to imagine. So why was she allowing them to overrun her house like this? For money alone?

The doctor stood behind the metal lectern. He held the clipboard at arm's length, peering over his glasses to read the printed words. Intermittently, he adjusted the controls on the hidden face of the lectern.

"Ninety-five... Ninety-six. Elevate to sixteen-oh-five." Turning to Covell, the doctor said, "Well beyond any normal lifespan." To Daniel he said, apologetically, "This'll be the last time."

The last time? How far forwards were they preparing to send him?

"Please," Daniel said. Covell glanced up for a moment but didn't respond. Florence bit her thumbnail.

Daniel twisted to face her. "Florence. Please don't let this happen. I'm scared. I don't know where I'm going." Where, when. It all amounted to the same thing.

Florence's head lolled. She rubbed at one eye with her sleeve.

The doctor retreated a step. He lifted a hand-sized object connected via a cable to the base of the chair. Unlike the trigger mechanism that Daniel had used, this new controller looked like a caricature of a dynamite plunger. Wile E. Coyote versus Road Runner. No subtlety, no precision. Push it down, wallop. All or nothing.

"They'll kill me." Daniel shuddered as he said it. He didn't understand the hows and whys, but he felt suddenly certain that this was the case.

"Don't." It was Florence who spoke.

The doctor's fingers tightened against the trigger. But he didn't push it.

All or nothing.

Daniel roared. His body spasmed. With unexpected strength, he ripped away the arm straps attached to the chair, lacerating his skin in the process. The doctor reeled, holding up the clipboard as if it might act as a shield.

The tracksuited enforcer lunged forwards.

Daniel lurched to one side as the man's spadelike hand hit against his shoulder. The collision jarred, sending arcs of pain all the way through his torso. Off balance, he struck against the nearest grey panel and ricocheted to the wall. His head hit the wooden dado rail with a dull crack. Somehow, he remained on his feet, desperately clawing at the bulky man closing in on him.

"Stop!" Covell shouted from behind. "Don't injure him, you fool!"

The enforcer hesitated, and Daniel grinned. A weakness. They needed him alive for their tests.

He grasped the opportunity and darted forwards, but the enormous raised arm dropped before he could pass underneath. A muffled bell tolled within his head. As he staggered forwards, something wet found its way into his right eye. He reached up and felt a sticky substance spread over his forehead.

Covell remained in the doorway. Both of his hands were raised in a 'stop' gesture more hopeful than threatening.

Covell, the root and cause of all his problems. Daniel sent him sprawling with a lucky punch to the stomach.

To his surprise, Florence stepped aside to let him pass through the doorway. Her expression contained a mix of horror and compassion.

His arms windmilled as he hurtled out of the room, through the lobby and, panting, into the forecourt. He dashed to the silver MG.

The keys were already in the ignition. His hands shook uncontrollably as he fired up the engine and threw the car into reverse, narrowly missing the doctor, who had emerged, shouting, from the Manor with the other men in tow. They shrank in the rear-view mirror as Daniel sped through the iron archway and hurtled along the curved driveway to the main road.

TWELVE

Lights flashed as he sped by.

He saw himself in the past and future. His past self was portrayed by William, with a face only subtly different to his own but frozen in his early twenties. His future was represented by grey, static Benfield, lost and trapped.

Refracted by the rain on the windscreen, the lights became long streaks that threatened to eclipse the road. The twin visions of William and Benfield separated like the parallel lanes of the motorway.

He saw his brother that final night. He felt William's hands clasp his own.

I'll do this for you, Daniel. But you have to promise it's the end.

~

He swung the car into the motorway services at Tebay and came to a halt in the darkest corner of the car park. Driving for an hour, as close to top speed as he dared, had left him exhausted. He peered into the rear-view mirror, then recoiled at the haggard face reflected there. The effect was worsened by the clotted continent of blood that covered his forehead and right cheek.

Four years. He had travelled four years into the future. His features, bloody and tightened like this, appeared correspondingly older even though he knew that he must not have aged a day.

He walked his fingers along his face to the temple, probing carefully. He spasmed as his index finger became embedded in sickly black mucus. His vision snuck away at the edges and he took deep breaths to clear his head. Blood began to ooze again from the wound.

He emerged into the cold air to search the boot of the car. It contained only a tyre jack and a green lumberjack shirt. Back in the driver's seat, he removed his T-shirt and pulled on the new one. It smelt of wood smoke and fit snugly.

In the glove compartment he found a pack of wet wipes. He spent several minutes dabbing at the dried blood on his cheek, avoiding his forehead. His old T-shirt ripped easily, but the resultant strip of fabric was tattered and uneven. He closed his eyes, resting for a moment before wrapping the cloth tightly around his forehead. Pain flashed through him. He shouted through gritted teeth.

The glove compartment also contained a flat tweed cap and leather driving gloves. Carefully, he positioned the cap so that it hid most of the improvised bandage. He pulled on the gloves, too, before leaving the car.

The distance across the car park to the petrol station seemed vast, but he was reluctant to drive to the garage itself. In all likelihood, there would be registration-plate recognition cameras. There was no telling whether the enforcers might have access to official databases. He collected and filled a petrol canister and then left it at the sliding door to the forecourt to stand, fidgeting, in the queue.

"Do you require any assistance, sir?" The purple-haired cashier glanced at the door, then frowned as she inspected his face.

"No," Daniel replied. "My, uh, brother will help me take it to the car. We broke down."

"I'm sorry, sir. That's not what I meant." The cashier touched her forehead, then looked pointedly above his eyeline. She squinted apologetically.

Daniel raised his hand. Warm blood had already begun to seep through the makeshift bandage, trickling past his ear.

He paid in cash, mumbling reassurances, and left. The petrol canister became heavier with each step. Beyond the halfway point, he resorted to dragging it noisily along the ground, leaving a rain of bitumen pebbles in his wake.

Once he had filled the petrol tank, he collapsed back into the driver's seat.

"Don't you dare sleep," he told his reflection.

The car spluttered into life. It pulled him towards the motorway.

Where was he going, anyway? Away from the Manor, certainly. He now relinquished any claim over the time machine. Covell and his investor friends paid for it, now possessed it again, and were welcome to it, so long as they let him alone. Whoever they were, they were far more dangerous than he had suspected. They would have no scruples in destroying him to protect their investment.

But, equally, he had no doubt that they would come after him. Even without the time machine in his possession, he represented a threat. They couldn't be certain that he would be unable to build a time machine of his own.

How much time did he have? Keeping to the main roads hadn't been ideal, but at least he had put a fair distance between himself and the Manor. And heading north was the best option, surely. With luck, his pursuers would have rushed south on the M6 towards Oxford.

He still hadn't answered his own question. Where was he going, exactly?

He dabbed at his forehead, producing an ache that made the car headlights on the slip road become blurred yellow smears. Before long, he would need to get the wound seen to, but checking into an A&E department was too risky. They'd require ID, and then Covell would have the means to track him.

Another issue nagged at him, too. Keeping to main roads might allow faster travel, but also opened up the possibility of his being noticed, either on CCTV or, if it came to it, police surveillance. He was still a murderer, after all. On top of everything else, he had killed two men.

Two or three.

There could be no going back.

So. Onwards and upwards. Sort of.

At the roundabout he yanked the car almost full circle, heading east along a single-carriageway road.

For two and a half bleary hours he threaded his way further east, then north, keeping to the narrowest roads. The central white lines skipped and alternated directions, usually racing towards him but sometimes, when his vision faltered, sweeping upwards from underneath the car and ahead into the distance. When his head lolled he placed his fingers on the window to let the cold refresh him.

Only when he passed the neon constellations of Newcastle did he dare to join the A1. The clock told him that it was just before midnight. The road edged slowly towards the east coast. At a village named Beal he turned the car fully towards the water. Soon, alongside warning signs and lights, the road itself dipped away into the sea.

He pulled to a stop in a layby. His head ached terribly as he left the car to pull cold air into his lungs. It was something of a miracle that he hadn't veered off the road during the journey. He leant back on the bonnet of the car and gazed out over the dark water. On the opposite side of the narrow strip of sea he made out shimmering lights, the only evidence of the few buildings on the island of Lindisfarne. A narrow, diminishing thread of stars across the water showed the positions of towers marking the causeway path, which was currently submerged. It was impossible to tell how deep the waters were, but the board at the roadside stated that safe crossing would only be possible after ten past five. Four hours from now.

His eyelids stuck more with each blink. The lights before him became a rope, the curl of a noose. He rubbed at one of the fingers of his left hand, marvelling at its smoothness.

~

To his surprise, he found himself blinking in the sunlight. His left leg, pulled under his body, had gone to sleep and prickled with pins and needles.

His surroundings had changed. Fear gripped him momentarily. Could the time machine affect him, even here? But then he recalled, dimly, crossing the causeway as the waters had finally parted, sometime before dawn. The ghost towers alongside the road had loomed like spectres. It had still been dark as he had pulled up outside the white-walled cottage. He had slid down to rest here against the wall after banging on the door to no reply. He was lucky that the morning was now bright and warm for September.

A middle-aged woman in hiking gear strode purposefully along the road. Her pace slowed as she noticed Daniel. One of his legs protruded onto the road surface. He squinted, hoping to recognise her. Weakly, he raised a hand. She hurried past.

The sound of gulls grew and lessened in volume with the changing direction of the wind. Here, though, Daniel was sheltered by the cottage and the single row of low buildings opposite. A red-leafed maple tree remained immune to the whooshing of air above.

He let his eyes close again.

A door opened and closed, far away.

"Daniel? Is that you?"

Groggily, he registered that the voice was speaking for the second time.

He peered upwards, shielding his eyes. A dog nuzzled against his leg. He pushed it away.

His eyes rolled back. Time passed.

The voice said, "You look like hell."

He felt hands latch under his arms and pull him upwards. His vision wobbled as they entered the relative darkness of the house. He sat at a wood-effect kitchen table. His eyes closed as the hands unwrapped his bandage and patted at the gash in his forehead.

"Done."

He opened his eyes. At the top of his field of vision he glimpsed the white bulge of the bandage. The wound throbbed no less than before, but the knowledge that it had been properly tended made the pain feel less severe.

He looked at the woman sitting opposite him.

The years, and the salty air of the island, had eroded his mother. Her hair had once been dark, but was now wiry and grey. Deep creases marked the corners of her eyes. But she still appeared striking. Like mother, like son. William's eyes had the same gleam of intelligence.

Daniel smiled.

His mother didn't reciprocate. "You're expecting me to ask about the head wound, I suppose. But I'd rather start with a broader question. What brings you here, Daniel?"

"Just felt like catching up," he replied. He was shocked by the weakness of his voice. A thought struck him. "So you haven't heard from me recently, then?"

Her eyes narrowed. "Sure. You were here just last week. You took me out for a belated Mother's Day lunch, then we watched Antiques Roadshow and did a jigsaw."

His smile wavered, only for a moment. "That's a joke."

"Yes, I'm joking. You're in a bad state."

"When did you last hear from me?"

She drew in breath. "Hardly seems like any time at all. It was just—what—eight years ago?" Her eyes showed no concern for him, only resentment. She stood and walked over to a counter to remove tea bags from two mugs. "So what kind of trouble are you in?"

It might take him all day to reply to that question.

A chocolate-brown Labrador padded into the room. Daniel pulled back his hand as he felt the wetness of its tongue.

His mother placed one of the mugs before him and nursed the other. "Some kind of substance, I'm guessing? Coke? Booze?" The tone suggested no judgement, only vague curiosity.

He shook his head. It was almost a relief that she imagined that his problems might be so straightforward. "Believe it or not, I'm clean."

"I suppose that was never your problem."

"I suppose not." He took a gulp of too-hot tea that stung his throat. He prayed for her not to bring up any of the episodes that had soured their relationship, even before the loss of William broke it off entirely. The pathetic justifications of his losses. Later, the cajoling, begging and stealing.

His mother took a deep breath. "So you're still down south? D'you see much of..." The forced conversational tone slipped.

He shook his head again. "Nope. I lost touch."

"Just me, then."

"Just you."

~

He slept all afternoon, waking at dusk due to an insistent pounding in his head. Dog hair covered the duvet of the bed. Ordinarily that might annoy him, but he found that it lent the room a sense of friendliness, with none of the sterility of his room in the Manor. Even so, he felt exhausted, as though he had tossed and turned the whole time he had been asleep.

After a minute or so, he realised that the thumping sound wasn't in his head. It came from the back yard of the cottage. He pulled on a jumper that lay on a wicker chair, then made his way downstairs and outside.

His mother turned from the pile of logs stacked in a tiny wood shed. She laid down the axe that she held. "You'll catch your death."

Daniel followed her gaze to his bare feet. He took a step back to stand on the bristled doormat.

"Sorry I didn't let you in last night," his mother said.

"You heard me knocking?"

She shrugged. "Look, I like living here on the island. And if you hadn't already guessed, part of that's the isolation. If I wanted people to come knocking on my door when it's black dark, I'd live in, I don't know, New York."

"Because that's what people do in New York."

"Well, I wouldn't know, would I? The point is that they don't here on Lindisfarne. But still, sorry. If I'd known it was you, and the state you were in..."

Daniel wondered how she'd finish the sentence, if she was being totally honest.

"I'm sorry too," he said. "For barging in. And for everything."

"Well, that's all in the past, isn't it? And the past's passed. Let's move on." She swept past him and into the kitchen.

He touched her arm and noted the slight withdrawal. "I'm serious. Mum. I'm sorry. It was a long time ago. I was a different person then."

"Stop it." She coughed. "Okay. Posh baked beans for breakfast. I know it's dinnertime, but your body clock must be all mixed up anyway."

'Posh baked beans' turned out to be a more substantial meal than Daniel had expected, with bacon lardons and butter beans in a thick tomato sauce. During their childhood, his mother had always ensured that he and William ate healthily, with few meals as indulgent as this. He ate with relish, realising with fascinated horror that he had no idea when he had last eaten.

His mother became quieter and quieter throughout the meal, only answering general questions about the island and her home. After dinner she offered him a glass of whisky. They drank in silence in the lounge and watched the fire that she stoked at regular intervals.

~

Daniel snuck out early the next morning, following a familiar path.

From a rock outcrop, he watched St Cuthbert's Isle dwindle to a thin strip as it yielded to the encroaching tide. This tiny mass off the southwest coast of Lindisfarne was barely an island at all. It was a moon's moon. Seeking contemplation, St Cuthbert had lived on that speck of soil marked with a plain wooden cross. He'd removed himself from the distractions of society.

That's what Daniel's mother had done too, years ago. He would never have known about her move to Lindisfarne, if not for a chance encounter with a family friend in Leamington Spa a few years later. But it made sense. They'd all holidayed here as a family, during his childhood. He winced involuntarily. Not just *his* childhood. *Their* childhood, his and William's. His mother had latched onto a location that represented a dialling back of the years.

Water slipped over the final ribbon of land so that the wooden cross was the only hint of St Cuthbert's Isle. Daniel turned in his rock throne halfway up the outcrop. He and William had often fought for possession of this spot, which they had named the Crow's Nest for its views. Below, on the opposite side, lay the ruins of Lindisfarne Priory. Its single remaining archway, a stone rainbow hanging far above the grass, defied the surrounding decay. This solitary strut indicated the grandeur of the original building.

Daniel shivered, even though the air was still and the sun warm.

He ought to leave. Onwards and upwards. The island was a literal dead end. But his mother knew nothing, and her lack of interest in him held enormous appeal. She was a wooden cross on this tiny island. A point of familiarity in his exile.

He rose to his feet and left the Crow's Nest. He climbed the ridge and skirted the priory to join a track that passed the village. Lindisfarne Castle appeared ahead on its grassy pedestal. He glanced back at the derelict priory and then again at the newer, restored castle. If one was to continue living in a building, it must be maintained. Abandon it for too long and decay must inevitably set in.

Beyond the castle, he passed the lime kilns. He had once imprisoned William here, barring the exit from the kilns with branches collected from the beach. As with so many of his childhood crimes, he had received no punishment. After William's eventual escape, Daniel had expected him to run to their mother. Instead, he had simply stored up the injustice, racking it up alongside all the others. As always in such situations, William just retreated further into his books. That night, Daniel simply stared at the TV, though unable to switch it on; his father had removed the power cord after claiming the holiday a respite from the modern world.

When had his father abandoned hope that Daniel and William might reconcile their differences? Years before he left, probably. Daniel remembered another scene from childhood, another one viewed from a third-person perspective. Another scene from a home video; perhaps he ought to search his mother's cottage for them. He saw himself from a first-floor window, his parents' bedroom, guiding William, who tottered on his BMX bike, new for Christmas. Daniel had one hand on his twin's back, propelling him forwards. Then, abruptly, he gave a sudden shove that sent William reeling to one side and onto the grass beside the pavement. Green stains on the knees. Daniel looked up, now in first-person, to see the camera. The camera watched his expression, his silent calculation. It saw William's resigned hurt. Daniel righted his brother upon the bike. He put his hand on William's back again, arm muscles tightening to keep him on track. They glided forwards.

Rather than investigate the lime kilns, Daniel pressed on towards the scar at the east coast of the island. The beach was littered with things washed up with the tide. He saw fishing nets and lobster cages along with other, less expected items. A child's red cagoule. A filthy, knitted toy octopus. Unlikely human memories alongside the litter of jellyfish and razor clam shells.

Two smudges further along the beach became his mother and Baxter, her Labrador. They paused to allow him to catch up. His mother's smile was cold. With only a nod in greeting, Daniel matched their pace as they continued walking north.

They reached the track that led through the sand dunes before his mother spoke.

"I'm not going to talk about him, you know," she said.

Baxter darted ahead and then back again to scurry around their feet.

"I know," Daniel said, "and I appreciate it."

"But you can't stay here. You understand that? I don't want you here. Not after everything."

"You mean William?"

"No."

"Because I can explain, Mum. It wasn't what you think. God, it was so long ago."

She slowed to a halt, watching Baxter worry at a stick. Her stiff posture seemed to require her constant concentration to avoid her bending with the wind. She had become so old while hidden here out of sight.

What did he have to lose, by explaining himself? What had he *ever* had to lose?

He took a lungful of salty air. "I owed money. More than before, a huge amount this time. And I couldn't pay it back. William knew."

Of course William knew. He had made it his business to catalogue each of Daniel's failures, to be digested and reconstituted as fake sympathy.

His mother still faced away, along the path that snuck through the dunes.

"Mum," Daniel said, more insistent now that he had made the decision to speak frankly. "Listen to me. I know you blame me. I know you think he'd still be here if not for me. And him dying doesn't excuse me running away, either. But once he'd gone, I had to escape. Not telling you where I'd hidden was part of the deal. I had to leave everything behind to start again."

"Stop," his mother said. "I told you it wasn't that."

Suddenly, Daniel realised that he had no idea how she felt. How had the loss of a son affected her, all those years ago? Or rather, the loss of both sons, given that Daniel had never returned home once William was found dead in the tennis courts, his face barely recognisable through the blood.

Too much time had passed. He wouldn't be able to appeal to his mother now.

He dug his feet into the sand, which pushed through the airholes in his trainers. "So what, then?"

She sighed. "It's because you're still you, Daniel. You're quieter, less brash. But that look in your eyes hasn't changed. I couldn't live with you nearby, even." She kept her eyes on Baxter. "I don't hate you. Put it this way if you want: it's not you, it's me."

"Except it isn't."

"Except it isn't."

"You were right about me being in trouble," Daniel said. "But you'll never—"

She held up a hand to stop him. "I already told you, I don't want to know. But it's obvious enough that you're torturing yourself about something. Do you realise you've been sleepwalking, like when you were a kid? Pacing up and down on the landing. You gave me a hell of a fright last night."

Daniel felt the muscles in his face tighten. He lapsed into silence as they plodded around the headland.

~

The next morning, his mother had become even quieter. Instead of serving breakfast, she just sat at the table, directing Daniel to the boxes of cereal on the counter. She sat stiffly with the newspaper open before her, but she barely glanced at it. After five minutes of silent chewing, Daniel could bear it no longer.

"What's happened?" he said.

She blinked and pushed wiry hair from her eyes. "Nothing."

"Come on, Mum. I know you."

She flinched. For the first time since he had entered the room, she looked at him directly. There was something new in her expression. Whereas previously she had seemed distant and unflustered, now he sensed something more raw. Uncertainty. No. Fear.

"Seriously, Mum," he said, "I can't bear this. What's going on?"

She pushed her chair away from the table. "Baxter needs fresh air. You stay here, okay? He's still not used to you being around." She pulled on her boots and jacket and left without saying another word.

Daniel drifted around the cottage. Being outside left him too vulnerable. Better to stay in here, with the fire and within the thick walls.

The image of his mother's panicked expression followed him from room to room. What had changed since yesterday? He thought again about her comment about his sleepwalking. When he had awoken that morning, his legs ached. Perhaps he had spoken to her in his sleep, too. What might he have confessed, semi-conscious, during the night?

Or perhaps it wasn't anything he had revealed himself. The island may be surrounded by the sea, but it was still penetrable. On a sudden impulse, he darted from room to room, searching for a phone. But there appeared to be no landline, and he hadn't seen his mother with a mobile since he had arrived at the cottage. It would be just like her to spurn the convenience of communication entirely. In many ways, she was even more of an exile than he was.

So it was something else, then.

He found himself in her bedroom. Small and sparse, it contained far less of her personality than the rest of the house. She must spend her days in the lounge, drinking by the fire.

"Typical."

His mother stood in the doorway to the landing, Baxter's lead hanging in her hand. She ushered the dog downstairs. Her face twitched with emotion.

"Go on, then," she said. "Do your best. Invent a plausible explanation for poking around in here."

Daniel stood frozen, ten years old again. "Look—" he began.

"No. You look, Daniel. You look."

Her eyes flicked downwards, just for an instant. Following her gaze, Daniel noticed something protruding from beneath her pillow. He grabbed it before she had time to move.

It was a small envelope, the size to hold a greetings card, addressed to his mother. He sidestepped as she tried to snatch it from him. He recognised the writing. It was his own. He couldn't begin to process what it meant.

His mother slumped on the bed where she had fallen. "Get out." She stood up, awkwardly. Perhaps she had twisted an ankle in her fall. "Daniel. You're ill. I don't understand, but it's obvious. You're very ill."

Daniel waved the letter in her face. "What is this? When did you get it?" He was shouting now.

He saw a trace of compassion in her expression. Her forehead creased in concern. She looked from him to the letter and back again, uncomprehending.

"Come any closer and you'll regret it," he said. He turned the envelope, slid his fingers along the top edge, then paused. "It's sealed."

His mother raised an eyebrow, partially restored to her usual cynical self. "Look at the postmark."

He turned the envelope again to study the tiny circle of print overlapping the stamp. *3 Aug 08.* The envelope slipped from his fingers and wafted downwards to rest upon the duvet. He leant heavily against the cold wall.

"I remember," he said. "I remember writing it. I was so sorry, Mum. I was convinced I'd destroyed you, somehow, along with William."

"Not sorry enough to show your face, though."

He grimaced. "You never opened it?"

"I didn't want to hear what you had to say. You were gone and, on reflection, I preferred it that way."

She took a step back as he reached to pick up the envelope. He tucked it out of sight again beneath the pillow.

She really had abandoned him, all those years ago. And if she had never read the letter, there was no possibility that she might hear his story now.

"It's all true, if you ever choose to read it," he said. But he knew that the envelope would never be opened. He walked to the doorway and turned. "I'm heading out. I need to clear my head. I'll leave first thing tomorrow, I promise."

THIRTEEN

"I can pay it for you, Daniel. I have the money. Work's good. Lorna earns more than I do."

"You'd love that, wouldn't you? Me, forever in your debt. Your debt and your shadow."

"Daniel. Look at me. How much do you owe?"

"Thirty."

"Thousand?"

"Yes. Thereabouts."

"And how's it to be paid?"

"Cash. Tonight. The tennis courts at the school."

"So they're kids?"

"Don't be an idiot. They're not kids. If they were kids I've have—
"

"But you owe this money, fair and square?"

"Yes."

"I'll bring you the money. Wait here."

"No."

"No?"

"No. I can't go there. You go. You take the money to them."

"Are you scared?"

"You really want me to say it? Bastard. I'm scared."

William had never asked how he had found himself so deeply in debt. And if he had, Daniel wouldn't have been able to tell him anyway. They were small amounts, here and there, just to tide him over. He had no drug problem, no expensive habits, just the occasional flutter. But he had no job either, most of the time, at least not one he cared to keep.

It was amazing that it could have racked up so high. Sixty thousand in six months.

Why hadn't he been able to admit the whole amount to William? If he had, perhaps that night might not have played out as it had. It was easy enough to imagine the scene. Those two or three men, one brandishing the hammer. William protesting.

I've brought your thirty thousand, in cash. No, thirty. No, I'm not Daniel, I'm his brother. I'm not him.

A quick shove into a wasp's nest.

~

Daniel's mind continued to churn long after he climbed into bed, preventing him from falling asleep. When he finally lost track of the passing minutes, he jolted awake to find himself on the landing, barefoot and shivering.

He concentrated, trying to locate a muscle memory. As far as he could tell, he'd been standing here for some time, wavering just outside his room.

Something nagged at him, just out of reach. Hadn't he been dwelling on something, when he'd finally drifted off? He grasped at the thread of logic. His gaze moved around the dark corners of the landing, passing over the door to his own room, then his mother's bedroom, coming to rest on a third door that led to a room at the rear of the cottage. He pushed it open.

The study was tiny and black. As he shuffled forwards his hip made sharp contact with something. He felt around to turn on a desk lamp. Its green stained-glass shade cast his eerie, elongated shadow onto the wall. The shape undulated as if it was trying to reach up to the window in the eaves. Daniel shuddered. He turned his attention to the contents of the room. Judging from the stacked piles of printouts, his mother had begun writing poetry. A chink in her tough armour.

An ancient laptop computer lay on the desk. A cable ran from its rear to a phone jack in the wall. Daniel winced. He had been wrong, then. His mother did have a method of communicating with the outside world. He edged around the desk and booted up the computer.

The computer desktop contained only a handful of shortcuts. He clicked on the internet browser. The homepage had been set to Outlook by default. Perhaps the computer might have stored his mother's email address and password? He tapped the 'S' key. No autocomplete text appeared in the login field. He tried other starting letters in turn, with no results.

On a half-formed impulse, he opened the top desk drawer and felt around. His fingers encountered a slip of card fixed to the front face of the drawer. He pulled it out. On it was written an email address and password.

He laughed. It was a family thing.

The inbox contained hundreds of emails, mostly spam. Daniel's pulse accelerated; the sender of the most recent email was 'C Jones Practice'. Its subject line read: *URGENT information regarding Daniel Faint.*

His fingers had become clumsy, so that he struggled to click on the message.

I am writing to you because you are, or have once been, in contact with Daniel Faint. I have been working with Daniel for some time, in an advisory capacity at my psychiatric clinic in Ulverston, Cumbria. In ordinary circumstances, these sessions would remain entirely private.

However, these are not ordinary circumstances.

Over the course of our sessions, it has become evident that Daniel is a deeply troubled individual. Matters, unfortunately, have come to a head rather sooner than I had anticipated. He has left the region, leaving me very much concerned and several others physically injured.

You may wonder why I am involving you in this matter. Simply put, Daniel has referred to you in one or more of our sessions. I fear that he may approach you in the coming days.

He must be located and our sessions reinstated, at the very least. If you have any information about him whatsoever, however trivial it may seem, please contact me directly. My details follow below.

Sincerely,

Covell Jones (MRCPsych)

Daniel scrolled upwards. The message had been sent two days earlier, the same day he had escaped the Manor.

He thought of the change in his mother's behaviour that morning. She had no real interest in keeping in touch with the world. In all likelihood, she had only read the email the yesterday evening, a day after it had been sent.

But would she have acted directly on it? Had she called Covell?

He closed down the computer, pulled its cable free, and tucked it under his arm.

On the landing he paused as he heard a faint noise.

He cocked his head. The dull, shuffling sound resumed. A distant clatter. Then, barely audible, a muttered voice.

The edges of the uneven wooden stairs dug into the soles of his bare feet as he clattered downstairs. At the bottom of the stairs he registered that the front door was still double-bolted. He spun around and threw himself into the kitchen.

His mother stood at the far side of the kitchen counter. She cowered backwards, jolting against an open drawer. Her right hand, raised to her cheek, held a mobile phone so old-fashioned that its aerial was as long as its body. It must have been buried away in the kitchen drawer, rarely used.

"You've done it, haven't you?" he hissed. "You've called him."

"You're scaring the hell out of me, Daniel. The unpredictability, the sleepwalking..." A flicker of regret crossed her face, then evaporated. "Even if you can't see it, you need help. And I want you away from here."

"It's not what you think."

"No? So should I ignore all this, because you're my son?" She shook with emotion. "Well, even that doesn't go far enough, Daniel. You were my son, once. You and William, my beautiful boys. But not any more. You both left me, and now you don't belong here."

Daniel rested on the counter, taking deep breaths to stay in control. "What did Covell say?"

Her eyes darted around his face. "I had to call. This is all beyond me."

"What did he say?" he shouted, struggling against the tightening of his throat.

After a pause she said, "That he's on his way."

Nothing meant anything any more. Survival was all that mattered. Daniel pushed away from the counter, aware that she still watched him closely. He slunk around its curved end.

His mother reached back into the open drawer. "Don't come any closer."

In place of the phone she now held a serrated bread knife. She pointed it like a rapier, at eye level.

Daniel smiled. She was tough, but not nearly that tough. "You're going to use that? You're going to knife your own son like a street thug?"

The knife waved, indicating that he should move back around the counter.

"I'm scared, okay?" his mother said. "You scare me. You always did." Her expression darkened, as if she was accepting this truth fully for the first time. "But now... Now it's another level entirely."

When he didn't move, his mother widened her eyes to reinforce the command. Daniel held up his hands.

The knife lowered, ever so slightly.

Daniel leapt forwards and to one side, pushing her arm upwards so that the knife jerked close to her own face. It spun from her hand to land on the counter with a sharp twang. Before she could react, Daniel snatched it up. He moved closer so that she was forced to lean backwards, awkwardly, over the counter.

He raised the knife.

Her eyes closed tight. Acceptance.

One quick shove would do it.

His grip loosened and the knife fell from his hand.

No. His mother wasn't involved in any of this. He had been the one who had arrived here, uninvited and unwanted. What kind of reaction had he expected? Was he going to punish her for being terrified of him?

Both of his hands went to his face. He groaned. When he removed his hands from his eyes, his mother still cowered, frozen in the same position.

Their eyes met. His mother glanced down at the knife on the tiled floor. She shook her head slowly from side to side.

Daniel drew a deep breath. When he stepped forwards, his mother didn't resist. He gripped her by the arm and led her to the back door. She whimpered, but allowed herself to be moved without resistance.

"You shouldn't have called them," he said.

His mother shivered as cold air blew through the doorway. She still wore just a dressing gown and slippers over her checked pyjamas.

"I'm sorry. I'm sorry," she whispered.

Daniel wrestled with the latch of the door to the tiny wood shed in the yard. He pushed her inside.

"You need help, Daniel," his mother said. She hugged herself against the cold.

Daniel closed and locked the door.

In less than fifteen minutes he had dressed and eaten a quick breakfast in the kitchen, all the time ignoring the muffled pounding from the shed.

~

If his mother had owned a car, he would have taken it. Driving the MG was an unfortunate necessity and would make him easier quarry. He tossed the stolen laptop onto the back seat of the car, along with his mother's mobile phone. The engine noise echoed from the row of cottages opposite. The neighbours would be furious, being woken at this hour.

The car hurtled away from the cottages and the ruins. Dunes rose to the right of the road, sheltering him from the wind. Daniel whistled a tune. Onwards and upwards.

Then he saw the causeway. Or rather, the lack of a causeway.

Only the towers and the tips of the guide posts suggested the route of the road beneath. If not for them, the connecting line between here and the distant blotch of the road rising from the other side of the water would have been invisible. With the tide fully in, the posts would be submerged entirely.

Four hours. Once the tide came in, the causeway would be impassable for four hours.

How long had it taken him to drive here from the Manor?

Four hours.

He pummelled the steering wheel with his fists, inadvertently sounding the horn.

A movement somewhere to his right made him turn. A lone figure crouched on the crest of the grassy dune beyond the road. Daniel forced himself to breathe. It was a tourist, a birdwatcher, that was all. The stranger turned to face the car. He or she held binoculars to his or her face.

Daniel jammed his foot onto the accelerator.

The undercarriage of the car howled as it slammed into the water. Glossy curtains of water burst up on both sides of the vehicle, arcing away in glistening rainbows. The body of the car rocked with thuds and a constant unhappy drone.

The steering wheel jerked beneath his fingers. He gripped it tighter as it swung from side to side. The car lurched left, almost hitting the nearest wooden guide post. He wrenched the steering wheel back again. The wheels of the car must be barely touching the surface of the road. The controls became loose and unresponsive.

Panicked, he glanced into the rear view mirror. The shore behind still loomed large in the reflection. Ahead, the road emerging from the water was little more than a smudge of grey. It inched closer, agonisingly slowly, as he struggled to retain control.

The car skidded wildly as the tyres bounced lightly on the submerged tarmac. Daniel yelled as the steering wheel was yanked from his grasp. Something bounced against the left side of the car. It must be one of the guide posts. Using his elbow, Daniel flipped up the door lock and bent low, trying to gauge the distance to the nearest wooden tower. If the car flipped, he would have to try and struggle free, swim to the tower, then simply wait. It was better not to dwell on what he would be waiting for.

He bounced in his seat as some part of the undercarriage pulled away with a groan. The left wheels juddered, hitting each tip of the guide posts in turn, but this at least gave them some purchase. He gritted his teeth and set himself to the task of positioning the wheels, now acting more as rudders, so that they continued to scrape against each guide post.

Finally, the car righted itself. He squinted to see ahead. The opposite shore was now startlingly close. Soon, all four wheels touched down once again onto the tarmac. A fine mist rose before the windscreen, thrown up by the skidding tyres. It hugged the car even as he sped up the dry tarmac that pulled up and away from the water.

~

His stomach heaved. He had pulled into a pub car park at Beal, once his adrenalin levels had subsided and his hands had begun to shake so much that it was impossible to steer. He pushed open the door and retched onto the gravel.

After a few minutes of producing nothing but rasping noises, he pulled the door closed. He rubbed his face, noting the stubble that had begun to grow on his cheeks. He couldn't remember the last time he had shaved.

At a loud trilling sound, Daniel spasmed with fright. Something electronic. He twisted in his seat to retrieve the phone from the back seat. Its screen was blank.

The ring came again, but not from the phone in his hand. His head cracked against the side window as he bent to locate the sound. His fingers closed around something hard within the door pocket. He pulled out a second, more modern phone. Its screen flashed with each ring.

This must be Florence's phone. Beneath a number he didn't recognise was a single word, *HOME.*

He shouldn't answer it.

Acting independently of his mind, his thumb swiped the screen. He held the phone to his ear without speaking.

"Daniel?" It was Florence's voice.

He mustn't speak, at least. He ought to hang up. Perhaps the phone made the location of the MG traceable. But if so, why had Florence rung it, alerting him to its presence?

"Daniel. Is that you?"

She lapsed into silence. Their breaths intertwined.

Finally he could bear it no longer. "It's me."

A quiet sob came through the phone's speaker. "You know that they know where you are. Don't you?"

"Yes. I know. I'm..." He considered his options. "I'm already far away. They'll not find me, Florence."

The speaker quietened again, long enough for Daniel to wonder if Florence had hung up. Then, with a static-filled sigh, she said, "That's good."

"You've got to get them out of the Manor," Daniel said. "Call the police. These are evil people, I think. They're dangerous."

He heard Florence's quiet breaths. "They're not evil, Daniel."

Why wouldn't she let him help her? "You shouldn't be mixed up in all this."

Silence.

He recalled the cautious way she had moved, the last time he had seen her. "God. I forgot. You're pregnant."

Silence.

He chewed his lip. He struggled to think of any questions that she might be able to answer. Florence understood nothing about the time machine or the real threat posed by Covell.

When she spoke again, Daniel had to strain to hear her voice. "My father died yesterday evening."

A jumble of thoughts hit him all at once. Grief, empathy, memories of other deaths, why them, why me? Why me?

"I... I'm so sorry, Florence. I met him. I'm so sorry." He thought of Benfield's skin, brittle like the sheets of notepaper pinned to the wall of his study.

"He was very old." Another long pause. "He asked after you, just before he died."

Daniel frowned. "Why?"

"He just did. You should check your mail."

"Florence. I don't understand. There's so much I—"

A distant click signalled that she had hung up.

He sat in silence, watching the irregular spurts of traffic on the main road.

After a few minutes, the phone beeped again. Not a call this time, but a text message. The screen identified the sender as *Florrie*. Daniel peered at the screen, unable to parse the words on his first reading.

YOUDONTBELONGHERE

All of his goodwill towards Florence evaporated in an instant.

She was stupid and smug, just as he had originally thought. She had nobody in her life, other than that bloated husband. Her father died and she decided to ring him, of all people! She must have thought they shared a connection, however twisted. She was that much alone. And yet, she clearly hated herself for it, too, at least judging by that text message.

He struggled to free himself from his seatbelt. He walked back to the point where the road flattened out to become the causeway. Deep puddles surrounded the road on both sides. Beyond, the waters were deep and murky.

With as much strength as he could muster, he hurled the phone into the dark water.

FOURTEEN

Daniel drove for as long as he could bear. It was only when the rain settled in and he began to struggle to distinguish the edges of the road that he allowed himself to pull over. At first he stopped in a layby and tried to rest but, realising that the car would still be visible from the road, he forced himself to continue for a few more miles to reach a small motel alongside a petrol station. With his remaining energy, he ensured that the MG was tucked out of sight before he staggered into the building.

He slept fitfully. On several occasions he found himself out of bed, his hands running the length of the curtains to block out the streetlights.

In the morning he was surprised not to be woken by the peacocks. How many nights had he slept in the Manor in total? He had lost all sense of the passing of time.

The mirror in the hotel room showed a man he barely recognised. The line of his jaw looked more like William's than his own. As he pulled on the scratchy green lumberjack shirt he wondered who had once owned it.

In the lobby, the receptionist pressed a lukewarm, foil-wrapped breakfast package into his hands. Without warning, the casual act of kindness made Daniel want to weep. His mouth twitched constantly as he went through the motions of checking out.

Outside, the dawn light glanced off the slick tarmac, producing sheets of colour that hung in the air. Daniel stood in the doorway, shielding his eyes.

He froze. At the far end of the car park, where the trees overhung the few vehicles, two figures stood beside the MG. Even from this distance, Daniel identified the shorter man as Covell and the taller one as his silent enforcer.

Acting on instinct, he flung himself low behind the cars closest to the building. He crawled on his hands and knees along the length of the car park, skirting around the two men. When he reached the opposite corner, he remained there, crouching and waiting. He raised himself just high enough to see into the wing mirror of the nearest car.

After a brief discussion, both Covell and his companion turned to face the motel. Covell took a couple of steps towards it, then paused as the enforcer gestured again at the car. Covell shook his head and, reluctantly, the taller man followed him across the car park.

Daniel leapt to his feet as soon as they had disappeared into the building. He reached the MG in a few long strides. A black BMW was parked alongside. He put a hand on its bonnet. Warm. He ought to slash its tyres, but had nothing to hand to do the job. There was no time to hang around. Better simply to get away as quickly as possible.

The tyres of the MG screeched as he swerved back onto the road.

He drove north.

Onwards and upwards.

~

The oncoming traffic bellowed and squealed. Trucks raised sheets of water that thudded down upon the bonnet of the car. At first Daniel flinched at each hammer blow, but soon the noise seemed to subside, becoming only as loud as the thumping within his head.

The rear-view mirror filled with ghostly images of the black BMW. A crow swooping low to the ground, wings spread as it sighted prey. A peacock with the power of flight, scanning the ground with its tail-eyes. Water rose in grey clouds at either side of the car and in a sharp cape of spray behind it.

As he drove, he saw his life as something small and hardened, manipulable in his mind as though solid and sealed. A new certainty dawned upon him. He had failed in all respects that mattered. What was life but a series of decisions? And all of his decisions had been flawed from the start. Nobody remained who would vouch for the path he had chosen.

He remembered something he had said to his mother the day before. *I had to leave everything behind to start again.*

No.

He had to leave everything behind and that was the end of it.

Let the bird find its carrion and pull at his flesh.

He flashed onwards to nowhere.

~

The traffic quietened again once he had crossed the Forth Bridge. The rain stopped, too. Without the distraction of the tunnel of spraying water, his mind became freer.

He must think like a scientist.

It couldn't be a coincidence that Covell had followed him to the motel. He thought again of Florence's discarded phone. Might the MG contain another tracking device? If so, it implied that Covell had been prepared for Daniel's reappearance. What other traps might he have set?

He realised that his bladder was full to bursting. After a few miles he pulled into a truck stop partially hidden from the main road by a line of trees. A huge articulated lorry provided additional cover. He entered a brick building containing a café and toilets.

When he emerged, yawning with relief, he pulled backwards in alarm. The black BMW, moving at barely a crawl, was just visible at the entrance to the layby. Daniel's breath came in short bursts. After counting to five, he sneaked another look. The car had disappeared.

He fumbled with the handle of the MG and tripped on the door trim as he flung himself inside.

Less than a mile further along the road he registered a black blotch to his right. The BMW pointed away from the main road as it made an awkward three-point turn in an adjoining lane. Daniel slumped low in his seat. The rear-view mirror showed the BMW entering the truck-stop.

So he had been right. Somehow, Covell was able to track him. Daniel would have to start from scratch to shake him off. Find a new car, somehow. Change his clothes.

But that wouldn't be enough. He would have to leave the country. Invent a new identity, go abroad. Somewhere far away. Portugal. Morocco. Australia. Nobody would be able to trace him. And nobody would miss him.

Except there was one person who had showed concern for him, recently: Florence Harrigan. He remembered her strange, disjointed manner on the phone. She had called Daniel to warn him that he'd been located. But there had been other details, too. Perhaps the situation at the Manor, and her grief about losing her father, had caused her to lose her mind a little. Regardless, she had tried to offer him help.

Why?

It must be something to do with her father. Perhaps she saw a resemblance. The old man's wiry hair might once have looked a little like Daniel's. She might have found similarities in the intensity of Benfield's research and Daniel's experiments at the Manor.

She had said that Benfield had asked after him before he died. Had she spoken to her father about him, enough to make the old man care a jot, in those final days or hours?

His fingers clamped on the steering wheel as he recalled the details of the phone conversation. Florence had said something else, too, unrelated to Benfield. Hadn't she given him a clear instruction?

You should check your mail.

Immediately, he pulled off the main road to wind through country lanes. Soon he reached a tiny village. It seemed to have no cafés or pubs but on its outskirts he found a dilapidated, red-boarded building with a sign announcing *Vacancies*.

The reception remained empty for several minutes after Daniel rang the brass bell. Finally, an elderly man wearing a grubby boiler suit appeared from a back room.

"Good afternoon!" he said. "Will you be staying long?"

Daniel showed his mother's laptop computer. "Actually, I was just hoping for a quick drink, and to use your wifi. Is that okay?"

The man frowned. "The bar's not open until five."

Breathe. Act normal. "In that case, maybe I could wait. But I'll need your wifi password."

"Are you from the hotel inspectorate? The AA?" The man glanced around, upset, as if seeing the clutter on the desk and the cracked walls for the first time. "What's this about a password?"

Daniel gritted his teeth and forced himself to remain polite. "For the internet. Wireless. I need to log on to check my emails."

"Ah," the man said, visibly relieved. "Oh, yes. One moment." He retreated through a panelled door into the back room.

Impatient, Daniel watched the road through the grimy window. A single cyclist passed, pedalling slowly to avoid coming into contact with the dog trotting alongside on a long leash. The cyclist tilted his nose to the ground as he pedalled. The dog mimicked the pose, a tiny facsimile of its owner.

The hotelier's voice echoed from the back room. "Brenda! Bren! Gentleman here wants to see our wiring. Some kind of password involved."

A woman's voice called in response, from somewhere upstairs. Daniel heard the sound of footsteps descending. His fingers rapped on the reception desk. He glanced at the empty road again. If Covell had tracked him this far, he might easily be in pursuit even along these country lanes.

Finally, he pushed through the door to the back room. The elderly man and a younger woman wearing a purple-spotted dressing gown both turned, showing only mild surprise.

"You can't be back here," the man said. "You don't belong here."

Daniel ignored him and addressed the young woman, presumably the hotelier's daughter or even grandchild. "It's very important. I must check my emails. Please."

The woman pulled her dressing gown tighter around her waist. Her wet hair had plastered to one side of her face. "We don't have wifi," she said.

"Then do you know where—"

"It's all right. We're not total luddites," she interrupted. "There are wired connections in every room."

He felt hot tears form in his eyes. "Then can I take a room?"

The woman watched on from the staircase as the elderly man guided him back into the reception. Daniel completed forms and nodded through the man's lengthy descriptions of hotel rules and regulations. Finally, key in hand, he stumbled up the stairs and into a cramped attic room. He yanked the ethernet cable from its retractable housing and crouched with the laptop on the bed.

He accessed Gmail and typed in his email address, then his password.

A message appeared in red beneath the login box. *The email and password that you entered don't match.*

He paused with both hands resting on the keyboard. He tried an older password.

The email and password that you entered don't match.

This was an unexpected setback. He thought of the period following his last use of the time machine, during which Jimmy had been killed. How long had that been, exactly? There was no way he might guess a password selected while he had been suffering drug-induced amnesia. It might as well have been somebody else entirely who had chosen it.

He stared at the screen for several minutes. He thought of Jimmy, the time machine, the Manor, Benfield's antiquated computer, Florence. Florence.

Florence had told him.

His fingers began to type before he had fully formulated the thought.

YOUDONTBELONGHERE

The login screen disappeared. The inbox opened.

It was almost entirely empty.

Daniel reeled. The deletion of his emails felt surprisingly invasive. He rarely used computers or the internet, having too few contacts to warrant it, but this still represented an erasure of part of his life.

Only one email remained. Its sender was Florence Harrigan.

The message contained no text, but a paperclip icon showed that there was an attached file. When Daniel clicked on it the browser disappeared behind a new window. A circular loading icon swung around and around, each sector in turn increasing in intensity.

A video began to play.

~

It took Daniel a few moments to recognise the man onscreen as himself. The facial features contained little that he recognised from his own mirror reflection or from photos. The eyes appeared wider, the mouth less pinched.

The onscreen Daniel glanced upwards, perhaps checking the recording status of the video. Behind him, Daniel recognised the cluttered pinboard in Benfield's study. To the right of the screen, shelves overflowed with Florence's sculptures alongside rows of hardback books.

He looks at home there. I do.

"Right. Okay then." The Daniel in the video window fixed his attention directly on the camera. On Daniel. He settled back into the armchair, producing a faint creak.

"This is not a good idea." Onscreen, Daniel's eyes lifted again. "We both know that."

Facing the lens again, he said, "This video is for Daniel Faint. You. If you're watching this video, something's changed. The plan. For some reason, we've decided that you ought to know the truth. I don't what the circumstances may be. This isn't my idea."

We? Daniel thought of Covell, then the enforcer, then the bald doctor, then Florence.

He saw himself rub at his face. The eyes flicked upwards. "I'm not sure I can—" He paused, then nodded slowly. "Sorry."

The Daniel in the video leant forwards slightly, as if he might reach out of the screen and take Daniel by the arm. "I'm you. Or you're me. I don't know. Either way, it's about time that we talked, so to speak. All these years and never a single word to each other. It's just not right. Right?"

Years? Daniel thought of his period of amnesia. That had been only days. Everything else could be accounted for in his own memories and his travels within the time machine.

The time machine. His travels. Daniel shook his head. His mind refused to begin to make connections.

"Maybe you've an inkling what's been happening," the onscreen Daniel said. "Maybe not. Maybe you're more of a fucking—" He sighed. "Look. This is really hard for me. I know that you're scared. I know that, because I've been there, I've been you, so to speak. The only difference between us, I suppose, is that I figured it all out first. But you'll never understand how strange it was for me, at the beginning."

Why was he talking as though they were not, in fact, one and the same person?

The onscreen Daniel cleared his throat before speaking again. "So. The time machine. It's not what you think."

He settled into his seat, feigning comfort. "It worked all right, at first, on the clay statues. On anything inanimate. It really did transport them into the future. But everything beyond that was a whole different matter. The machine can't cope with anything organic, anything with a mind. Just think of that peacock. It didn't disappear—it just freaked out. Got all weak and confused until it came to its senses again. Until it got its mind back. I know *exactly* how it felt, in that short time in between.

"Before we entered the machine, there was just one of us. Okay? We're no superhero, nothing special. Just a thief with a machine we never understood in the first place. And then we tried it out on ourselves. As far as you were concerned, you jumped forwards in time. Remember?"

Of course Daniel remembered. That was exactly what had happened. He had seen the sun jump in the sky.

"But that's only half of the story. Your half. For me, that first time, that first squeeze of the trigger, nothing happened. Nothing at all. I watched the clock, I tightened connections, I waited. And then—" He took a deep breath. "Then things got confusing.

"The clock changed. It worked. Except... except I hadn't pressed the trigger. Could've just been a delayed reaction, I reasoned. Who knows how time machines work? Especially a stolen, half-finished one. But then it happened again. Time jumped past in an instant, without me having done a thing."

No. That's not how it happened. Those things hadn't happened to Daniel.

The eyes of the onscreen version of Daniel darkened. "I didn't try using the machine again. You've got to have a control test, right? And I was scared. I'd meddled with something I didn't understand, just once, and the repercussions were beyond me. I stayed in the Manor. I paced around the building, I cooked, I called Clark Benfield at his care home in some attempt to find a kindred spirit, I..." His eyes glanced upwards again and a blush coloured his cheeks. "I wanked furiously, anything to act as a distraction. And I avoided the machine.

"But it kept happening. I'd be in the middle of something, then in an instant—" He clicked his fingers. "—I'd find myself suddenly sitting cross-legged in that tube in the middle of the machine. Terrified. It was only when that knackered old computer showed up on the carpet beside me that I called foul on the whole thing. I can't tell you how alarming that was. If I didn't put it there, who did? Of course, I know the answer now. But at first I considered memory loss as a possibility, until I watched the webcam video. I saw you. You, starting the video, sitting in the machine."

No. The video hadn't recorded. For whatever reason.

"Are you getting there yet? I deleted the video. I was terrified. I guess even back then I could tell we weren't the same, instinctively. We were already acting subtly differently. Moving differently. And I understood what it all meant, you see, long before you had even a sniff of the truth. We'd branched off. That was how I thought of it. Like that monkey puzzle tree. One trunk, two branches, leading onwards and upwards. Two independent people but only one body between us. It was the only explanation. But it *killed* me to think that, during the hours and days I lost, you were still out there, living life instead of me. Living while I disappeared."

Daniel gripped the edges of the laptop. It began to shake along with his hands. He thought of those first days in the Manor, after he had used the machine for the first time. His uncertainty about the passing of time, the sun changing position even when the clocks denied the passing of time. The hollow hunger in his belly, then his confusion about when he'd eaten. The events of his night with Nic, the—

YOU DON'T BELONG HERE.

The message, scrawled on the wall. The handwriting had been familiar. Not Nic's. His own. Almost. It had been the handwriting of this man shown in the video, written drunkenly as he began to glimpse the truth.

"I can almost picture your expression right now." The onscreen Daniel peered up at him. "That thing's no time machine. Sure, you woke up in the future. But the truth is, your body stayed put. All that happened was that you switched your mind off, temporarily. And that allowed mine to switch on. I only existed when you used the time machine, when you vacated your body. When you're gone, *I'm* the house-sitter."

But. No. But. Yes.

Brightness flashed at the edges of Daniel's vision as though the machine held him even now.

"So, what would you do, armed with the information I had? Now I knew that you'd been showing up, taking control of our body, continuing to muck around with the machine. Squeezing that trigger again and again, like an ape in a psychology experiment, oblivious to what you'd set in motion. I had to think fast. You understand the quandary, don't you? I'm not a monster. I understand that you consider yourself the real Daniel Faint, the original. But I'm Daniel Faint too. I'm just as much the definitive article. I share all your memories from before the first use of the machine, our life when we were one and the same. But now it's all different. We have nothing in common. When you're in control, I disappear. Not even limbo. Just nothing. You're the invader, not me, or at least you might as well be." His eyes glanced upwards again. "And that's as much justification as I'm going to give."

Daniel thought back to the biggest mystery: the inexplicable way that the lounge in the Manor had reset itself and the time machine had ended up hidden in the swimming pool. It hadn't been Jimmy, after all, then.

"I can almost hear the cogs turning in your mind." The face cracked into a broad, easy smile. "I can read you like a book. You never spotted how much time had passed with each jump, did you? I changed the clocks and calendars, of course. Simple. I answered Harrigan's phone calls and made the arrangements for his visit. I hid the machine in the pool.

"I know you're puzzling over that one. Why didn't I just destroy the thing? But think about it. I needed the machine even more than you did. I was alive for only brief periods. Hours at first, then days, but then longer periods of being switched off, so to speak. I needed to make certain you'd use the machine again, because if you didn't... well, there'd be no more me, ever." After a meditative pause, he chuckled. "God, how I laughed when I heard the stories about you at the hunt. I like to think I'd have handled the situation with a little more grace."

He paused, tapping the fingers of his right hand on the back of his left. Daniel glanced down and saw that his own hands were held in exactly the same pose. Was it really possible? Could this man, so like himself but so different, have filled in the gaps in his own life, all this time?

The voice quietened, becoming more contemplative. "But we're not the same person. Not now. It's about nurture, not nature. Experience maketh the man, more than the DNA you're born with. I've learnt nothing about time travel, but that's one thing I have learnt."

His voice became brittle. "And I had one experience that you never had." He rubbed one eye with the heel of his hand. "Christ. I actually miss him, the bastard."

Daniel spoke for the first time. His voice sounded absurdly loud in the tiny hotel room. "Jimmy."

"Jimmy," the other Daniel agreed. "I know what you assumed happened to him. And it eats me up. Despite how I feel about you, it genuinely hurts that you believe I killed him."

He looked to one side as if gathering courage. "Look, here's the truth, for what it's worth. I panicked about Jimmy appearing, just like you did. More so, I suppose. At least you had some warning. For me, he was just *there* one day. He was after the machine for himself, of course, or at least a cut of the profit. He was untrustworthy. Sure, he even drugged you just to get you into the machine, which was more than a little impolite. But he was harmless, at the end of the day, and it's not like you and I ever had a surplus of friends, you know? Still. I guess my relationship with him was different to yours. He and I were the underdogs.

"So. I was there, climbing Pavey Ark with him that day, scrambling up Jack's Rake. And he just fell. Maybe you still won't believe that, but he fell and I had nothing to do with it."

He pinched the bridge of his nose. "Actually, scratch that. You *do* believe it. You know it's true. And the fact that Jimmy's death wasn't murder grants you nothing. No get-out-of-jail-free card. I'm not saying my own reaction was respectable. I got scared, of the police, of the guys who built the machine, of you. Tosh agreed to cover for me, that loveable old lunk. He offered to spin the story so it'd be as though I was never out there on the fells. Even the police understood my knee-jerk impulse to hide the fact, after a bit of questioning. They could see that there'd been no foul play."

Daniel jerked backwards on the bed as the image of himself drew closer to the camera. "Oh, but you were far worse, weren't you? I know things about you. At least, I have my suspicions. You did it, didn't you? You actually went and killed Tosh?"

The hotel room seemed to darken. With a start, Daniel realised that it was his own field of vision that was closing in. He was close to passing out. He shook his head to clear it.

The onscreen Daniel paused as if waiting for his attention. "And there, m'lud, I rest my case. You killed Tosh. Right there and then, you forfeited the right to be the one of us who gets to live. And this isn't even corporal punishment, nothing as medieval as that. I'm the one who gets to live, and you just... stop. Christ. You let yourself become a monster. Is it any wonder that I hate you? There. I said it. I hate you, Daniel Faint."

Daniel felt immobile and powerless. He imagined himself wrapped in towels and covered in wasp stings.

The other Daniel's tone of voice became dry and factual. "Emails have been sent out to everyone we've ever known. You're a threat to them all. There's nobody from the past that you can trust now. They don't trust me either, of course, but the difference is that I can handle that. I have a future. As we both know, there can be no going back. Perhaps you've tried it, moving around the country to approximate time travel. Run straight to Mum maybe, sobbing about William. Yeah, we still share that shameful episode from our past. There's no changing that. The difference is that I'm trying to make amends.

"But you'll be found. Covell knows us better than we know ourselves. My years of therapy with him achieved that, I suppose, but it's more than that. He's my best friend. Never thought you'd have one of those, did you? And you never will. Covell loves me like a brother, and he wants me returned, safe and sound. Me, and not you. You, he hates, because you showing up means my death."

Daniel clenched his teeth. Covell, motivated by brotherly love? He turned the thought in his mind, unable to make it click.

The other Daniel laughed. "You should see Covell's dossier. The stuff we've been working through on his psychiatrist's couch is far from the usual therapy. We've spent four years working together. Accounting for the future, not the past. He's scoured my memories, searching for patterns, impulses, tendencies. He knows me inside out, and that means he knows *you* inside out. We've traced all the possible routes, all the options you'll consider. We've prepared for years for your return. Covell's intent on—no, he's obsessed with—dragging you kicking and screaming back to the Manor. You'll go into the machine. He'll squeeze the trigger. You'll vacate your body for good and I'll take over again. This time, you'll go further than a lifetime. When the machine tries to bring you back, there'll be no body to receive you. I'll not be your house-sitter anymore, Daniel Faint. I'll be lord of the fucking manor."

The onscreen Daniel took a deep breath. His eyes darted from side to side. "Except, if you're watching this, something's changed. I don't know what. I've given you all the information you need. Clearly, now you have the upper hand. But here's something else you need to know. Covell will not stop. I'm not here to help you. I can't stop him now. There's nowhere left for you to run."

No, Daniel thought. Experiences maketh the man. I could go anywhere.

"Try it," his own voice said from the screen, almost sounding warm. "Try running. Try setting up a new life in Portugal or Morocco or Australia."

Daniel flinched. He recalled considering those exact locations as potential hideouts.

"Covell will be one step ahead. He'll find you. And then we'll be me again."

The image of Daniel leant towards the screen again, reaching forwards with one hand. Daniel saw a glint in his eye, something that he'd never recognised in himself, something harder. Conviction.

The screen went blank.

FIFTEEN

He drove, hurtling south, afraid that each car heading in the opposite direction might contain the man who wanted him erased from the world. Being pursued by the police, or by the enforcers of impossibly wealthy investors, or by revenge-fuelled research scientists, these were all threats that Daniel could imagine battling. But Covell was compelled by the desire to ensure the safe return of his friend. Simple, fraternal love. An unknown quantity.

He thought again of those other, preferable threats. Covell hadn't been sent by the machine's investors or its research team. So, in fact, nobody had traced him north from Oxford, other than Jimmy. All this time, he had got away with the theft of the machine. His plan had been sound, up to that point. He had disappeared into the Manor, and the Cumbrian fells had risen to embrace him, hiding him. All this time, and it had been only himself that he had been running from, ultimately.

He slept in the car, only leaving it for brief periods to urinate and to collect food. He stopped at petrol stations. What did CCTV cameras matter now? The MG didn't belong to him, and he no longer feared the police.

Once he left the motorway, he slowed, not due to caution but due to the pleasure of roads familiar from his journey to the Manor, the first time, all those weeks ago.

No. Not weeks. Years.

The car slowed still further. He let his body take over while his mind wandered. Somebody had once tried to explain to him the paradox of Achilles and the tortoise. It was something about distance. Halving the distance to one's destination, halving it again, but never reaching it. He wished that it were the case.

But there could be no going back. Only onwards and upwards, creeping inexorably forwards in time, whether using the machine or not.

It seemed to him that the car, unaided, navigated the remaining distance. An arrow arching towards a target. A vector tracing a fixed course.

The car took an alternate route into Broughton-in-Furness and came to a halt outside a long-abandoned outdoor sports centre. Daniel left the MG with its door hanging open.

He took the track that led towards the Manor. Orange sunlight drew sepia-striped patterns on the dust. Walking this route, as familiar by now as any location from his childhood, made him relax, almost. He waved at the old woman hanging out her washing. He whistled a meandering tune. *The farmer's in his den.*

The golf course appeared before he had fully prepared himself. His fingertips danced upon the dry-stone wall. Cloud shadows dreamily deformed the Old Man of Coniston. He slowed his pace, concentrating on each heavy footstep that carried him along the fairway. When he reached the copse, he ducked low to the ground. The Manor was visible now through the thinned trees lining the driveway.

He should watch and wait before approaching any further.

He crept into the copse. Light strobed through the gaps between the narrow tree trunks. As he entered, he realised that his breathing had, until then, been shallow and almost painful. Now, within the damp darkness, the air came more easily.

With a hand resting on one rough trunk, he let his body sink down until he leant against its base. His arms encircled his knees. It was peaceful here. Even the birdsong came muted from outside the clump of trees. Perhaps they never entered the copse. Perhaps nobody did.

Nobody. No body.

With this thought he raised himself to all fours on the mulch and bark.

He searched for signs of Tosh.

Nothing. He laughed. Had he expected to see flowers growing from the grave? Monochrome ones, nodding dog daisies, to mark the location of the gardener's corpse. But there was only dirt.

"I wasn't to know, Tosh," he said. "It was a misunderstanding. An accident." The words 'I'm sorry' repeated in his head, but he didn't say them out loud.

From here, if he positioned himself just so, he could make out the front door of the Manor. The windows of the building were black. Blind. He waited, crouching on his haunches, and watched and watched.

The day grew darker.

If he stayed in the copse any longer, he would have to sleep. The thought wasn't unappealing in itself—it was peaceful, after all—but that wasn't why he came, was it? For some reason the sense of urgency, the threat of Covell's return, had become difficult to fix in his mind. All the same, he pushed himself to a standing position and threaded through the trunks to emerge, blinking, from the copse. He prowled with hunched back towards the Manor, using the driveway trees as shelter.

On the forecourt he paused, remembering a dark shadow that had crouched here, once.

He cupped both hands over his eyes to peer into the window of Benfield's study. He saw the diagrams pinned to the wall. He remembered Florence's words: *He asked after you, just before he died.*

No. Benfield had asked after Daniel Faint. But not this Daniel Faint.

Some half-conscious impulse made him turn abruptly. The sense of being watched was overwhelming. He squinted along the fairway leading to the copse. Wasn't there a figure there? Tosh? Jimmy?

William?

No, only shadows. But those shadows seemed to gather and draw closer.

He sidestepped with his back to the wall of the Manor, towards the door, still watching the nothing that seemed to come closer each second. His hands snuck behind his body, gripping either side of the doorframe.

He watched. The light-dark nothing-figure watched, too. Peacocks yelled from somewhere hidden.

He found that he could no longer move. The shape— no, only the *suggestion* of a shape—reached the tarmacked forecourt. It moved closer at a pace that suggested hesitancy.

Abruptly, the security lamp switched on.

Daniel jerked backwards, reeling as the door sprung open beneath his weight.

He bent double in the doorway, struggling to breathe. He looked out at the Victorian lamp, then back at the forecourt.

The thing had disappeared. The nothing had become truly nothing.

He turned and entered the Manor.

~

He passed through the darkened lobby and into the kitchen. Outside the wide window, three peacocks shuffled lazily beneath the monkey puzzle, billowing their wings and dipping their beaks into the last warmth of the sun.

In the garage, the neon strip light buzzed and flickered, animating the racks of tools that lined the walls. Whoever had succeeded Tosh must perform a greater variety of tasks; whereas previously only the sit-on mower had been in regular use, two newly-installed benches were strewn with pots and soil and hardware halfway fixed.

Beneath laden shelves, metal hooks held hanging tools. Previously they had been haphazard, but now they had been arranged carefully in order of size. Trowels at the left, saws and hammers at the right. Daniel moved to the right-hand side.

He swung the sledgehammer at his side as he re-entered the main house. Its heavy head acted as a slow pendulum.

The steel door to the lounge gleamed.

As Daniel raised the sledgehammer above his head he took a step backwards to stop its weight from toppling him. The machine, hidden behind the door, hummed its encouragement. His elbow wrenched painfully as he brought the hammer down upon the silver door handle. A dull clang reverberated around the lobby. The sound redoubled as it echoed up the stairwell.

He bent to examine the handle. He hadn't made even the slightest mark.

He swung the sledgehammer again. His neck crunched with the violent impact.

Again, nothing.

All this distance. All this time. For nothing.

One more try. He raised the sledgehammer above his shoulder once again, then hefted it higher still.

"Four. Six. One. Three."

Daniel whirled around. Florence Harrigan stood halfway up the wide staircase.

"You only had to ask," she said. "Four, six, one, three."

Daniel opened his mouth but struggled to speak. He lowered the sledgehammer and turned to the keypad beneath the door handle. He concentrated hard to keep his fingers from shaking as he pushed the buttons. Four, six, one, three. It was the local phone number of his childhood home. It was no secret. Nobody was trying to keep him away from the machine. On the final key press, the door sighed open. The machine, crouching in the shadows, breathed a welcome.

Florence watched without moving down the staircase.

"Who else is here?" Daniel said.

She spread her hands. "Nobody. Just me. Just you and me. You watched the video." It was a statement, not a question.

He stared upwards. His position relative to Florence reminded him of the way his onscreen self had looked up above the camera, while filming his piece. The flush in Florence's cheeks eclipsed her freckles. Daniel looked at the bulge in her belly, protruding through the gap in her loose cardigan.

He remembered the way she had held that belly, when he had reappeared. The way she had looked at him. The grief.

"Oh God," he said.

Florence's expression softened. She glanced down at her belly, too. Then she nodded.

Instinctively, Daniel touched a smoothed section of skin on the fourth finger of his left hand. Florence noticed. She held up her own hand, displaying her wedding ring.

She had married him. The other Daniel.

"What about Harrigan? Ian?" he said.

"We divorced years ago," Florence replied, "and Daniel and I started things even before that."

It made sense. Nic must have known about the two of them. *I want you to know that nobody else knows.*

Florence worked the ring with the fingers of her right hand. "We've worn these for two years now. You took yours off as we neared your return date. I mean, he did. My Daniel."

"So that I wouldn't suspect."

"Exactly. He wore the same jeans and white T-shirt every day for the last month, too, knowing you could appear at any moment. A charade for your benefit."

Of course. A charade to keep him placid, until the doctor could arrive to operate the machine. "Except now you've told me the truth."

She sighed. "I'm not a monster. And neither is my Daniel. He's desperate, we both are. Others, too. We all want him back. Even my—" Her expression hardened.

Daniel completed the thought: even her father, were he still alive. He thought of Benfield asking after him before he died, and his mysterious phone call. So that was one more person who loved this other version of Daniel.

Florence gathered herself again. "But I can't see it through. I can't allow you to be murdered."

Daniel choked at the thought. Yes, that was what this was. A murder plot. "No matter how much you want your Daniel back."

"No matter how much."

So Florence had insisted that the other Daniel record the video confession, to use in precisely these circumstances, in case she had these qualms. But that wasn't enough to save him. "But Covell doesn't agree with you. Covell won't change his mind."

She nodded slowly and gave a wan smile of agreement. "They might as well be brothers."

Daniel pressed at the bridge of his nose with his free hand. He realised that his right hand still gripped the shaft of the sledgehammer. He lowered it to the ground and took a step towards her.

"You're not afraid of me?" he said.

Florence stood her ground. "Not a bit. I was. But now I'm not."

"Why?"

"Because I knew that you'd come back here once you knew the truth."

She followed his gaze as he glanced at the sledgehammer resting at his side. She lifted her hands from her belly, drawing attention to it.

"I know you won't use that," she said. Daniel noted the strain beginning to show in her voice. "You won't destroy the machine."

"Why?" he said again. His own voice had become hoarse.

"Because you're Daniel Faint. Not *the* Daniel Faint, not mine. But I *know* you. You're closer to the person I married than any person could ever be."

Close, but not close enough. Daniel's eyes stung. "I'm so scared."

He shuffled forwards. Florence descended a couple of stairs and leant down to take his hands, raised as if in prayer, in her own. "I know. I know that you've tried to be good. It just went wrong, somewhere along the line."

Tears flowed down his cheeks now. In the semi-darkness, Florence's long face appeared as luminescent as the steel door. She was beautiful, he realised. Objectively, astoundingly beautiful. Her thin fingers traced his cheekbones, smoothing away tears.

He nodded slowly. "I can change. You're right, I see it now. I can get back on track. Me and him, we're the same."

Florence's fingers stopped moving. Now she cradled his face without tenderness, as if simply supporting something inert.

"No," she said. "That's not what I meant."

He stared at her, pleading silently.

"You've enough of him in you," she continued, "that I knew you'd come back to the Manor. You're confused about the reasons why you're here. But you'll do the right thing."

"Please?" His voice had become little more than a croak. "I can be him."

Florence pulled her hands away. Daniel wavered on the lowest stair once the contact with her skin broke.

"You can't," she said. Cloud cover dimmed the glow of her face. "Never. I know what you did to Tosh. To others too, maybe. My husband could never have done that. You'd already changed so much, by that point. Whereas he'd turned a corner. He could never have lived with having done what you've done."

"But—"

Daniel found that he had no words to finish his objection. So the fact that he had lived on, managing to come to terms with his crimes, was enough to sentence him. Each of his decisions had seemed rational, in context. Now, the lines of reasoning became a tight tangle.

Florence watched him with an expression more of encouragement than hatred.

"You're closer than twins," she said, "I know how he felt about you, and how he would have felt about himself in your situation. The guilt plagues you." She spoke the last statement as simple fact.

Daniel wiped his eyes.

She was wrong. Guilt didn't plague him, only frustration and fear.

But he could put an end to the fear, at least.

If there was no machine, there could be no other Daniel. No house-sitter.

His life could be his own again.

But.

What then?

This other Daniel had friends, a wife. *The wife wants a child.*

What did he, the real Daniel, want? What did he have, now?

Florence stiffened as he turned to lift the sledgehammer again. With a sleepwalker's slow plod he dragged it along the carpet of the lobby, through the doorway and into the lounge.

The machine crouched at the far end of the room. Shutters now blocked all light from the wide windows but the grey panels shone with some internal glow. It hummed happily, welcoming him back, but gently mocking him too. With sudden conviction, Daniel understood that it had a soul. He sensed some latent intelligence, or perhaps the other Daniel, waiting.

"I hate you," he said, addressing the machine.

He said it again, louder this time.

Before Florence could follow, he heaved the sofa to one side, blocking the door.

~

Florence's fists and wrists ached from pummelling at the steel door. With shaking hands she tapped the keycode once again, then rattled the handle, but the door wouldn't budge.

All of her calmness evaporated. These next few moments would decide everything.

"Daniel! Oh God. Daniel!"

She realised that she was addressing somebody that she would never see again. Not *her* Daniel.

Sounds came muted from within the lounge. A long, low moan, then a muffled shout.

She slumped down to the floor with her arms encircling her belly.

She said to her belly, "I'm so sorry."

The door trembled against her back with vibrations that increased in magnitude. The dull shouts from inside the lounge mingled with another sound, neither human nor mechanical.

Her breath caught. She clambered to her feet again. Was that what the machine sounded like in operation?

"Please, let it be," she said in a quiet voice.

A churning sensation in her stomach matched the woozy, whirring sound. She pressed herself against the cold door and she prayed.

Come back to me. I hear you.

Yes. The machine is bringing you back, after all.

But the sounds became sharper, fractured. Her stomach felt hollow. She pictured the sledgehammer crunching against the grey panels, fragmenting them like fibreglass, shattering them into sharp jagged splinters that clacked and bisected as they hit each other.

Then the noise subsided so that Florence could hear only a faint, ragged wheeze.

A softer sound came from somewhere close to the door. The sofa was being moved. Florence held up her arms but realised that she had no idea whether it was in order to push or pull, defend or grasp.

She watched the handle turn.

The door opened.

A figure stood in the doorway. She found that she wasn't able to look at his face.

Behind him, as she had expected, the time machine lay in pieces. The stubby feet of the grey panels only hinted at their usual height. They looked like the struts of a ruined building. Smaller, sharper shards from the panels had become embedded into the carpet like lightning bolts made solid. The walls of the slatted tube lay in tiny crumbs and hints of curves.

So that was that.

She forced herself to look at the dark, blurred-edged shadow before her. His body was sodden with sweat.

And.

And he was smiling.

She mouthed a wordless question.

Daniel moved towards her, raising his arms to take her into an embrace.

ACKNOWLEDGEMENTS

Firstly, I'd like to give huge thanks to Emma and Anna at Snowbooks for having faith in this book.

Thanks to the Online Writing Workshop crowd, and to Rob Graves in particular for his insightful comments on an early draft.

Enormous thanks to Kate Jonez at Omnium Gatherum for publishing my first book, *Carus & Mitch*, and to Adam Roberts, Lynda Rucker, James Everington and many others for supporting it so wholeheartedly.

Thanks to James Paul Wallis for the joke.

The epigraph features lyrics from 'Farewell to the Gold', written by Paul Metsers, published by Topic Records – Paul's recording is available on the album 'Caution to the Wind'. Thanks so much, Paul, for allowing me to use these lyrics here and within the novel. Your introduction to the song when performing it live, "to all those who have never struck it rich", is an apt dedication for this book, too.

To Gwenda Major, for giving me the writing bug in the first place, and Mike Major, for proudly photocopying and distributing my first short story, twenty-five years ago.

Most of all, to Rose, for her encouragement, support and love from start to finish.

Tim Major

January 2016